DEMON
OF
UNDOING

Andrea I. Alton

A Baen Books Original

Baen Publishing Enterprises
260 Fifth Avenue
New York, N.Y. 10001

First printing, June 1988

ISBN: 0-671-65413-6

Cover art by Kevin Davies

Printed in the United States of America

Distributed by
SIMON & SCHUSTER
1230 Avenue of the Americas
New York, N.Y. 10020

To my parents,
Charles A. Moore & Ruth W. Moore
and to my husband,
Richard.

CHAPTER ONE

The Chalig warriors, still howling their war cry, retreated from the white walls of Fen, taking their wounded and dead with them.

Wrong-handed Fenobar, Commander of the Temple Guard, hastily slid his sword into the scabbard at his back as he lunged for one of his warriors, pulling the palecrest back as he was about to go over the battlements after their enemies, too far gone in battle lust to listen to Fenobar's shouted commands. Fenobar slammed him up against the stonework with enough force to get his attention and held him there with his good hand.

The warrior twisted his head, snarling at his commander over his shoulder, ears flat and eyes slitted with fury. In the brown furred hand the sword shifted toward Fenobar's unprotected stomach, but then the glazed eyes focused on Fenobar's white crest and sanity fought a return in the light green eyes. Sullenly the palecrest lowered his sword, shamed that he had so far forgotten himself.

Fenobar let him go, his duty toward the older

1

male done. He turned away to move down the wallwalk, anxiously checking the rest of the troop along the portion of the wall for which he was responsible. It was proving more difficult than he had anticipated to maintain his authority over the warriors, even with the winter months spent in training. It was just a minor problem, he told himself desperately, as his bad hand started to twitch. He would not let himself think of the dishonor which would be his, if he were unable to call the troops back from their battle madness, and they went harrying off after the enemy, leaving a dangerous breech in the defenses.

The nervous knot in his stomach lessened slightly when he saw that the other temple warriors had themselves well in hand. They were taking advantage of the brief respite to slip off helms and slump down against the battlements to rest. Sekhur, Fenobar's lieutenant, waved to him from the shade of the watch tower at the other end of their section. So. It went well there.

They had not done so badly for a troop made up of the old and the maimed. Unlike the younger troops, his warriors were experienced fighters and fewer of them were down than in other troops along the wall.

Wishing he dared follow his warriors' example and stretch out on the walk, he braced himself against the slight angle made by one of the crenels. His legs trembled from weariness, but he wouldn't even let himself sit down. All his life others had been on the watch for and quick to take advantage of any show of weakness. He could not afford any further loss of status or honor with death so near and his place in the Void at stake.

The shield dragged at his bad arm and his whole left side ached. Was there enough time to unbuckle it before the next attack? A glance over the wall assured him the Chalig had all pulled back to the Chawnelg River, beyond arrow range. It looked as if they were planning to stay there a while. Reassured, he propped the buckler up on a convenient ledge and pulled at the fasteners holding it onto his arm. As the weight came off the muscles spasmed, twitching uncontrollably, taking their revenge for being overused. He had expected the cramping; he absently massaged the pain away as best he could through the padding that helped conceal the twisted bones. Dressed as he was in his chain mail, with its padded left arm, there was nothing to show he was crippled except the twisted, clawlike fingers in which that arm ended. His left hand. The sword hand.

Those fingers were bloody. Surprised because he didn't feel hurt, he looked down his slender length. He was liberally splashed with blood, none of which was his own. The grey surcoat with the temple crest on the chest was rent and filthy, hanging off him in tatters. Blood had somehow gotten onto his helm and into the crestwell and was matting down the long crest hairs, gluing them to the metal, an irritating pull and tug. A pair of browncrests were edging along the wooden wallwalk carrying an injured warrior between them. He flattened against the stone at his back to give them room to pass and the toe claws on his bare feet rasped across the wooden walkway, leaving pale, splintery gouges.

Thirty feet below, the promenade between the town wall and the blank walls of the male circle was full of movement. Darkcrests hurried here and there tending the injured crest-kin lying under the striped awnings which in more normal times protected the scent and flower peddlers. The worst of the wounded were being taken off to Butcher Square, where the implements for crude surgery were already at hand.

The dead fared less well, being simply rolled off the narrow walkway. The Fenirri were fighting for their lives as a Clan and there was no time just now to give them the proper death rituals.

It seemed strangely silent with only the moans of the hurt and dying where the Chalig and Fenirri war horns had filled the air with clear, brazen voices. But the shouts and the cries, the sharp clang and clatter of sword against sword and shield against shield still rang in his mind. Behind his eyes he could still see sharp-fanged mouths opened in yells and howls under battle helms, the rise and fall of arms and feel of blows he had given and taken.

It was all terrifyingly different from the challenge circle or the practice ground. There was more blood, for one thing. And the battle songs never mentioned this bone-crushing weariness in the aftermath of a fight. Perhaps he felt like this because he knew there was no hope of winning against the Chalig. Defeat was always bitter.

Above the sounds of the wounded, clear and sweet, came the chanting of the females and young from the Goddess Garden. Fenobar's ears perked upright under the helm guards, swiveling against the cold metal as he strained to listen. The Goddess Garden was the unchanging center, the heart of the Clan, and the sounds represented stability, order and calm. Juxtaposed against the reality of what was happening outside the walls the chanting suddenly took on an eerily alien quality. Along his back, light brown fur tried to rise under the weight of his chain mail.

He shifted again, trying to throw off the mood, and looked past the crenel at the masses of Chalig resting in the churned remains of their best pasture. The dull, silver glint of armor seemed to go on forever. Nearly every adult male warrior in the en-

tire Chalig tribe was incorporated into the personal
retinue of Thenorig the Mad, and had spent the last
two years being marched mindlessly up and down
Chalig territory. Until this spring, when Thenorig's
wanderings had finally taken him across the border,
directly to their gates.

His eyes studying the Chalig camp, he let his right
hand stray across the picture painted on the inside of
his shield, where no one but himself could, or would,
ever see it. He did not need to look at it to trace the
outline, raised slightly from many years of repainting.

The image was of a strange, alien male. Less heavily muscled than most Imkairans, it was furless, except on its head. In spite of being male, it had no
head crest. It had five long and sinuous fingers on
each hand, instead of the Imkairan four. Its fingers
ended in flat nails instead of claws. It had wide
shoulders and narrow hips, which gave it a decidedly
triangular shape. The eyes were small, the face flat.
The mouth had wide lips. The ears, so small and
round as to be almost useless, were hidden under
the fur on the sides of its head, instead of being on
top like a person's ought to be.

Most people would have considered the creature
ugly past bearing. If Fenobar had once thought so it
was so long ago he no longer remembered. Familiarity had robbed the creature of strangeness, and over
the years he had discovered an integrity of form and
balance in the creature's shape which gave it its own
kind of beauty.

It was a Demon of Undoing, a servant of Chaos.
Once the Demons had walked among the Imkaira,
and where they passed, change followed. They al-
tered entire clans, sowed deviant ideas as a plowman
casts seed upon the ground. Wherever they appeared,

the old ways, which had been good enough for thousands of years, mutated into something else. Life fell into confusion and disquiet. It took centuries before the turmoil sorted itself out and customs stabilized.

They were undeniably powerful beings, but their power was so subtle that it was hard to pin down just what they had done. They were not cruel or arrogant; indeed, they seemed genuinely distressed at the results caused by their presence, as if they felt the trouble they caused was a matter for dishonor. They retreated from the world and were seldom seen again.

The Kings and priests watched them leave with a feeling of profound relief. One thing was agreed on. No one wanted them back. Afraid to speak their name lest one of the Demons take it for a summons, priests, when they were forced to speak of them at all, did so in whispers and in language so circumspect that it was almost impossible for an outsider to understand what they were discussing.

So to carry the picture of one into the Temple of Shaindar was an act not likely to endear one to priests or acolytes. Had they ever learned that Fenobar not only called upon the Demon but was in the habit of thinking of him as his ranking whitecrest, they would have been horrified. Had they been told that Fenobar firmly believed the Demon answered his requests for aid they might well have gone catatonic.

A warrior's status and honor was dependent upon the status of the whitecrest who was willing to take him as an ally. This held as true for the younglings as it did for the warriors. But not until Fenobar was fourteen and nearly full grown did one of the older whitecrests at Bokeem see his value as a fighter and take him, for the first time in Fenobar's life, into a war band.

Fenobar's survival up to that time had not been easy. He owed his life to his belief that he was under the protection of the Demon of Undoing. Fenobar learned of the Demon of Undoing from an obscure book in the library at the whitecrest training school of Bokeem when he was ten. Fenobar had never had much hope of being accepted by a Ranking Whitecrest and had a pretty good idea of what his life was going to be like without the protection of a troop around him. The longer he stared at the picture of the Demon, the more he felt there must be a bond between it and himself. The demons were the authors of change and strangeness and surely he, as different as he was, was under their protection, or he would not have lived as long as he had. Fenobar even looked a little like them, for he was built along slight lines for a warrior of the Fenirri, and the Demons were more slender than Imkairans.

It was desperation that first put the notion in his head. He was barely surviving a regimen that gave no quarter to one crippled as he was, and the instructors had yet to get seriously down to the business of teaching them war skills. He needed a strong ally. Here was a creature so strong even the priests were afraid of him.

He could ally with a Demon. He knew he could. No one had taken a Demon over-lord in the hundreds of years since they first appeared. His offer of allegiance must be valued on that count alone, even as weak and crippled as he was.

Carefully, he considered what might happen to him if his teachers or the other cublin learned of this alliance—and knew, even before he started, that he had nothing to lose. There was no other choice open to him.

So he fasted and prayed and, on the fourth morning, weak and dizzy from hunger and lack of sleep, he heard the Demon speak to him. He could not make out the words, but it did not matter. He had his sign. He lay the tip of his sword in the honor fire and when it glowed red he pressed it against the inside of his wrist. Distantly, feeling no pain, he watched the puff of smoke rise upwards from burned fur, and so the bond between them was made, accepted and sealed.

The image he painted on the inside of his shield, a copy of the picture in the book, was at first only a focus for his mind as he sought contact with his Demon to discover and use the subtle changes the Demon wrought on his behalf. Over the months and years the strange creature grew ever more real to him, evolving from something remote and godlike to a friendly presence to talk with in the dark; a solace for long, lonely days.

It was not easy having a Demon for an ally. He learned the hard way that it had a trick of giving with one hand and taking away with the other. Not for nothing were they called Demons of Undoing. As he grew older and his skills something to be reckoned with, he asked its help less and less. Indeed, so wary had he become of asking the Demon's aid, that not since the day he walked through Bokeem's gates to find his way back to Fen had he called on his Demon for help of any kind. He had held to that until three days ago when they first learned that Thenorig was coming. And even then he did not ask for himself, but for the clan.

The image had become a trifle chipped and faded. A bit guilty at his neglect, and feeling vaguely that the Demon would be stronger and more willing if he repainted it, he found some colors and set to work. He'd picked the head fur out in gold, not having any silver at hand to give it the white crest of power, and hoped the Demon would not be offended. Because his dye had not been good, the eyes, which he'd always made the color of the sky, as the old descriptions said, had come out gray, ringed with black, the eyes of a direhawk. But other than that it was the best likeness he'd ever achieved, right down to the rounded nails on the long fingers.

Gently he touched the image, careful not to mar the paint with his claws. Had HE brought the Chalig down on the Clan? Had the Demon felt his hatred for the stifling life of the temple and brought the Clan to this as a way to free him? It was, he acknowledged wryly, the kind of double-edged response his Demon was capable of—to give him his freedom by destroying the Clan. It was the fear of just this sort of solution to his problems that kept him from calling on the Demon. If he died today, how much of the blame for destroying his clan would the Old Sisters assign him?

No matter. Whoever was to blame, it could be Undone. He would worry about the price he would pay for the Demon's aid later. He closed his eyes and rested his fingertips lightly on the image. Never had he been as passionate in his inarticulate pleading as he was at that moment.

Horns rang above the town roofs. Fenobar's eyes snapped open as his head jerked around. It was Challenge. One King to another. But Black Fentaru, King of Fen, did not have the status or personal power to win against Mad Thenorig. There was no one who could win against Thenorig. The number of warriors in his retinue attested to that. Had his sire been pushed into madness by imminent defeat? Was THIS his Demon's response?

Even as the thought crossed his mind he heard

footsteps approaching from behind and with a quick, practiced shrug of his shoulder swung the shield onto his back, where the image of the Demon was hidden against his body.

"My Lord?"

Fenobar turned around. The speaker was a darkcrest wearing Black Fentaru's House Badge on the breast of his tunic. Fenobar dipped his crest in acknowledgment against the pull caused by the blood-matted hairs.

"The High Priest requests the Commander of the Temple Guard to accompany him to the Challenge circle as witness to the challenge between Thenorig, High King of the Chalig, and Black Fentaru, King of Fen."

"I will come immediately," Fenobar answered. He started past the darkcrest, seeking Sekhur, to tell his lieutenant where he was going. As he did so he reached up and impatiently ripped the long white hairs of his crest free of the blood gluing them to his metal helm.

The Challenge horns were still calling musically and all along the wall warriors were stiffly rising to lean over the crenels, striving to see the King's gate and the ancient challenge ground in front of it.

Sekhur was waiting for him at the tower entrance, his white-muzzled face calm as ever. "You will be needing a mount," he said before Fenobar opened his mouth. He jerked his head toward the street below.

Fenobar followed the line of the brown chin to see red-furred Ropsha, one of his palecrested warriors, looking up at him, his light brown crest held at a respectful angle. In one fist he was holding the reins of a riding tatarra. The purple hide was spotted with rosettes, a sign it was from the King's stable. But the long, narrow head was drooping and the feathery scales were dusty.

Fenobar decided not to ask where they had gotten it. Fenobar turned to Sekhur but that old warrior composedly forestalled him again. "Do not fear for your honor. I will see to all, Lord."

Whatever needed doing, Sekhur could be relied upon to do. So Fenobar tipped his crest at him, both salute and acknowledgement, before ducking through the low door of the tower, finding his way down the steep, narrow steps more out of instinct than by the light from the few narrow arrow slits.

Once at street level he took the tatarra's reins from Ropsha and swung up into the saddle, exhaustion forgotten. Eyes bright with excitement, he sent his tired mount clattering down the flagstoned promenade toward the other side of the town. He came into the wide plaza in front of the King's Gate and slowed his animal to a walk. The market was full of the walking wounded, who had been drifting toward the gate since the first sounding of the horns. They formed a wide arc around the massive, heavily guarded King's Gate. Silently they leaned on their weapons, watching the King, who was mounted on his war tatarra and waiting in front of the gates.

The King was a tall, broad-shouldered figure. His black war helm was held under his right arm, leaving his head bare. His crest was a long fall of shimmering white. The black chain mail shone like fish scales against his black fur. The white surcoat with the King's badge, the Black Axe of Monghan, embroidered on the chest, seemed doubly bright against the sable hue of his armor. The long orange and red cloak thrown back over his shoulders swirled lightly with every movement, like a fall of flame, now obscuring, now revealing the black and silver sword sheathed at his back.

If he was feeling any fear or doubt, it did not show in the lifted head and the squared shoulders. He sat his great purple tatarra easily, not showing any signs of the fatigue he must have accrued during that long and brutal morning.

Fenobar, well acquainted with Black Fentaru, who was his sire, curled his lip at the bright cloak and clean surcoat, but privately thought his sire looked magnificent. He urged his tired mount forward through the press of warriors, conscious of a little lift of hope. Black Fentaru was a notable warrior and no fool. If anyone could beat Mad Thenorig, it would be him.

Beside the King, on a tatarra stallion so ancient it was white, sat Shont, the High Priest of the Warrior God Shaindar, less colorful, but just as regal. Allowed only the color gray, Shont's tunic and overrobe was so thick with silver thread and moonstones that he shimmered like a fall of stardust. Under the rich material his muscles were age-thinned, and the once-white crest had turned yellow and brittle. In spite of his infirmity there was no one, not a single warrior in all of Fen, who would have challenged him. Who would risk the wrath of Shaindar by removing from this earth one He had chosen to be His Spoken Word?

Fenobar picked distastefully at the blood on his surcoat and shrugged. This was a battle. They would have to take him as he was.

Six palecrested temple acolytes came trotting into the marketplace from Maze Way carrying the litter bearing the Eyes of Shaindar on their shoulders. The Eyes were a small image of the Warrior God in the temple. Fenobar reined his mount aside as the crowd parted hastily to let the Eyes of Shaindar through. The acolytes hurried toward the gate to set the image down in front of Shont, who acknowledged the presence of his God with a bowed head and dip of his crest, as did Black Fentaru. Fenobar and the other warriors present gave the three-way salute as the Eyes passed them.

Pushing their way forward in the wake of the Eyes came two whitecrested warriors as blood bespattered and as tired as Fenobar. As they came abreast of him Fenobar's nose identified them before he could make out their features behind the nose guards of their war helms. They were Felingar, and Fegulum, two older sons of his sire. Felingar was favoring his shield arm and Fegulum had a white bandage tied around his left leg below the knee. They smelled him nearly at the same time and their crests jerked in surprise, although they did not acknowledge his presence. Fenobar had expected that. He was dead to his House since being sold into the temple. They were higher status than he, so he courteously waited to let them go first before following them to the gate, where the King and the High Priest were growing impatient.

Black Fentaru was watching their approach, and his large golden eyes narrowed when he saw Fenobar behind his two sons. The acrid smell of battle fesen clogged the air. The hair rose along Fenobar's backbone even as his crest started to flatten in appeasement. He forced his crest erect, reminding himself that he was temple bound and not under his sire's authority.

Fenobar stopped the proper distance from the ranking males and saluted, open hand to crest. He had to use his right hand, not his left, of course, which always made his salutes look awkward.

The King turned to the High Priest, his crest jerking with suppressed fury. "I asked for Commander

Fangbor, not this crippled cublin! What game are
you trying to play, Shont?"

Serenely, Shont's dim, age-filmed eyes met the
King's golden ones. "You asked for the Temple Commander. You have him."

"If I had known . . ." the King started furiously.

"The result would be the same," the High Priest
interrupted calmly. "As ill as you like it, Fenobar is
the Temple Commander. The Temple Commander,
whoever he is, is present at the Challenge of a King."

Black Fentaru glowered at them both. "Stupid
custom." He reined his war mount around and waved
imperiously at the guard above them on the inner
tower. With a protesting squeal the inner door was
raised. The King and High Priest entered the narrow
space between the inner and outer gates, followed
by the acolytes carrying the Eyes of Shaindar, Fegulum
and Felingar, and last of all by Fenobar.

The space between the inner and outer gate was
called the regt, which in the old tongue meant "trap."
Fenobar had always thought that was a singularly apt
name for the place. Being there made him feel acutely
uncomfortable, and especially now with the heavily
reinforced outer gates closed and the inner ones
coming down behind. High above them the walls
were darkly patterned with arrow slits. Movement
showed in the slits now, as the bowmen leaned forward to get a look at their King and High Priest.

Deep inside the gate towers came the clash of
chains being tightened, and the groan of the winches,
as the huge bars were pulled back. Warriors rushed
forward from the gate towers to push the ponderous
doors open just wide enough for the King and the
High Priest to ride out side by side.

The wind switched around, carrying with it the
sudden stench of a multitude of unwashed Chalig.

Fenobar's nose pinched shut in distaste, and his ears flattened under the upright ear guards of his helm. The scent had been in his nostrils all that morning. He'd taken it for the smell of battle, and here all the time it had only been the smell of Chalig.

The road down to the ancient challenge ground was narrow and twisting. The banks of the hill on either side of them was close set with trenches and stakes. The ancient challenge ground was a circular flat spot beaten into the hillside, so it was said, by the great Fen himself. Within the grassy plot was another circle, outlined in curbing stones of the same yellowish granite the town walls were made from.

Leaving the Eyes of Shaindar and His attendants at the edge of the grounds, the warriors rode forward to the challenge circle and spread out. Felingar and Fegulum took places to the right of their sire, careful to stay out of his line of sight, for Black Fentaru was not entirely sane just now. A warrior readying himself for a challenge fight was only a crest-hair away from attacking anything that provoked him.

Fenobar took his place to the left of Shont, as was proper, leaving the two ranking males to sit side by side. Shont was the only one here with enough rank to control the King if he went berserk before the time was right.

The five of them sat staring down the long, gentle slope at the massed ranks of Chalig drawn up beside the river. Considering the state of battle readiness he was in, Black Fentaru was terribly calm. Fenobar puzzled over Black Fentaru's patience, until he caught the King casting a surreptitious look at the sky. It was no more than a swift upward shift of the large golden eyes, but Fenobar understood instantly.

The air was still. No cloud marred the clear spring sky. The signs were perfect for the coming of a jekbet. But no flock of birds wheeled blackly against sun, seeking the safety of their roosts among the trees by the river. That was a pity, because the flocks of mountain rioles were always the first sign that a killing north wind was about to come whistling out of the teeth of the mountains. It was a blast of air so cold it could freeze a young tatarra colt as it nuzzled for milk at it's mother's flank. The Chalig were from the more hospitable southern forests and were standing out there in nothing but their armor, unaware of the danger Fentaru wished on them so ardently.

Shont broke the silence with a comment to his King. "You cannot win this challenge."

"I know," the King said shortly. His yellow eyes glittered with a hard light, and the scent of his battle lust suddenly took on a new, disturbing odor.

"Then why did you make it?" Shont's words might have been taken for rebuke, except the tone was so bland as to be disinterested.

"Because no matter what we do we are going to lose. The only thing left is to choose how."

"You are the King. You ARE the Clan. Your honor is the Clan's honor. If you are disgraced, the Clan is disgraced."

"That is what the Second Warrior Rank has been telling me. They think we should fight to be the last warrior and sing our defiance while the town burns around us as our funeral pyre.

"But I ask you: Did not the Clan exist long and honorably before I was born? Should it not exist long and honorably after I am dead and gone?"

Under his helm guards Fenobar's ears were twisted as far as they could go in the King's direction, gathering every word. From the corner of his eye he could see a strange expression on Shont's face as he pondered the King's question.

"You are saying that the Clan is more important than you are?" Shont hazarded.

"Should the Clan exist to uphold the honor of a single warrior? Or does the King uphold the honor of the Clan? You are more learned than I and have the ear of the God besides. Tell me what Shaindar says," Black Fentaru demanded impatiently.

In a slow voice that showed how far his mind had turned inward, searching through his memories, Shont replied, "The teachings say only that the honor of the King and the Clan are one."

Black Fentaru tilted his crest in satisfaction. "I say the honor I have accrued in my little life is meaningless beside the honor the Clan has acquired over hundreds of years. My honor is already part of the Clan. It cannot be removed. The Honor of the Clan is so vast it will hardly notice the defeat of one of its Kings, so long as the Clan lives. And that is the difficulty, Speaker for Shaindar. There is only one way for the Clan to survive Mad Thenorig, and that is for me to challenge him, even if I lose. For then the law forbids him to enter the walls."

"I have never heard any King speak like this," Shont said respectfully. "It has always been accepted that the honor of the Clan is subservient to the honor of the King. Shaindar has heard your words and judged them truth. They will be written down as part of the laws. I salute you now as forever."

This was the ultimate in praise and the King was at a loss for a moment. Then he tilted his head courteously to Shont's salute and turned eyes front again.

Fenobar let his ears relax to a more normal position and spent the next few minutes committing Black Fentaru's words to memory for later pondering. No doubt, he would find the time as they followed Mad Thenorig around the countryside. Black

Fentaru's conviction that Clan was more important than he was certainly novel. How had the Demon sold his stolid and pragmatic sire on such an unconventional idea in so short a time?

There was a disturbance in the front ranks of the massed warriors beside the river. They parted to permit a helmed and surcoated warrior passage to the Fenirri waiting above. He was huge, fully a head taller than Black Fentaru, who was nearly the tallest warrior in Fen, and wide—nearly twice the width of Black Fentaru. Curiously enough, the only armor he wore was a battered war helm. Only a few tatters of a whitecrest showed through the crestwall to hang limply to one side. The sword that protruded over his shoulder was so big, most warriors would need two hands just to lift the thing. The once white surcoat, torn and dirty, bore the King's Clan badge . . . the red banner.

Fenobar leaned forward on his saddle horn, breathing heavily. So this was Thenorig.

Mad Thenorig was riding a patuz. The Chalig King set his clumsy animal to a trot and it lumbered toward them through the spring grass, pounding the soft earth with huge, round feet. There was nothing graceful or particularly beautiful about a patuz. They were big and heavy, and they stank.

As Thenorig came closer. Fenobar began to appreciate just how big the Chalig King was. It was entirely possible that Thenorig rode a patuz because there was no tatarra anywhere that could carry him and walk at the same time. Nevertheless, that did not seem reason enough for Thenorig to sit the animal as if he were a sack of wheat. Thenorig had no warrior bearing at all.

As Thenorig's animal climbed the gentle slope toward them, Black Fentaru deliberately raised his crest, flashing a white challenge. A fraction of a second later, the rest of the Fenirri did the same, even old Shont, who, Fenobar thought, was past such things. Behind Thenorig the Chalig returned the challenge, but the white flickering was disjointed and listless. Their hearts were obviously not in it. Just how deep was the bond between the Chalig King and his retinue? A low status palecrested warrior would have received more support.

But Thenorig did not seem to notice, or if he noticed, did not care. There was that look about him . . . not the uncaring of pride, which is above such things, but the disinterest of one who is far removed from what is going on around him.

Fenobar shivered. He'd seen that look once before —in a sick tatarra just before it died.

Half hidden behind the patuz trotted a meek-looking browncrest on a small tatarra. He was wearing a richly embroidered tunic with a matching cape of shimmering silk. The presence of a browncrest at a challenge was unheard of. There was something lacking in the dark-crested males that made them content to serve. They were NEVER close companions to the warrior kind.

Fenobar's bad hand started to twitch where it lay on his thigh. Everything about this meeting was WRONG. What was his Demon up to?

The browncrest brought his tatarra up beside Thenorig's huge animal and, reaching out a hand for the headstall, brought the patuz to a stop the required ten feet from the waiting Black Fentaru. It put Fenobar irresistibly in mind of a keeper putting a bull tongue through its paces.

Up close, Thenorig's small, heavy-lidded eyes looked sleepy. It was impossible to tell what he was thinking, if anything. Under the filthy surcoat his brown fur was dull, patchy and liberally scarred. He still had not returned Fentaru's challenge.

Black Fentaru's nostrils were flaring at this insult. He was as still as a statue, a sure sign he was close to losing control.

The little browncrest stretched upwards a bit to whisper in Thenorig's ear. The heavy eyes blinked and then, seemingly with great effort, the Chalig King lifted his sparse crest. The challenge flash made a pitiful showing. Then, indifferently, Thenorig pulled off his helm and tucked it under one enormous arm.

There was a collective gasp from the Fenirri. The right side of Thenorig's head was caved in, a mess of red and white scar tissue thinly drawn over crushed bone. What was left of his right ear was a misshapen, hairless lump.

Black Fentaru was the first to recover. "I challenge by King right. Your retinue to come to my authority if I win." His words, stated in a loud, ringing voice carried well to the Chalig beside the river, as he intended. Let no one say there were any illegalities about this meeting.

Thenorig answered . . . something. His voice was so deep, thick and guttural it was impossible to understand him. From his position beside Thenorig, the small browncrest spoke up, not at all humbly. In fact, Fenobar had never heard a browncrest so smug before. "The Lord Thenorig demands you surrender to his authority or suffer."

The Fenirri stiffened in outrage as their hands went for sword hilts. Even Shont had gone to his shoulder after a nonexistent sword.

Black Fentaru's ears went flat to his skull; his crest rose slowly and then tilted stiffly forward—signs of a warrior about to go berserk.

Breathing heavily through flaring nostrils, Shont

hissed from between long, yellow teeth. "You are an outlander. By what right do you assume the rights of a High King over a clan of the Monghanirri!"

Thenorig didn't seem to be aware that the High Priest had spoken. But the browncrest blinked in surprise and then his ears went to the side, anxiously, as if some well-rehearsed ritual had developed a wrinkle he was unprepared to handle.

The darkcrest whispered to Thenorig. In Thenorig's small eyes some sort of understanding dimly came to life. The heavy neck swelled and his scarred hands clenched fiercely at the reins before one heavily muscled arm went back over his shoulder, seeking his sword. Before he could draw it, the browncrest threw himself upward and hung onto his arm, whispering frantically into his one remaining ear. Thenorig went still, and then settled, calm, once more.

Fenobar's bad hand was twitching madly, but he scarcely realized it. His eyes were on Black Fentaru, who had also gone for his sword, but stayed his hand when Thenorig did not draw. Fenobar let go a breath he had not known he was holding. Had swords been drawn, it would have changed the challenge from a simple hand-to-hand combat between whitecrests, to one between malin—Thenorig's warriors against all of Fen.

Thenorig growled . . . something. The darkcrest said, "The High King agrees to the challenge right of personal combat. The winner to take the other's warriors."

The answer was not strictly according to proper ritual, but Black Fentaru, running his eyes over Thenorig's thick, battered body, chose to ignore the irregularity. Contempt lifted one lip as he turned to say something to Shont. And suddenly Fenobar realized Black Fentaru was seeing himself winning this fight. Seeing himself as King of the entire Chalig nation. There was that about him.

Wait! Fenobar wanted to cry out. There was something badly wrong here. Hadn't either of the ranking warriors noticed that Thenorig's crest had not risen in challenge as he went for his weapon? Indeed, it had gone flat in submission. A cold chill of fear ran down Fenobar's back as, chewing on a claw in frustration, he listened to Black Fentaru conclude the preliminary ritual and dismount. Only Shont could get Black Fentaru to listen to him now and it was doubtful Shont would see any danger. His face was wearing nearly the same exultant expression as was his King.

He looked again to this sire, searching for any sign that Black Fentaru knew something was desperately wrong, and saw only a whitecrest tempted beyond sense by the greatest opportunity of his lifetime. Fenobar shifted his shield to his shoulder and, bracing it on his thigh, traced with desperate intensity the picture of the Demon of Undoing.

CHAPTER TWO

Fegulum, the eldest of the King's whitecrested sons, dismounted, to make sure the challenge circle was free of rocks and sticks that might trip up a fighter. Meanwhile, the King's other whitecrested son, Felingar, was helping his sire out of his armor.

Sword and kalnak, the right-hand daggar, were not permitted to touch the ground. Felingar took them reverently from his sire's hands and hung them from the pommel of the King's saddle by their harness.

In the meantime, Thenorig had hauled himself off his patuz and was slouched against the animal's broad, leathery side.

Divested of helm, ringmail and linen undertunic, Black Fentaru took his position outside the stone circle, armed with nothing more than his teeth and claws. Only then did the Chalig King finally rouse himself enough to remove his sword, which he dropped heedlessly onto the wet grass, and toss aside his stained surcoat. He shuffled opposite Black Fentaru only after the browncrest motioned him forward and stood with hunched shoulders, staring morosely at the ground.

Shont raised his arms, his gray sleeves like shimmering wings, and called a low invocation to the war gods. As he finished and lowered his hands, the two Kings stepped into the challenge circle.

They eyed each other across the space between them. Black Fentaru was fully alert, measuring his opponent with the experience garnered form twenty years of status fights. His golden eyes sparkled beneath the nervously flexing white crest. Fesen was high in Black Fentaru. But now, when he needed it, there was no battle madness in Thenorig at all. The Chalig King was . . . indifferent.

With a sudden, beautifully athletic spring, Black Fentaru was in the center of the ring, claws out, uttering his high-pitched war challenge.

In reply, Thenorig shuffled forward, hands raised. Fesen still had not risen in him. Without it, no matter how good he was, he would be no match for a beserk battle warrior.

Fenobar bit through one claw on his good hand, spat it out, and started chewing nervously on the next one, waiting for the trap to snap shut on his sire.

Black Fentaru circled in a feint to one side, which Thenorig moved clumsily to block. Black Fentaru slowed and stepped back, looking a trifle worried.

Fenobar breathed a little easier. The King was using his head still. Battle lust was not blinding him.

Almost gingerly the King danced around his huge opponent, barely tapping at the massive chest and the heavy, muscle-laden shoulders. Carefully, he kept out of the way of the clumsy arm swings, the bull-blind rushes. Thenorig was not just a slow fighter, he had no battle reflexes at all. It was as if he had never been battle trained. Ponderous and heavy footed, he was a patuz in Imkairan shape.

Black Fentaru moved, a flash of dark power. Awkwardly, Thenorig turned to face him, a sash of red, welling blood running from shoulder to thigh. They all knew then that Black Fentaru could kill the huge Chalig at his convenience. It might take a while, simply because Thenorig was so padded with muscle and bone, but Black Fentaru had all the time in the world to whittle away at his enemy, and he set to it with a will. Thenorig howled from the pain of his wounds and shuffled after Black Fentaru as fast as he could. But Black Fentaru was never within reach of those huge arms and sharp claws.

The Fenirri whitecrests had relaxed, but Fenobar's stomach was contracted into a tight knot of tension. He had abandoned claw chewing to hold his wildly twitching bad hand down. Thenorig could NOT be this inept a fighter and have taken all of the Chaligirri in battle. Fenobar edged his mount close to the Chalig browncrest, and, leaning on the pommel of his saddle, bent over to say confidingly to the other, "From the scars on your Lord's body, I would say it is difficult for him to win challenges."

The darkcrest was intent on the battle and answered absently, "Oh, he doesn't win." Then, seeming to realize what he'd just said, he shot Fenobar a glance of pure loathing. Raising fingers to his mouth, he whistled, a piercing, demanding blast. Thenorig, who was swaying slightly now, his fur gone from brown to red, dropped to the ground, curled into a ball and mewed, keening like a frightened, despairing infant.

Fenobar nearly fell off his tatarra with shock. But the effect on the King, who was slashing down at Thenorig's unprotected back with all the force of his considerable strength, was even more violent. He aborted his blow with a quick twist of his body, throwing him to his knees. Eyes wild, he scrambled away from the keening Thenorig, shocked completely out of battle madness. He went right over the curbing in his flight and once on the other side, slowly straightened, staring at Thenorig as if he were some kind of monster. Witlessly, he backed away, until he came up against Shont's tatarra, where he stood and shook.

No adult male can kill an infant. It was an instinct as old as the species. But no adult male can keen like an infant. They CANNOT. But Thenorig was and Black Fentaru was no more able to tear out his throat than he could stop breathing. While the Fenirri sat stunned, staring at Thenorig, the browncrest, with a triumphant flick to his crest, was motioning to a small group of mounted Chalig warriors. Two whitecrests started toward them.

Fenobar was numb, yet he had to concede, in all fairness, that the Demon had done exactly what he had asked of it. The Clan would live. And it was Black Fentaru, not himself, who had had to pay the price this time. The King had stepped out of the cirele. Mad Thenorig had won by default.

The two Chalig whitecrests were among them now, their tatarra as thin and unkempt as they themselves. Their manner grim, they set about their tasks without meeting any eyes. Fenobar was sitting his tatarra only a few feet from where the two Chalig were hoisting the still huddled Thenorig onto his patuz and strapping the huge body in place with ungentle hands and practiced efficiency.

While one Chalig whitecrest led the patuz back down to the river, the other gathered up Thenorig's belongings. Head bent, the Chalig murmured, "Thenorig will demand the Spirit of your Clan. Once he has it, its power will go to feed the Red Banner.

Shocked, Fenobar stuttered, "But . . ."

"If the Spirit is not given into his hands, the town of Fen will be reduced to rubble, as happened to Charne."

Fenobar glanced up at the other, saw the device on the Chalig's surcoat—a gold tatarra above a ripple of blue. It was a simple device, unmarred by family badge insets—the mark of a king. "Charne was yours?"

The other's crest lowered in shame. He turned away without answering, to grab up the reins of his tatarra, and swung into the saddle only slightly hampered by the weight of Thenorig's helm and sword. Without another look he rode off after the patuz.

Slowly Fenobar rode back to the High Priest, chewing meditatively on one claw.

Black Fentaru, already in his mail, was standing with his helm under his arm, staring at the walls of Fen with a lost look in the large golden eyes. It was just past midday and the sun was flooding down upon them with eye-searing brilliance. The sky was blue. The grass was green. Somewhere a bird fluted. The breeze was cool and carried with it a hint of pifir spice from the mountains. The world went on its measured path, irregardless of the disasters that befell the Fenirri.

It did not seem fair, somehow.

The acolytes bearing the Eyes of Shaindar were already trotting up the hill, hurrying to take them back to the temple. The King waited, giving the Eyes time to reach the gate. It would not do to come too quickly on the heels of the God.

Saluting the High Priest, Fenobar said baldly, "The Chalig will demand the Clan Spirit."

"To add to the power of the Red Banner Clan."

Shont half closed his eyes as one finger stroked his cheek. "We had heard of this . . . sacrilege. The Chalig will never recover from the things Mad Thenorig has done to them."

Fenobar stifled an urge to damn the Chalig to the outmost limits of the Void. "How are we going to protect the Black Axe of Monghan?"

Shont's yellowing crest twitched in gentle amusement. "We do not."

Fenobar clamped his teeth shut over sudden temper and forced his ears up. The High Priest was baiting him. Fenobar could never get as much amusement out of these encounters as Shont did and found it less exacerbating to his pride to keep hot words inside his mouth.

Oddly enough, it was the King who explained to the temple commander. In a lifeless voice he said, "There is a duplicate Axe. That one we will give to Thenorig."

"And what of the real Axe?" Fenobar asked worriedly as they began the ride back up the hill to the town. He was the temple commander, and the protection of the Axe was his primary concern, no matter what the King's privileges were.

"That you will take to the Royal Clan at Mone for protection."

"You cannot remove the Clan Spirit from the Clan!" Felingar cried out, shocked, from his place on the far side of the King. He came under the withering look of the two ranking males of his clan and lowered his crest, mumbling an apology.

"Well, Fegulum," the King said, turning to his other son. "What do you think of removing the Axe?"

Fegulum, no fool, said merely that if the warriors were not going to be inside Fen's walls, it probably wouldn't matter where the Axe was kept. His reward was a derisive look from his sire and a dry, "So true."

"I will take the Axe to Mone?" Fenobar asked in a small, stunned voice.

"Can't you do it, Wrong-Hand?" the King asked instantly. "I can find someone else . . ."

"No! That is, I was just surprised, My Lord. The Axe will be safe in my care."

"That's what My Lord Shont said, so there are two of you in agreement." Black Fentaru's brittle tone was not encouraging. He twisted around in the saddle to favor his youngest whitecrested son with a long, brooding look.

Fenobar forced himself to keep his eyes steady and his shoulders straight under the weight of it. He was suddenly acutely conscious of the twisted bones in his left arm.

"Well," the King said at last, "to have survived Bokeem there must be more to you than meets the eye. But not even such a paragon as yourself can survive outside the clan without a retinue at your back. You will have Stells and the best squad among my personal war troop to accompany you."

Fenobar's ears went down and stayed there. Stells was Black Fentaru's sholstan, his left-hand warrior, the highest ranking palecrest in the clan. The least member of the King's war troop had more status than a temple commander. He was going to be the titular head of a troop of warriors all of whom outranked him. Had he ever asked his Demon to help him gain a war troop of the finest warriors of Fen? He couldn't remember, but he probably had—it was such a youngling's dream. Well, he'd gotten it with the typical Demon twist to the gift. When would he ever learn!

The outer gates were flung open, and they entered Fen for the last time through that narrow, stone-walled passage in the thick walls. It was cool and the confined air smelled of tatarra dung and sweat. While they waited for the inner gates to be cranked up, the gate commander leaned over the battlements and called down to the King. "My Lord, they won with a trick. We think we should fight them anyway."

Black Fentaru looked down at his hands on the reins in front of him before lifting his head finally and calling back. "Not this time, Morliu. We are not yet ready to be food for the ker. Send a runner to the warehouses and warn the sister-groups to hide the seed corn. Send a runner to each gate with this message: 'Tell the Chalig whatever you like, but they are not to enter any gate but the King Gate.' Morliu, I charge you not to let any Chalig enter until the second hour past high noon. Sound the Assembly horns now, Morliu!"

Morliu gave a quick, involuntary glance over the wall where the Chalig waited. "Yes, my Lord."

The inner gate ground upward. As they passed under it, Fenobar heard the high, sweet notes of the horns, pealing forth Black Fentaru's command for all warriors to meet in the plaza in front of the King House.

The gathering of warriors in front of the gate had grown while they were gone. The wounded leaned on spears or on each other. Ears were down and crests were held flat. They all knew what that call meant. In silence Black Fentaru walked his war mount through the clan-crests, for more than warriors were there. Darkcrests too were among the crowd silently waiting to bear the word back to the inner maze where the females and young dwelled.

Alone, Black Fentaru made his way through the crowd to the steps of the King House to give the hardest speech of any in a long life. Shont did not wait. He kicked his aged tatarra into a slow trot and headed down the nearly deserted promenade toward the temple with Fenobar at his side.

Only the temple guard were exempt from the
King's summons, for their service was to the God.
The old warrior who met them at the foot of the
south steps to take their mounts was clearly unhappy. His eyes, Fenobar noted, kept turning uneasily toward the King Gate, as over the House roofs,
the clear, silver notes of the Assembly call continued
to sound. Old habits are hard to break, and the
warrior clearly felt drawn to answer that call.

The High Priest had already dismounted and was
halfway up the long flight of shallow steps, seemingly
unbothered by the weight of his embroidered and
begemmed overtunic. Fenobar hastily ran to catch
up with him before he disappeared into the depths
of the temple.

He caught up with the old warrior when he stopped
behind the first line of inner pillars to let his eyes
adjust from the midday light to the cool shadows.
The temple was a long, hushed dimness forested
with vaulted stone pillars of soaring perfection, stretching upwards to meet the great spreading vault of the
high, arched ceiling. Seated in a single shaft of sunlight at the far end was the great, brooding presence
of the Warrior God, Shaindar. Before Him, on a
raised dias, had been placed the Eyes, and the two
figures seemed to be exchanging information in godly
converse beyond mortal hearing. To either side of
the Eyes, small and insignificant, priests and acolytes
crouched on the flagstone.

The High Priest moved to the wide center aisle
and saluted the God. He turned his head to look into
the deep shadows at the back of the temple. From
the darkness near the priest door that led into the
living quarters, a small darkcrest scurried forward.
"Bring Elsdor to me," Shont ordered.

The darkcrest hurried down the aisle toward the

genuflecting priests at the altar. Shont looked at the priest door again and another darkcrest scuttled forward. "Bring Commander Fenobar's old surcoat from the storeroom, a heavy cloak and provisions for three weeks. Hurry!" The young darkcrest was off like a bolt from a bow. The door into the living quarters opened with a flash of torch light and slammed shut behind him as he disappeared.

The first darkcrest was bending over a priest kneeling somewhat forward of the rest in front of Shaindar's image. The priest leaped to his feet and, casting aside the measured tread of priestly dignity, actually hurried to meet the High Priest. Shont slowly paced up the main aisle between the carved pillars to meet him. Not having been dismissed, Fenobar came along behind.

As Elsdor approached, a hand signal from Shont sent Fenobar back several steps, leaving the two ranking priests of the temple a space for private conversation. Shont spoke softly to his second-ranking priest as he moved toward the altar. Elsdor nodded once, sharply, as Shont finished speaking and stepped to one side, dipping his crest to his High Priest. He retraced his steps to the altar and, calling to two of the older priests to attend him, vanished behind a carved wooden screen beside the God Image, which hid the secret door into the temple treasury.

Shont made his slow way up the long aisle, past the humped, gray-clad backs of the temple priests and acolytes, until he was standing directly in front of his God. He tilted his head back and his dim eyes met the stone orbs of Shaindar.

Fenobar, standing one step behind and to one side of the High Priest, pulled off his war helm and thrust it awkwardly under his bad arm. His attention shied away from the God, with whom he was not on the best of terms, to what lay across the lap of the seated image. It was an immensely old war axe, nearly as long as Fenobar. The double blade had been chipped by a master's hand from a single block of obsidian. No easy task, for obsidian is fragile in its way. Strike it wrong against something and it would shatter into thousands of deadly, knife-edged shards. The bright sun streaming down from the roof and over the God's shoulders struck squarely on the Axe. The conchoidal chip marks along the Axe edge were filled with dark rainbows.

On either side of the God's feet candles were burning, pale leaves of light against the sunshine. Candles had burned at the God's feet day and night since the hour the Axe was put into Shaindar's keeping, a thousand years before.

Shont turned away from his communion with Shaindar and held up his arms. The embroidered tunic winked and shimmered in the light. The priests and acolytes sat back on their heels. Their gray robes made them difficult to see against the general darkness. When Shont was sure all eyes were on him, he spoke. "Hear me, those in the God's retinue! I am the Voice of the Warrior God. As I say, so let it be!"

"So let it be!" the priests answered.

Fenobar mumbled the response softly from his place beside the High Priest.

"This is a time of great trouble for the Clan. You have heard the horns. You know what that means. The priests will go from the Clan also—all but the oldest ten. To those who remain is given the charge of advising the Elder Sister-Group, who will take over the business of the Clan while the King is away. Leave now to make all ready. I will not speak with you again."

The priests and acolytes silently paced away be

tween the tall pillars into the dark at the far end of the hall. A low buzz of excitement erupted as the first rank reached the priest door and filed through into their quarters.

Under cover of the susurration of bare feet against the stone, Shont said softly to his commander, "Black Fentaru is the best King the Clan has ever produced. There is much of your father in you, youngling. You have his faults as well as his strengths. Make them work for you because much is going to rest on you before your duty is finished."

Fenobar, listening to these low-voiced comments, let his grey-green eyes go wide with astonishment. He had never come much in the way of the High Priest, in spite of his duties. He had thought the old warrior, at best, was indifferent to him. Had conjectured that the reason Shont was so insistent that the Temple Commander accompany the Axe was to uphold the honor of the God and the Temple. Now he was telling Fenobar that the responsibility for the Axe lay not with Stells, who was the highest ranking palecrest in the Clan, but with Fenobar.

By this time they were alone in the temple and Shont turned to face Fenobar. "I know you are ambitious for rank and status. You would not be your sire's son if you were not. I also know how these two years in the temple service have eaten holes in your soul. Had you been born with two good arms you would have been the next King of Fen. As it is," the High Priest paused and shrugged his gem-covered shoulders, "Shaindar alone knows what He has destined you for. But it is not temple service." His last words were spoken with a good deal of feeling.

"You are free to make your way in the world now. Listen well to the advice of one who in his time was a warrior. A whitecrest's rise does not depend on his ability in arms. It only helps. The most important thing a whitecrest must have is a wise and loyal palecrest to be his sholstan.

No matter how clever he is, a whitecrest cannot rise in rank without the right kind of help from his sholstan. You have intelligence. Use it to find yourself the kind of sholstan who will give you the help you need."

Fenobar was soaking up these words as if his mind were a dry sponge. Shont was giving him the kind of advice the valued sons of a House receive from the ranking male before an important status fight. Unaccustomed emotion, which he could not name, tilted his crest at a strange angle and closed off his throat, so that he could barely whisper, "I hear and will remember, Most Honored," which is what a youngling answers when his elders have taken the trouble to give him advice.

A flash of light in the depths of the temple announced the opening of the door to the priests' quarters. There was a quick patter of bare feet over stone before they saw the young darkcrest trotting toward them between the pillars with Fenobar's old white surcoat over his arm. He stopped in front of them, saluted the God and bowed to the High Priest. "The provisions are with the Commander's tatarra. The Commander's retinue has come and is awaiting the Commander at the eastern edge of the steps." It came out all in one quick rush.

"Commander Fenobar, I release you from your duty to the temple. Take again the white surcoat of your House." Shont motioned to the darkcrest, who moved forward instantly to help Fenobar remove his harness.

He pulled the grey temple surcoat over Fenobar's head and deftly tossed Fenobar's old white one, with the Black Hand badge on the breast, over the commander's head. A moment more and he had tied it at the sides and removed the tangle of belts and buckles from Fenobar's hand. Within seconds he was straightening the scabbard at Fenobar's back. Finishing with a last twitch to straighten the kalnak at Fenobar's waist, the darkcrest scooped up the gray surcoat and darted away between the towering pillars.

Fenobar watched him leave, a bit limp-crested with surprise at the adroit result of a whirlwind of movement. Unaided, it usually took him a good ten minutes to get into his harness. He was just beginning to wonder why it had never occurred to him to have one of the temple darkcrests help him arm when Shont stepped forward and lifted the Axe off the stone knees. He turned to Fenobar, holding it out in both hands. "Take hold of the portion of shaft between my hands."

Fenobar reached up with his right hand and reverently took hold of the haft. He felt a small tremble in the ancient weapon, for it was heavy, and it was no small task for the old High Priest to hold it out the way he was. Fenobar tightened his hold and took as much of the weight as the High Priest would permit.

Shont looked him in the eye and with terrible intensity said, "The God and I commend the Spirit of the Clan to your care. See it comes to no harm."

"I swear by my honor and by my place among the dead, I will see the Axe to safety." Fenobar meant it with all his heart.

Shont released the Axe into Fenobar's hold and the younger warrior shifted it so it lay on his sound shoulder. The Axe was heavier than Fenobar had expected, but beautifully balanced. Hampered as he was, with his helm still under his bad arm and the Axe on his shoulder, he could not make a proper

salute. He bowed instead, and Shont never realized
it was to the High Priest rather than to the God that
he made this last obeisance.

Time was spinning away from them, and at Shont's
dismissing gesture he whirled about and trotted down
the side aisle toward the stairs, suddenly feeling as if
no further delay dared be permitted.

Halfway through the temple he heard a sound
behind him and turned his head. Another Axe lay on
the lap of Shaindar, and Elsdor was helping Shont
remove the costly embroidered robes he was wearing. A red robe—a sacrificial robe . . . lay draped
across the stone altar in front of the Warrior God. As
Fenobar ran out from between the pillars into the
sunlight, he knew he'd had his last sight of Shont in
this world. It was possible for a High Priest to die of
old age, but it didn't happen very often.

To his left, two hands of mounted warriors waited
at the bottom of the steps where the tall pillars
holding the colonnade roof ended in enormous blocks.
Stells was halfway up the stairs, obviously coming to
look for him. The King's sholstan was big, a hand
span taller than Black Fentaru, his shoulders a shade
wider, his fur just as black and shining. But his crest
was gray and gray also his eyes, a color so pale they
were like twin pools of water. Fenobar had heard
that Stells and Black Fentaru had both been sired by
Fenthath, the old King of Fen, and had had the
same mother.

The big sholstan reached for the Axe with anxious
and proprietary hands, and Fenobar let him take it.
In his short walk through the temple he had already
realized that, one-handed as he was, he could not
carry the Axe and guard it at the same time. And to
use it as a weapon was unthinkable. He could give it
up to Stells without jealousy now, warm with the

inner knowledge that both the God and the High Priest held him in esteem.

As he came down the steps behind the sholstan, Fenobar was aware of being closely scrutinized by the eight waiting warriors. They all bore marks of hard usage from the morning's battle, and he felt the signs of war he carried on his own person were being coolly assessed. Suddenly he felt like the greenest of untried cublins.

But he knew his abilities. *Let us get used to each other,* he thought with an unaccustomed surge of confidence. *They will see how good I am, and once they learn to respect me, I will lead in truth, and not just by the right of the whitecrest I bear.*

Hidden behind the huge pillar footings at the foot of the steps were four laden pack animals and a spare war tatarra. It was a beautiful shade of purple, marked with the darker rosettes that showed it had been bred in the King's stables. Its dainty, cloven hooves were shiny black and as hard as steel. Drawn to it like a magnet, Fenobar reached out his hand and touched the feathery softness of its scales.

"That is your mount, youngling," Stells' deep voice said behind him. "I sent that slug the temple thought a riding tatarra back to the stables."

Fenobar didn't say anything. That casual "youngling" told him clearly just how unworthy Stells thought him to command such a troop. Fenobar might be the whitecrest, but it was going to be Stells who was in control. Or so Stells thought. Fenobar knew how to be patient. Sooner or later Stells was going to learn the quality of the whitecrest he had to deal with. Fenobar shoved his helm onto his head and swung up into the saddle.

The young darkcrest came running down the steps,

holding out an axe sheath and harness of the plainest leather. He pushed it into Stells' hand, gasping, "Here! The new High Priest says you must have this!" Then he was galloping back up the steps and vanished between the pillars.

Stells had accepted it without a blink, and was now slipping the leather over the Axe head and tying it in place.

Fenobar ran his hand down his mount's faintly iridescent neck. The stallion turned its liquid black eyes toward Fenobar and whiffled softly in its throat, a sound of interest.

Stells slipped the harness over his head, where the Axe jostled for space with his sword. Gathering up his reins, he swung up onto his own mount. "We are ready to leave any time, my Lord," he said, cocking his ears toward the other side of the city. "The sooner the better. It won't take long before even That Lump realizes the King is stalling and why."

"We'll use the north postern gate," Fenobar said, putting his tatarra into motion. Stells gave him a glance. It was the kind of indulgent look a grown male listening to a very young and precocious cublin would give. He sighed behind the nosepiece of his war helm. It was going to be a long, long trip.

CHAPTER THREE

Clan Fen dwelled on the plain below the foothills of the yellow Halejek mountains. The Monghanirri royal clan was to the northeast, deep in the heart of those same mountains. Not encountering any stray Chalig to sound the alarm, Fenobar and the little troop of Fenirri warriors plunged into the forest-covered slopes and headed northeast. An hour later, with the first of the red-banded foothills piling up around them, the Fenirri stopped as one accord to look back at their city.

All around the distant walls was the glint of mailed and armed warriors swarming like sheer beetles on a dead carcass. Bags of grain and dried meat were being tossed over the walls to them by the Chalig troops within.

After a time, the Chalig fell back. A single figure on a grey patuz moved out in front of the Chalig warriors and headed west along the river. The Chalig fell into place behind him, one clan after another. A cloud of yellow dust, kicked up by the marching feet, gradually rolled upwards, obscuring their outlines and coating them into uniformity. With distance the whole toiling mass of them merged into the appearance of some monstrous, sluggish centipede.

Fenobar was suddenly exhausted to the core. The fighting he had done that morning along the walls was part of the weariness, but under that was the sheer, unreasoning terror of knowing he was without the power of his clan behind him.

Added to that was the crushing responsibility for the safety of the Axe. Though he did not doubt his ability to get it to Mone, he was just then profoundly grateful to have Stells with him.

Intermixed with everything was a thread of personal grief at the loss of Shont, who had given him, however briefly, the feeling of being valued.

There was a sudden twitch in his bad hand, which escalated quickly into full-scale spasms that shook his whole arm. Afraid the war troop would think he was shaking with fear, Fenobar pinioned it fiercely against his chest and looked around defiantly at the others. Crests in the entire troop were as flat as the crestwells on their helms would permit.

This would not do, Fenobar decided. Flashing his crest to get the war band's attention, he started his mount toward the uplands.

Behind him, still staring down the hill toward the town, Stells said bitterly, "If Peleth doesn't guard his back, I'll have his hide tanned and used for a rug."

There was no doubt in anyone's mind who "he" was. Stells had been sholstan to Black Fentaru since they were cublin together playing in the streets of the women's maze. For Stells there was only one "he."

As the huge black sholstan ranged his mount up beside him, looking so much like Black Fentaru it made his crest twitch, Fenobar asked, "How long will it take us to get to Mone and return?" He wanted to remind them all that this exile was not permanent. After they put the Axe into the keeping of the temple at Mone, they would try to rejoin Black Fentaru. Even walking in the dust among the Chalig was preferable to the almost insurmountable odds of trying to insinuate themselves into a clan not their own.

Stells threw him an enigmatic glance before answering. "It should take us three eight-days. If nothing goes wrong."

They headed deeper into the foothills, and until nightfall, that was the last exchange of words between any of them.

The spring rains had barely started and already the new green shoots were emerging beside the dried remains of last year's grasses. The sere skeletons of rollabout bushes were tangled up in odd corners where the winter winds had left them. They would soon be beaten down by storms to furnish the hairy-leaved yachaboy a place to set its roots and bring into the world those small golden pods which were such a delicacy.

It was doubtful any of the riders noticed these small signs of abundant life. Tired and depressed, they watched their backtrail, and for the rest, kept their unhappy thoughts to themselves.

They followed the Singing Water, a tributary of the Chawnelg river, for four days, until they were at Wifton Notch, the doorway into the Halejek Mountains. Here the Singing Water plunged a hundred feet in a smooth curtain at Wifton Falls.

The Halejek Mountains became increasingly more barren, for the rains that fell this deep among the peaks were few. The Fenirri spent their days scrambling up and down desiccated mountain slopes as they followed the dim trail through a harsh, yellow-hued landscape. Low-growing bushes and gnarled trees with slender dust-green leaves grew sparsely in sheltered ridges. For the rest, the slopes were covered in shale, rocks, pebbles and rock dust. Only occasionally did they come upon some watered place where masses of wildflowers bloomed in vibrant colors.

Sometimes they could ride, but more often they led, pulled or pushed their reluctant lowland tatarra up the arid mountain sides. Only a few days after leaving Wifton Notch, Fenobar had used up his store of invective and was reduced to shouting "move" and slapping his beast on the rump with a leafy branch.

Qurngar, a warrior of middle years, with a merry disposition, surprised them all, especially those who had known him for so many years, by showing an unexpected turn for inspired cursing. There were times during those long days of travel when they would all fall silent and respectfully listen to Qurngar chivying his animal up a trail. Once at the top of a ridge, he would stop, look around at his war mates and dip his crest in acknowledgement of their appreciative hissing. Several of his mates thought so highly of his performance that they voluntarily raised him in status until he was only two places below that of Rondar, who was troop leader under Stells.

For Fenobar the days were not the hard part of their trek. He was, if anything, in better physical condition than the rest of them. Nor was the lack of water anymore troubling to him than to the others. It was the nights they spent sitting huddled in their cloaks around their meagre fire that tried him the hardest. For it was then, more than any other time, that he felt shut out from the fellowship of the war band.

The night after they left Wifton Notch, he sat with the others at the fire. They always left a space to either side of him, even if it meant they had to sit touching shoulders. Suddenly the sense of being apart grew too much for him. Getting quietly to his feet, he walked away into the darkness, wrapping his cloak tightly around him as he did so, for the night was freezing.

Twenty paces away, the fire and the dark shapes around it were hidden by a rocky outcropping. He sat down on a boulder and stared up at the sash of bright stars cutting the sky in half. A little breeze stirred his crest hairs. Over the years the Demon had become so real to him that it took very little effort to summon up his image. The strange shape seemed to hover on the edge of sight. It drifted nearer, and settled on the rock beside him, just out of sight behind his shoulder. The pain around his heart grew bearable. He WAS part of a war band, even if it only consisted of the Demon and himself. Hugging his knees to his chest under the cloak, he said, "I haven't had a chance to talk to you for a while."

The Demon nodded noncommittally. Not having a crest, he had to use head movements like a female. He put one shadowy hand on an equally shadowy sword at his side, an invitation to practice.

Fenobar removed his cloak and drew his weapon. Facing the Demon he saluted and took his stance. The Demon was right-handed, as was Fenobar. He was the only practice partner Fenobar had ever had with whom the sword moves could take on the flowing patterns they were meant to, albeit in reverse.

As he parried and thrust against the insubstantial weapon the Demon wielded, Fenobar, as was his long-time custom, held a running commentary on their performance, suggested alternative moves and spoke of the day's happenings. He was deeply immersed in this routine when a harsh demand abruptly yanked him back to reality. "Who are you talking to?"

The steel-edged voice spun Fenobar around to confront Stells. Not far away stood the black-furred sholstan, face and crest alike rigid with fury. He was holding Fenobar's shield and he slowly turned it around, the little image on the inside glimmering palely in the starlight.

Fenobar straightened up, breathing a little heavily from his exercise, and coolly sheathed his sword. "I imagine you already have some idea or you wouldn't have asked like that." He spoke with deliberate hauteur. He was a whitecrest, by all the gods, and no palecrest, not even Stells, had the right to use that tone to him.

"This is a DEMON OF UNDOING!" Stells fairly spat at him.

"Yes," Fenobar agreed in a dangerously level tone. "I would like to know why you were meddling with my equipment?"

Stells looked a little taken aback, but he wasn't going to let go of his grievance. "How could you bring something like this around the Axe! You know what the demons can do!"

"I know what it is *said* they can do," Fenobar replied evenly.

"Don't try to split hairs with me, youngling. Before those imps of Chaos first appeared on Imkairan soil, life was simpler. The clans were evenly matched, and every male knew his place. It was a better, a cleaner time.

"Then the Demons came. For a time they walked almost hidden among us, only the priests and the kings were aware of their presence. Protected by them, for as the Demons walked they dropped a word here, a word there. Made a suggestion in a willing ear, asked a question. Made the powerful ones think in new ways. Made the powerful even more powerful. And you know the outcome of that. It was in your history lessons at Bokeem."

Fenobar dipped his crest in acknowledgment. "But by the time they withdrew to the Smoking Lands, they had given us reading, writing, the clan schools, improved weaponry, art . . ."

Stells roared, eyes flashing. "Clan was set against clan as males forgot their places and their duties. Males left their own clans, fought their way into others, bringing their own special brand of contagion with them, until our entire race was an uproar. Fighting and mayhem everywhere, because there was no agreement on status for these new things. No acceptance for these new things among the ranking. Why do you think the schools were started? To train younglings? Hah! There was nothing you learned in Bokeem that Black Fentaru or I could not have taught you better. No. It was to contain those with new ideas. To pass judgement on their accomplishments. To control any change unleashed into our world.

"It has taken three hundred years for the fur to settle and the blood to cool. Three hundred years to regain our balance. Three hundred years to forget."

"Three hundred years of stagnation," Fenobar said softly. "Nothing new has ever come out of the schools."

Stells glared at him, visibly reining in his temper.

"We are not going to argue the decisions of the priests!" He shook Fenobar's shield at him. "You deliberately brought this Demon, this agent for Chaos, near the heart of the Clan!"

"It wasn't planned. I had no time to remove it." The words calculated to turn aside Stells' rage, also dared the palecrest to ask why he had such a thing at all.

Speculation had replaced some of Stells' anger. He had not been in charge of training Fen's palecrested warriors without coming to know something of young-lings. So he didn't ask the question. He grabbed Fenobar's left arm instead, pushing up the mail and undertunic so he could see the wrist. It was bare of marks. He dropped it, baffled.

Outraged, Fenobar pushed down the tunic and straightened the mail. "Have you finished your list of insults or did you have more indignities planned?"

Stells' crest twitched in spite of himself. "You sound like your sire." Encountering a burning look, he held up one hand. "No, don't get your crest hairs in a swivet. I don't want to know how far this thing has gone with you, but as long as you are traveling with me you will never call on the Demons . . . and you will get rid of this image." He dropped the shield at Fenobar's feet. "Now!" Without waiting for an answer, he stalked back to the fire.

Fenobar picked up the wood and leather buckler, using his bad fingers this time to trace the outline of the image, and breathed a sigh of relief. He had always known discovery was inevitable. As it was, it had not gone so badly. What would have happened to him if Stells had thought to look on his *right* wrist for the bonding mark? War bands had been known to get rid of unfit commanders. How much easier it would be for Stells to kill him when there was not even a bonding between them to make the act dishonorable.

Finding a sharp-edged piece of stone, for he did not want metal to cut at the Demon, he began, with many apologies, to scrape off the paint. As he bent over the work, it seemed to him that the Demon came once again, to sit just behind his shoulder and keep him company. He brightened. Perhaps he did not need the image to call the Demon.

The war band ignored his return to the campfire. He replaced his shield against his saddle and sat down. The space they left between him and them was wider than before. He laughed to himself, a mirthless twitch of his crest, as he stretched out to sleep.

They moved into the mountain peaks, leaving behind even the short, twisted trees and dried up shrubs. Underfoot was nothing but wind-scoured rock. The mountain plant life tended toward a sparse assortment of camouflaged barbed and sword-edged plants growing among the flaking boulders. Usually, the Fenirri discovered their existence by painful accident.

On the seventh morning after leaving Wifton Notch, they were climbing up a mountain shoulder, with the high peaks rising all around them. Fenobar was pulling his tatarra up a steep-sided ridge, covered with slippery rock chips and patches of paw-like, spine-covered plants. The effort made him dizzy.

Once at the top he stopped, unable to breathe properly, his vision obscured by the spots that were forming in front of his eyes. He sank on one knee, panting for breath. When his sight cleared somewhat, he found himself staring down into a wide

valley filled with misty green depths. Tracing a winding path through the heart of that greenness was the
silver flash of a river. It was beautiful.

He smelled Stells not far away, coming up behind
him, and forced himself back to his feet, trying to
breathe normally. Automatically, his bad hand slid
out of sight under his cloak.

The older warrior came up beside him, breathing
heavily, one mail-clad arm thrown over his tatarra's
shoulders, frankly leaning on the animal. Together
they stared down at the valley and then upward at
the ever-rising peaks, each one larger than the one
in front of it, snow-tipped at their summits. Between
them ran the sharp spines of ridges, like causeways.

From Stells came the first words spoken to him in
six days. "It's going to take longer than I thought to
get to Mone."

Obviously the sholstan wasn't appreciating the
beauty of the wild scenery. Fenobar's heart lifted
ridiculously at these few words, but he kept his crest
still and merely nodded.

Stells pointed his chin toward the east. "That is
Kaymath territory. They are hereditary enemies of
the Monghanirri."

Fenobar switched his reins to his bad hand as he
tried to think of something to say in response. But
before anything occurred to him, Stells straightened
up and, wrapping the reins around one big hand,
pulled his tatarra after him as he started across the
ridge.

Still holding the reins in his bad hand, Fenobar
prepared to follow. The stallion shook his head as a
flying insect buzzed his eyes, roughly yanking Fenobar's
arm to one side. The weak muscles cramped and the
distorted claws sank through the thick leather and
stuck there. Fenobar's crest lifted in a surge of rage

at thus looking so foolish in front of warriors who already thought ill of him. He fought to control his temper as the rest of the warriors moved past him. When safely alone, he brought his hand to his mouth and carefully freed his claws of the leather. Ruefully, he examined the slits they had left. One good yank below that spot and the leather would tear. He sighed, took hold of the reins above the weak spot and started after the troop.

As the thin air took its toll, the warriors spread farther and farther apart. Fenobar let himself lag behind the rest, not caring if he was the last. He plodded along and only looked up as the footing changed abruptly from yellowish rock to gritty black sand and pebbles. He raised his head just in time to see the last of the war band disappearing into a forest of great dark slabs.

He was quite a distance behind the rest when he finally led the stallion among those close-set, towering black blocks. It was as close and as cold as a tomb within the narrow aisles. He heard nothing beyond the crunch of his own footsteps and those of his tatarra. He could not hear the wind, though he could see dust and small leaves blowing over the tops of the walls.

It was like being under an enchantment. He didn't like any part of it. It made him nervous to have to rely solely on his eyesight and nose. He found himself hurrying in a most undignified manner, straining to hear sounds from the retinue ahead, but only the scent of their passing proved to him he was not alone.

He turned a sharp-angled corner, seemingly no different from many others, and saw, to his relief, a slice of sun-bright slope framed between two of the blocks. Eagerly he hurried forward, pulling his stallion with him, intent only on getting out of that confinement. The scent of breeze-borne fesen hit his nose like a blow, stopping him abruptly in his tracks. His war mount bumped into him from behind. The stallion's head stretched over Fenobar's shoulder, black eyes intent on the opening. He knew the scent of battle madness as readily as Fenobar.

Without taking his eyes off that patch of slope, Fenobar reached up to the saddle and took his shield on his arm, his fingers busy strapping it in place before he was fully aware of what he was doing. Sword out, he ran toward the end of the maze. Eerily, he could see and smell warriors fighting and dying before he heard anything. Stells and the troop were fighting for their lives against at least ten hands of strange warriors.

When he left the last of the rocky maze, the world opened up with shocking suddenness into blue and green glare, as he stepped into a snow-fed meadow. From out of the knee-high grass a dark-furred warrior jumped up, sword ready, eyes blank with battle fesen. Fenobar slashed, right-handed, his sword catching the other's weapon. They hung there, shield against shield, and he had a moment to see and recognize the sunburst device on the warrior's surcoat. He was of the Kaymathirri.

Confused to be finding himself facing a sword instead of a shield, the Kaymath stepped back. Fenobar followed, pressing his advantage. Then something rammed into him from behind, shoving him sideways. Fenobar staggered, raising his shield in a fruitless attempt to protect himself. But it was his war mount rising above him, screaming tatarra defiance as iron-shod cloven hooves aimed killing blows at the Kaymath warrior.

Feeling his feet sliding out from under him on the slippery shale, Fenobar let go of his sword to let it hang by the wrist strap and grabbed desperately for the reins dangling from the stallion's head. As his weight came onto them, the leather parted above his hold. As he fell backwards, Fenobar had a glimpse of the meadow pocket filled with fighting warriors, the ever-rising granite mountain wall and an intensely blue sky. There was nothing under his desperately seeking feet but sliding shale, and then there was nothing under his feet.

CHAPTER FOUR

Fenobar was sliding head first down the mountainside on his back. His body hit an easier slope, covered with gravel, and instinctively he flung out his shield. The edge dug into the pebbles and pulled him to a halt, swinging him around.

He opened his eyes, which, somewhere along the line, he had closed. He lifted his head, the movement accompanied by a riffle of disturbed stones sliding past his shoulders. Framed between his downward-pointing feet was a steep slope of slippery gravel that went down . . . and down . . . and down, in a smooth sweep to a cliff edge. And far, far below that was a blue-hazed valley of green trees and verdant meadows.

He thought he heard someone whimpering.

Turning his head ever so slowly, he looked upwards, past a sweep of gravel to smooth rock, rimmed at the upper edge with green. Out of his sight above him they were still fighting because he could hear the clang of sword against sword, war howls and a differently pitched cry as someone was hurt. He had to get back there. His war band was outnumbered. Living or dead the result would be the same. They would be plundered of their arms, and Stells was carrying the Axe across his back.

His good hand was still gripping the ends of the reins and he forced his fingers to turn them loose. His sword was half buried in the gravel, still attached to his wrist by the leather loop. Gingerly he pulled it free of the rocks, the stones falling away past his feet with a roll like death drums. With the tip he dug into the gravel and felt marginally safer.

His bad arm was bent excruciatingly above him. Using the sword, he tried to push himself higher to take the weight off his shoulder. The pebbles gave way under the pressure as easily as slicing through a rotten dilk fruit. His shield was simply not made to support the full weight of a warrior, and this last little tug proved too much for the inside straps. There was a popping sound as the rivets came loose. Fenobar flattened himself against the gravel, digging in sword, fingers and heels. He slipped a few inches and his world thundered to an uneven drumming which he belatedly realized was his heart.

Slowly, at first, against the press of elbows and heels dug into the shifting gravel, he started downwards. Then momentum took over and his slide became ever faster until he was at the core of an avalanche of gravel and rock, enveloped in a cloud of dust.

Suddenly the ground dropped away beneath him and he had a sudden vision of that long, long distance to the hazy valley floor. Then he hit something with bone-crushing force and jammed, while all around him gravel, sand and small rocks continued their slide off the cliff edge. Small rocks and gravel contin-

ued to bounce off his armor, piling up around him,
half burying him as he lay stunned. When the last
trickle of rock slithered past, and a huge silence
reigned, he lifted himself slightly, felt with one bloodied and battered hand at what had stopped his fall,
and discovered he was curled up against a half-buried
boulder. His next thought was for his sword. He had
not let go of it. He could still feel it under his
fingers, but his right hand and arm were buried in
gravel. Painfully he dug his arm out, breathed a
prayer of gratitude to see the sword in one piece,
and quietly collapsed with the hilt against his chest.

When he opened his eyes next, it was dusk. Moving was the most utterly painful experience of his
life; it took all his willpower just to pull himself to a
sitting position beside the boulder. It rocked under
his weight and he felt his heart lurch. He scrambled
back from it, and in doing so, got his first good look
at what lay between himself and a dubious safety.

In front of him, the slope of gravel and small rocks
ended at a steeply tilted shield of bare rock, scoured
clean of everything except cracks. Lose his footing
and he'd shoot off the mountain like a greased glingail
hitting a mud slide.

To one side it was about a hundred foot lengths to
a rock ledge and what looked like a fairly easy climb.
To the other it looked like a hundred and twenty-five
foot lengths to a crumbling, banded cliff, a narrow
ledge and a stiff climb to the top among boulders and
bushes.

"Demon?" He could feel that shadowy figure somewhere beside him nodding encouragement. He looked
at the nearer edge, a bit wistfully, knowing the only
way to safety was to inch his way off the slope on his
stomach, spread out flat like a skinned mardook,

using his toes for support. In that position, with his bad arm even more useless than usual from the mauling it had taken, he could only go in the direction of the longer crawl—the one ending in a wall to be climbed.

He tried to slide his sword into his back sheath, and when he found nothing there, noticed for the first time that most of his harness had torn away during his wild slide. All that remained of his surcoat was a tattered ring of cloth around his neck. His armor was shiny, the rings worn thin along the back, and a few of them had broken. His feet and legs were badly bruised, as were both hands. It could have been a lot worse.

Moving painfully slow, he turned over until he was flat against the slope, with the acrid scent of rock dust in his nostrils. Pushing the pain out of his mind as he had learned to do in battle practice, he started to inch crabwise across the treacherous scree, refusing to look down, refusing to think of the consequences of slipping as small bits of rock turned under his weight, sending him slithering downwards.

Little by little he moved, forcing badly swollen fingers to grope for new handholds. Three hours it took him to traverse that one hundred and twenty-five foot lengths. At the end of that time, exhausted, he found himself against the cliff face. He worked his fist into a deep crack in the reassuringly solid rock and gave a great sigh of relief. The sandstone and limestone layers were rotten and crumbling, forming a kind of stair. "Demon," he whispered, "grant me the strength to climb to safety."

He looked over his shoulder to find a firm place for his feet and felt the blood drain out of his face at the single body length that separated him from a smooth slide into oblivion. His feet scrambled of their own volition against the rock face, found some small support, pushed him upright, and the next thing he knew he was on a wide ledge, lying flat on a thin carpet of leaves and new grass, trembling.

It was well past high noon of the next day before he stumbled once again into the meadow where they had been ambushed.

His noisy entrance through a line of screening bushes disturbed the ker at their grisly feasting. They rose with a loud flapping of shiny black wings, chorusing their indignation in the hoarse calls which gave them their name.

Four of the Fenirri lay there—Balrig, Dinoth, Culmor and Rondar, the second squad leader. The earth was churned and trampled throughout the small area. He looked around him, reading the signs. The Kaymath had been camped here and had been surprised by the Fenirri. The Fenirri hadn't taken all the deaths. There was more blood than could be accounted for by his own dead. It had been a good fight, as to be expected from the best warriors bred to Clan Fen.

The surviving Fenirri, the tatarra, the provisions, and of course the Axe, had been taken away. The Kaymath had not feared pursuit and had left a clear track. He smiled to himself, the merest baring of fangs. Crest jerking, he followed that trail with his eyes. But he was not yet free to start that hunt.

Limping to where Balrig lay, he knelt stiffly to straighten the twisted limbs, and found hidden beneath him his kalnak, the warrior's right-hand knife. He pounced on it with an exclamation of pleasure. His own kalnak had been lost on the scree. He searched, but no other weapon or shield remained behind.

On Culmor's body he found a pouch containing a firestarter. He took Rondar's cloak—it was the least bloody of them all.

From Dinoth he took his surcoat. It was torn and bloody, but the badge on the shoulder was that of Fenobar's House. He did not feel right wearing it, but to wear no badge at all was to proclaim himself outcast from House and Clan. Everything else he had borne, but he would not take that onus on himself. No. He would wear Dinoth's badge and be grateful for it.

He pulled the bodies together. There was no wood to give them a proper pyre. Laboriously, with only his one good hand, and that one much bruised and swollen, he gathered a small pile of dried grass and twigs and set them afire. As they burned he intoned the Words for the Dead, invoking the power of the Axe to lead them through the Void and protect them on their never-ending journey. Having no death drum he used his sword, beating on the blade with a pebble. One-handed, he could not produce the complicated rhythms. He stopped only when the small fire had burned down to ash.

Gathering up the ashes, he tossed them onto the bodies, scattered a few pebbles over them in token of the cairn they deserved, but which he had not the strength to build, and turned away, his duty done as best he could manage. It was fully dark by then, but he would not rest there. He started up the trail the Kaymath had left, staggering with fatigue and the beginnings of fever.

He woke early in the sheltered place he'd found not so very far from the meadow. Thirst drove him to his feet this time. Every step was pure, undiluted misery as his swollen, infected thighs rubbed pain-

fully together. His back was a sheet of fire and his
feet were bruised. But water was not so far away. He
could smell it.

He struggled along over the rocks and slid painfully down the steep side of a ravine. At the bottom,
a knee deep, icy stream chuckled merrily over moss-
covered boulders. With only enough sense left to
drop the cloak well up on the bank where it would
not get wet, he waded in. Little yelps escaped him
as the cold water rose up around swollen limbs and
invaded hot wounds. He drank his fill and then,
finding a convenient rock, slowly eased himself down
on it until the clear water could lave over his thighs.

He rested for a long time, but finally drove himself
to his next task. Taking out his kalnak, he folded the
leaves of the leather and mail skirt away from his
legs. The fur was coming out by the handful, leaving
bare skin along the wounds. Delicately, using the
sharp knife tip, he opened the worst of his sores,
letting blood and other matter swirl away down the
stream.

Time passed. The sun moved through the sky and
the stars reeled overhead. One day or two? He wasn't
sure. When the cold water became unendurable, he
would climb out onto the bank and wrap himself in
the cloak. But the pain always drove him back again.
The pain in his shoulder was something he would
have to learn to accept. He would not, not even to
stifle that agony, lie down in water with his armor
on. And he could not get it off as injured as he was.

He woke in sunlight, calling for his Demon, and
when he realized what he had been doing, wondered
at himself, for he was far beyond the age of asking for
help from another male. But his head, at least, felt
clear, the fever gone. His legs were greatly im-

proved. As he lay wrapped in Rondar's cloak, he heard a rustling among the sparse grasses on the other side of the stream and a brown, furred body moved busily among the rocks, collecting new leaves. Hunger sprang to life from a belly knotted tight with emptiness. His good hand closed over a rock and slowly he lifted his arm. There was a shrill squeal as the rock thudded home and Fenobar rolled to his feet, wading eagerly across the water to collect what he'd brought down.

A plump rock cald lay there, leaves still in its mouth. He snatched at it with eager claws and devoured it there, where he stood. He felt much better when he'd finished. Sucking at a leg bone, he tidily buried the pelt and uneatable feet. As he rinsed bloodied claws in the water he saw a small finor tree growing on the mountainside. All parts of the finor tree were used to make poultices for wounds. Climbing up to the finor tree he scooped up dried leaves and clawed out a handful of dirt from among the roots. Carrying his booty to the stream, he mixed the finor leaves and dirt into a paste and plastered the concoction over his thighs. He spent the rest of the day setting snares. By nightfall he had five more rock calds. Two he ate immediately and the others he scorched over the fire to be eaten the next day.

In the morning his legs were much better. His shoulder still pained him when he moved, but that couldn't be helped. It would be months before those torn muscles healed. He made another poultice of finor leaves and sacrificed the hem of his cloak to wrap around his thighs. After a last deep drink of water, he wrapped his few possessions in the cloak and, munching a cald leg, started off in pursuit of the Kaymath.

It was said that if you took the badge, and therefore the name of another, they would appear to you demanding redress of their honor. But no ghostly presence appeared to reproach Fenobar, stalking at his shoulder, demanding to know why he had stolen another's place in the world. Fenobar was a bit disappointed. He would have appreciated the company, at that point.

Four days later he reached the top of a small rise, and there, spread out before him, was a valley, green and perfect and cut into fields. Against the far end the Kaymath stronghold was backed up against the mountain. He squinted against the midday sun to see it better, for the town had been built of the same yellow rock as the mountains around it and the edges had a tendency to fade into the background.

Alarm at being so close to his enemies sent him off the path, into the scrub. He lay hidden a long time, sniffing the air and watching. It wasn't until dusk that he dared to steal cautiously around the rim of the valley. At daybreak he was on a jut of the mountain face above the town. He climbed out onto a smooth dome of rock, where a crooked tree cast a narrow-leafed, shadowy veil over him.

Stretching out, he settled himself to study the place. The town was built right up against the mountain, around an ancient, hollow, square fortress. Used now as the residence of the King and training ground for the warriors, it lay at the back of the town. Perhaps that fortress had once housed the entire Clan, for inside the square rose the crowns of several tall trees, the remains of a Goddess Garden.

The new Goddess Garden was built far to one side of the town, with a cluster of female huts surrounding it. The shapes of the roofs troubled him until he realized that, unlike the rounded female houses in

Fen, these were sharp-angled, shaped like the mountains around them.

The temple of the Warrior God, Shaindar, lay opposite the Goddess Garden, with the main road, rather like an extended market, running from the main gate straight through the town to the wide portals of the King House.

Prisoners would be kept in the punishment cells, under the King House. Once he found his warriors, he would try for the Axe. But how was he to get inside the Kaymath town? A strange whitecrest walking into the town, no matter how battered, or with what kind of a tale, would only end up in the punishment cells with Stells.

A strengthening breeze brought him beautiful food smells from the cooking stalls in the Kaymath market. Involuntarily his eyes closed as he pictured the darkcrested servants in the barracks at home bringing in platters of steaming meats. His jaws made little biting motions. Swallowing, he opened his eyes and sighed. Gods, but he was hungry!

He thought wistfully of how a darkcrest could march right into that enemy town and not be given a second look. No one noticed a darkcrest, not even other darkcrests. A darkcrest could go right up to the food stalls and buy whatever meats and pasties his whitecrested commander wanted. Fenobar wished he had such a servant here with him. . . . But wishing wouldn't get the sword sharpened.

He turned over on his back, hand behind his head, staring up at the sky through the thin canopy of leaves above him. A trick of memory brought him a scene long ago when he was just a cublin. He had laughingly accused one of Black Fentaru's war band . . . grey-crested Sornel, it was, of being a whitecrest in disguise. Sornel's outrage had been so towering he'd never dared tease a warrior in that way again. Of course, no whitecrest would ever lower himself to the status of a common warrior, no matter how inept he was as a leader. He'd kill himself first.

Certainly no darkcrest could pass himself off as a warrior, no matter how light he died his crest. He simply didn't have the right instincts. But . . . Fenobar's thoughts wandered idly. A whitecrest, with his higher intelligence and training, could pass himself off as a darkcrest, if he could stand the loss of status and rank.

The last thought hung formless in a white fire of inspiration. *Dye his crest?* he asked himself in horror, as his empty stomach tried to curl up into a knot. *Never!* And yet . . . it did answer the problem of how to get into the Kaymath town without getting himself killed. He shuddered, closing his eyes, throwing his good arm across his face, and moaned. If the Demon was responsible for giving him this idea, he was going to redraw the image darkcrested, with a squint in the small eyes.

It did not matter if it was the Demon or the War God who had given him the thought. The idea was there, sitting in his brain like a thousand clawed markik, and refused to be dislodged.

The color of a male's crest was a reflection of what he *was*. How long, he wondered uneasily, would it take before he was caught forever in the slow-moving thoughts of a darkcrest? How long would it take him to lose his warrior skills and fesen?

As stiffly as an old, worn-out warrior he slipped off the rock. His bad hand was twitching and he held it tightly with his other. He did not know where he was going to find the necessary plant dye. Surely the ones he was most familiar with did not grow at these altitudes?

His ears were flat to his skull and his crest was perfectly limp with misery as he started up the trail toward his little camp. He slipped and landed heavily on his good arm. Just in front of his nose was a thrung root. There was no mistaking it. He squinted at it in acute dismay. Once the God has His claws in you, He does it with a vengeance.

Thrung root made things brown. Dark brown. Feeling uncommonly grim, he drew his knife and dug it up.

CHAPTER FIVE

By filling the crestwell in his helm with leaves and mud and then lining it with a corner of his cloak, he was able to use it for a pot. He filled it with water, while setting rocks to heat in a small, smokeless fire. When they were red hot he dropped them into his makeshift pot along with the peeled thrung root. Glumly he stirred the mixture with his knife. When the murky liquid cooled to a bearable temperature, he took a deep breath and plunged his head into it.

Ten minutes later he was a darkcrest.

He felt awful.

Fenobar spent the next hour erasing all signs of his camp, and anxiously evaluating his fesen levels for any sign that they were lessening. He didn't *feel* any different, but perhaps the change took time.

Never would *this* story be sung around the hearth fires. No one would remember that Fenobar the Wrong-handed sacrificed his honor and status for his clan. What he was doing was not heroic, only embarrassing. Great songs were not made of embarrassing moments . . . except the comic ones. He grimaced at the thought of warriors seated around their fires, laughing at his story for the next thousand years.

He tossed aside the leafy branch he'd been using to erase some of the more obvious marks of his presence, and as he did so, the chain and leather leaves of his armor skirt swung forward. He stared down at himself, realizing suddenly that the accumulated woes of this day had not yet ended.

A darkcrest does not wear armor. In taking off his armor—which was going to be sheer agony because of that bad shoulder—he was going to have to take off his undertunic, with its padded left arm. Not since his second year at Bokeem had anyone seen that arm uncovered.

Setting his teeth, he tried to ease out of the armor. That was impossible. No matter what position he took, pain lanced sharply up his back, through his chest, and caught at his heart. He took three long, deep breaths and endured a short, fierce struggle. It ended with the armor in a pile at his feet, half inside out. He was sick and shaking, but it was done.

The linen undertunic would be easier to get out of. It laced up the front and all he had to do was unfasten the ties. But he couldn't move just yet. He slumped down on a rock, fighting nausea, cradling his left arm. Who would think such a twisted, useless thing could cause so much hurt? His good hand rubbed gently at the thin muscles, fruitlessly trying to ease the ache. Finally he got up and slipped out of the undertunic.

He found himself staring down at an incredibly filthy piece of fabric at his feet. How long had it been since he'd taken off his armor? Two hands of days? Or longer? Long enough so that he felt strange without the weight of his mail around him. He started to bundle up the surcoat and paused, spreading it out

on the grass. A nice wide piece of cloth would not
only support his arm, but would serve to hide it as
well. With a little apology to Dinoth, he ripped a
wide strip from the bottom of it and fashioned a
sling.

Making armor and weapons into one somewhat
awkward bundle, he set it on his shoulder. It took
him a while to work his way down the hillside and
into the fields, where a wandering darkcrest would
not look out of place. Following a narrow track beside the river he saw bright squares of material on
the far bank; someone's washing stretched out upon
the cafu bushes.

He looked around, nose working furiously. He was
alone. In a moment he had splashed across the shallow sand banks, snatched up a plain brown tunic of
the kind a darkcrest would wear, and was back among
the thorn bushes, examining his booty. Excessively
pleased with himself, he pulled it on, settled his sling
around his shoulder again, and set boldly out to the
main road. He was a field hand going into town on
an errand for his lord.

Halfway to the road he heard the tinkling of little
silver bells and the patter of hundreds of tiny hooves
behind him. He glanced over his shoulder and saw a
large flock of ghaido, with their herder, coming from
behind a stand of trees. They turned onto the path
and headed in his direction.

This was it. Someone was actually going to see him
as a darkcrest. He gulped, and with every bit of
self-discipline he possessed, kept ears and crest up.
As it turned out, it wasn't the herder he had to
contend with first. A flood of animals overtook him,
and in an instant he was up to his knees in long-
haired, white and tan ghaido. They bumped him

from behind, stepped on his bare toes with hard, round hooves, and milled around him, blatting mindlessly. The air reeked with their hot, musky scent and his mouth started to water.

The herder waded cheerfully through his charges, encouraging them forward with a long stick from which hung myriad tinkling bells, sisters of the little bells fastened to the ear tips of each animal.

Fenobar tucked a shoulder shyly between himself and this blackcrest. On the shoulder of the herder's sleeveless field tunic he bore the Family badge of a running ghaido.

"It's late to be going into Kalbeyo," the blackcrest called cheerfully to Fenobar. "I'd have been earlier coming this way myself, except these children of Tyvai took it into their heads to scatter and not listen to me all this afternoon." His voice changed a bit as he caught up to Fenobar. "You are far from your friends, for I do not think I recognize you."

Fenobar looked into the friendly green eyes, suprised. He'd never heard a darkcrest talk that way before. "I'm from the other side of the valley. I'm visiting Family," he added, giving a toss of his head to indicate the direction from which he'd come. The herder could take it to mean anything.

"So you're related to the Daksall?" the darkcrest asked, openly studying the badge on Fenobar's shoulder. "I see you're a temporary, since they didn't bother to change your badge." Then his eyes went to the bandaged shoulder, the scars on the legs, the limp Fenobar was trying to conceal. In quick sympathy the herder said, "Must be hard, outworking like that. You aren't protected from the warriors like you would be at home." His cocked ears invited confidences.

Uncomfortable, Fenobar muttered, "It's not good to be in the courtyard when the warriors are practicing," remembering a few times in the temple when the warriors, letting fesen rise during practice, had turned on the darkcrested temple servants. None had come to much harm because he had been there to keep his troops to the correct actions.

"Speaking of warriors, do you smell whitecrest around here?" The herder was sniffing the air in long, deep draughts.

Fenobar's heart took a leap and his crest started to stir. Deliberately he flattened it, keeping it firmly under control. He'd never known . . . never . . . that darkcrests could smell the difference between themselves and warriors. He flicked his ears in a laugh, and pointed his chin at the bundle he was carrying. "I am taking the Lord's armor into town to be fixed."

The darkcrest twitched his own ears to show he appreciated the joke. Jingling his stick at the flock, which had started to wander off the lane into the fields, he said, "Our warriors are high on fesen these days, and blind to what their swords damage." He was harking back to what was evidently a favorite topic. "It was not like this when my mother was young. The old King kept his warriors to the line with iron teeth. Not like this cublin who sits in his place! Hunh! He thinks he can dispossess the Monghanirri Royal Clan and not have every Monghanirri clan rising up against us. And all because that Monirri female and her malin sisters refused him as a mate. He calls it dishonor. I call it pure luck of the Good Goddess that he was not accepted, but these snowtops never see things that way. So this madness starts." He shook his head. "Whitecrests gone wrong are worse than any ten troops of fesen-mad warriors."

Fenobar mumbled something noncommittal.

"Of course it would be nice to get some good pastures from the Monirri," the garrulous herder continued. "But it's going to be a high price we'll be paying for them, even though Kaylin has some secret tucked in his crest to help us win."

"Secret?" Fenobar looked around, ears pricked.

The herder laughed in surprise. "You have not heard? Some say it is a demon, and some say it is a great black Axe. At least, that's the newest rumor." He shook his head. "They say this Axe is a Spirit of one of the Monghanirri Clans. They plan to turn it against the power of the Monghanirri tribe and funnel strength from our enemies to our own Clan." He shook his head half ruefully and half proudly. "Puts one in mind of the old stories when warriors made a habit of spirit snatching. But no one's snatched a Spirit in centuries."

"They haven't forgotten how to do it, though," Fenobar commented, a bit more grimly than he intended.

The herder laughed, his crest bobbing happily. Ahead of them, the ghaido were trotting gaily down a side path toward a distant cluster of red-topped buildings. The herder jingled his stick at Fenobar. "Well, this is where I leave you! Farewell!"

Alone once more, urgency prodded Fenobar's steps to a quicker pace. Soon he came to the main road, finding it deeply rutted and uneven underfoot, not much better than the path he'd been on. He moved over into the grassy verge, where the tall weeds whipped at his legs and tangled around his feet. The bundle of armor was growing heavier. No amount of shifting seemed to find a place where something wasn't digging into either his neck or shoulder.

There was some puzzle here, in that the Kaymath King had looked outside clan *and* tribe for mates . . . why? He had been turned down by the Monirri females. Again, why? It was a very high honor to be chosen by a King—even one of a different tribe. But even stranger, Kayrell had not let the matter go, but challenged the Monirri and through them the entire tribe of the Monghanirri in order to regain his status and honor. Why had Kayrell felt so shorn of prestige? It was all very puzzling, but such speculation wasn't going to help him get the Axe back.

While he was lost in thought, he'd come around a copse of trees to find himself in a stretch of lane bounded on both sides by impenetrable hedges. Behind him came the lurching rattle and rumble of a heavily laden wagon. Four heavy draft tatarra came into sight around a curve, pulling a big wagon piled high with boxes and bales. At the reins was a female, and perched beside and behind her were three other females. A Kalbeyo sister-group, Fenobar realized with a gut-wrenching twist of fear. He hid his head behind the bundle on his shoulder until he could get his crest under control.

He did not know how a darkcrest behaved around females. He, himself, had not had contact with any since he was a very young cublin. His bad hand, hanging from the sling, was twitching like a mad thing. He pulled at the fabric with his teeth until those twisted fingers were covered. His rather desperate hope that the sister-group would pass him by with no more than a glance than if he had been a rock, was frustrated at the onset by a friendly hail. The team slowed, matching his pace. One of the crestless females, in a blue pleated tunic, smiled at him.

"So, little brother, you have had a weary way with a heavy burden," she said in a friendly voice, the kind of tone they seldom, if ever, used to the warrior kind.

Fenobar risked a quick upward glance, keeping his crest flat to his skull. If he were discovered . . . A female who chose to use her claws against a male could not be fought, only endured. Immutable instinct demanded the warrior kind never raise a claw or a weapon to a female.

She was waiting, kindly still, but with growing impatience for an answer. He murmured something in a low voice, pitching his words so they were lost in the groaning of the wheels beside him.

"I do think this one must be shy, Marless," the female said to the driver merrily. She leaned from the wagon to touch a forefinger to the badge on his shoulder. "Hard to believe *that* House could breed any such. I've never been so importuned by darkcrests as the day we stayed there."

The other females laughed, and the one addressed as Marless said something Fenobar couldn't quite hear. Fenobar had a cowardly urge to hide, but the hedges closed him in. The female leaned toward him again, asking in a gentle, interested voice, "What is your name?"

Fenobar's mind went blank. No darkcrest would dare have a name that started with the name of a Town, even an enemy town. He shut his mouth with a snap of teeth, gulped and tried again, his mind moving frantically among possible right sounds.

Warriors had names that started with explosive sounds, like "b," "k," "d" and "g." Many also used the "s" or "f" sound, since it was close to a hiss. But none of those would be used by darkcrests. "Hebnor," he gasped out at last. And wondered what tricks his Demon was playing to hand him in his extremity the name for a kind of hand axe.

"Your mother had hopes for you!" the one called Marless chuckled.

Then the female beside Fenobar asked the others, "Shall we let him ride with us? See how tired he looks and how he limps? It is a heavy burden he carries, one armed as he is. You must talk with your sister, Marless, and find out why they permit their darkcrests to be so abused in that House!" She was quite indignant.

The driver pulled the tatarra to a slow walk. "If you can find room in the back, Hebnor, hop on."

Fenobar scrambled for the rear of the wagon as if he were seeking protection from a mountain pumnor's vicious teeth. With a mound of boxes and sacks between him and the too-interested female, his heart finally slowed to normal, but his crest, released from the hold he'd kept on it, twitched uncontrollably for a long time.

He sat swinging his legs off the end of the wagon, while the yellow dust thrown up by the wheels settled on his feet. The fear he had experienced worried him. Could it be that his fesen levels were starting to deteriorate? How long did he have before he turned completely darkcrest? Hidden in the sling his hand started to spasm again, and he rubbed absently at it as he watched the countryside.

The fields grew smaller the closer they came to Kaymath. The eccentrically wandering stone fences that marked their boundaries threw long, fantastic shadows across the growing grain as the sun grew closer to the horizon. The rhythm of the jolting slowed, and he craned his head around to see they had reached the town walls. Two hands of humorless guards were preparing to close the gates for the night, and impatiently waved them through, giving Fenobar only a cursory glance, thinking he was with the females.

Fenobar studied Kaymath's defenses with professional interest. The city's main portal was an old-fashioned single gate guarded at each side by a high stone tower. Easy to break through. The walls, too, were neither as high nor as thick as those of Fen.

Moments later he was surrounded by the busy life of Kaymath as the wagon rolled up the main street. Some shops were still carrying on business, but most of them were closing up the fronts for the night. Food vendors hawked their savory meat pasties at every corner. Warriors lounged in front of their House, eating. All reassuringly normal.

The sister-group was craning their heads this way and that, looking up the side streets, searching for either someone or some place. Fenobar figured he'd better leave before they found it. He hopped off the wagon when it turned into a narrow side street. With his burden on his shoulder he still managed to be unobtrusive as he slipped between two empty wagons and a stall, to become just one more darkcrest going about his business.

It was starting to rain; the soft, persistent rains of Spring. A cold mountain wind had come with the rain, whipping around the corner where Fenobar had taken shelter under the roof overhang of a shed near the King's kitchen. From where he leaned he could watch the servants and guards hurrying in and out of the yellow square of light that marked the open kitchen door.

He had hidden his armor in the smithy near the

stables. The fires had been banked for the night and no one would come near until the smith started work again in the morning. By then Fenobar would either have recovered his war band, the Axe and his armor . . . or he would never have need for any of them again.

Fragrant cooking aromas swirled past his nose, and somewhat to his disgust, set him drooling. Blotting his mouth on the sling, he tried not to think about what bliss it would be to bury his face in a plate of chopped liver. He stayed where he was, and not much later his patience was rewarded when several groups of darkcrests entered the courtyard on their way to the kitchens. Fenobar could make out at least three different House badges and there were very likely more. He'd been counting on that—that even in this alien tribe the Houses and Families were responsible for seeing any of their people who were in the dungeons were fed. The King would provide the food, but the Houses had to show their responsibility for the actions of their members by taking it to them.

He pushed away from the damp wooden wall, quietly following them into the bright light, heat and clamoring business of the vast kitchen with its four great ovens, and the three fire pits running down the center. Between ovens and fire pits were the long tables, piled high with cooked meats and breads. Cooks and helpers worked at the tables, hovered over the cavernous ovens. Kettles steamed, meats roasted, cleavers flashed in the light and came down in rhythmic thunks. Overpowering smells mingled with voices indistinguishably rising and falling like sea waves against a beach.

He joined a line, picking up a tray in his strong right hand, awkwardly using his crippled left to set the filled dishes onto it. The darkcrests he was following took their heavily laden trays and made for an inner doorway giving into a side corridor. He followed after as they all turned left. The hall ended in a heavy, brass-bound door. The first of the servants reaching it turned and hit it with his shoulder. It swung open on silent hinges and a stench poured forth into the hallway. Only one thing produces such an unsavory upwelling of foul odors . . . the dungeons. Mindful of their burdens, the darkcrests picked their way carefully down a flight of winding steps which were badly lit by torches set into iron wall rings.

A cold blast of air snapped Fenobar's attention in the opposite direction. Rain gusted across the flagstones as two warriors wrenched open the outer door and stamped into the building. They leaned their war pikes against the wall while they removed their leather rain cloaks. The taller of the two, with a brownish crest, said, "I tell you, Dagess has it in for us. Name me two other warriors who have stood guard as often as we have in that mud patch they call an outpost."

"It is because of those Fenirri in the lower level," the other said, "Kayrell is afraid Monghan clancrests will try to get them out."

"Bah! The Monghanirri don't even know we have them. If you ask me, it's something else he's afraid of. . ."

"Like what?"

"Like what might try to free that *thing* he has in the second level."

"Bah! You've been listening to Parnath again. Beerpot fancies! Kayrell has some prisoner he's keeping secret and suddenly everybody thinks there's a monster down there."

Several darkcrests had come up behind Fenobar and were protesting the way he was blocking the hall. The warriors looked around at the small commotion and the taller one snapped, "Here, you! What are you listening to! Begone!"

Fenobar forced the instinctive snarl off his lips and moved toward the dungeon door, forgetting the obligatory submissive crestbob which was a warrior's due. The darkcrested servants, frightened at what they saw as his defiance, hurried him forward as quickly as possible before the warriors became aware of the omission and decided to do something about it.

Fenobar turned a deaf ear to their scolding, his attention on the food he was holding. There he was with all that food under his nose and unable to pop a single succulent morsel into his mouth. Even the smell of the dungeons couldn't curb his appetite as they passed through the narrow door and started down the steps. He added this torture to the list of grievances he was already holding against the Kaymath.

At the bottom of the steps was another door, heavily bound with iron, but with a small, barred window set in the upper half. It was open, and inside the guard room four warriors crouched around a dicing grid scratched into the flagstone floor. Helms had been laid aside and weapons were sheathed. Crests bobbed over intent faces as the players called encouragingly to the dice, patting at the stone floor in supplication to the Gods of Luck. Engrossed in the game, they ignored the line of darkcrests passing through the guardroom to the first-level holding cells.

Although the smells had been getting progressively worse, Fenobar was unprepared for both the sound and heavy stench which now assaulted his senses. "Waugh!" he cried involuntarily, and shoved his face into the sleeve of his stolen tunic.

A darkcrest grinned, not unkindly. "You must be new to this duty. This is nothing. Wait until you must bring food to the second level."

There were only two holding cells, one on each side of the room with a wide corridor between them. They were full of warriors, rival retinues, hurling vocal abuse at each other. The darkcrests were spreading out, ignoring the noise and handing their bowls of food in through the bars to eager hands.

Fenobar drifted to the far end of the room, where he'd seen another door. It was closed, but unbarred. Peeking in through the small window, he saw an unoccupied guard post with the door on the far side standing wide open, showing part of a flight of badly lit steps. Beside him a warrior was cursing his slowness, demanding to be fed. He shoved his tray of food into clawing hands. In the moment of surprised silence when the warrior found himself clutching a tilting tray, he grabbed up a dish for himself, opened the door to the lower levels and slipped through.

The heavy door shut behind him, muffling the din in the upper level. Three strides took him to the opposite door and he stood there a moment, listening, before taking a deep sniff. "Waugh!" he cried for the second time, and stuck his nose into his armpit. The darkcrest had been right. The smell *was* worse down here. But that wasn't going to stop him from eating . . . and then, with a fingerful of minced meat at his mouth, he realized he couldn't clean his bowl down to a shine because he needed the food as an alibi in case he ran into any guards. They would not question a darkcrest with a full food bowl, but one carrying around an *empty* dish was going to be highly suspicious.

He sighed dolefully, feeling profoundly sorry for himself, and started down the steps. His ears swiveled first one way and then the other as he listened for the guards. At the foot of the stairs was another corridor lined with small cells. Each cell was a granite cubicle with an iron-bound wooden door and a small barred window set into it. At wide intervals a torch was set into holders so that the passage was dimly lit. He didn't bother looking in at any of the cell windows. His Fenirri warriors were not being kept here. The guards had said the lowest level. If this were the lowest level it would not be called the second level. Quickly, Fenobar ran the length of the passage, looking for another flight of steps leading down.

At the far end, the corridor branched left and right. He flattened himself against a cell door and stealthily peered around a corner of roughly hewn rock. To the left, the hall passage ended in a low doorway with a set of stairs leading downward. It looked as if it had been cut right out of the bedrock. To the right was another of those double-doored guard rooms. Feeble torchlight from the open door did little to lighten the general gloom of this side hallway. The light shifted unevenly, casting weird shadows as guards moved in the room beyond, out of Fenobar's line of sight.

There was the steady clicking of one of the interminable dice games so loved by the warriors. A mutter of conversation lifted for a moment and died.

Fenobar chanced a look around the corner, saw no one, and sped lightly for the steps. Flattening himself to the curve of the stairs, out of sight of the open guard room opposite, he stopped to listen and catch his breath. He dared to stick his head around to check the guardroom. The back wall of the guardroom was an open barred cell, and in the deep darkness behind those bars came a shuffle of movement and the clank of a chain as something large stirred in the piled straw. There was an odd scent, like fermented sajawa juice, running under the pervading stench. A pair of long-fingered, pale hands gripped the bars and behind them, a strangely shaped but familiar outline, as *something* watched him. A guard cursed the prisoner, beating on the bars with a war pike until it moved back into the shadows.

CHAPTER SIX

He sank down on the steps feeling as if all the wind had been knocked out of him. *It couldn't be.* Yet it was. A Demon. In the flesh. Alive. Here.

He looked down at the bowl of food in his hand and pushed it into a corner. He wasn't hungry anymore. Scrubbing his good hand through his crest, he tried to figure out where his duty lay, and what was expected of him. It did not matter that he had never thought to see his Demon—or any Demon, for that matter—in the flesh. His hand began to jerk. Nevertheless, he should have suspected it would happen sooner or later, the Demon being what He was.

One thing was abundantly clear. Fenobar had taken the white-crested, blue-eyed Demon as his Ranking Commander. He owed him an under-commander's duty. Since the creature in the cell was a Demon, if only a darkcrested one, he had to assume it had been sent to him for a reason.

He hunched up, pulling absently on his crest and staring sightlessly down the gloomy steps. The Demon was his. What he did with the creature might change history for all time. If that was so, then it would have to be carefully guided so it would do as little damage as possible. He was determined the one thing it was not going to do was run amok, spreading change wherever it turned. He had had plenty of practice second-guessing his Demon. If anyone could handle a Demon it would be him.

He gathered his feet under him and looked down the long flight of uneven stone steps, to where they disappeared into absolute blackness. The world and responsibility for it was awaiting him . . . but first, he needed a torch. Cautiously, he peered around the corner again. It was still clear. Moving as silently as a hunting pumnor, he removed one of the torches burning in a wall ring just outside the guardroom. He knew the prisoner could see him, and dared to bob his crest at that dark cell in acknowledgment of the prisoner's silence.

The rough-cut steps grew progressively slimier as he descended. His toe claws scrabbled for a hold on the uncertain footing, leaving scratches which quickly filled with water. Halfway down, Fenobar let out a breath he had not known he had been holding, took another and gagged. The air here was thick with a miasma which made the upper levels smell like a flower garden. It was a foulness made up of old death, decay, and raw sewage. He buried his nose in his armpit and tried not to breathe. His crest could not go any flatter, and he wondered how his warriors could still be alive, breathing what passed for air down here.

With his torch held high he continued down, into the profound darkness. The place was alive with the gentle sound of moving water. The flickering light gleamed along the walls in wavering streamers. Icy rivulets running silently down the rock picked up the glow, carrying it with them across the steps and down again into the all-consuming dark, out of which came the steady, quiet plinking of water droplets falling into a puddle.

From out of the stygian depths Fenobar heard a voice . . . a snatch of dolorious song . . . and stepped off the last step into two inches of ice-cold water. He gave a startled yelp and the singer stopped. A fist beat on a thick wooden door and a deep voice, one Fenobar knew well, shouted, "Let me out of here! I demand to speak to the King. I challenge for right of passage!"

Fenobar slogged through the black water, in which floated formless lumps. Inadvertently he stepped on one and it turned into disgusting mush under his toes. He tried not to think about it. Finding the right door, he shoved the torch into the ring on the wall saying, "Save it, Stells. It's only me."

"My Lord! Is it you in truth?" Stells' astonished, black-furred face pressed up against the small, barred opening in the door. Light-grey eyes squinted painfully against the feeble light from the torch. "We saw you go off the mountain and thought you were dead!" Behind Stells the surviving members of the war band crowded up. Fenobar could just make out an ear here, an eye, a chin, a line of jaw in the dark.

"It will take more than falling off a mountain to kill me," Fenobar replied a little airily, fumbling at the heavy wooden beam securing the cell. The wet had warped it badly and it would not move under a one-handed grip. "Can you fight if you must?" he asked, crouching to get his sound shoulder under it.

"Yes," Stells replied grimly. "Qurngar is wounded in the leg, but he can still walk. Exdem is coming down with a fever."

"I can still fight," Exdem said shortly.

"Pelgir and Gartol only have nicks in their hides, as do I. But no wounds that could keep us from raising a sword."

It would be a while before Fenobar realized he was getting a field report from the King's sholstan, tactfully giving him his due as commander. At the moment, more than half of Fenobar's attention was on trying to free them. The bar was clinging stubbornly to its position. Gritting his teeth he pushed upwards, disregarding the awakening, throbbing pain in his back as torn muscles protested this use to which they were being put.

Stells fell silent, watching him struggle with the bar, not knowing, perhaps, if the slightly built Fenobar would be able to free them.

Slowly, slowly, the wood gave way to him. Then with a shriek like a diving gayun bird, it gave way altogether. There was a new jangle of pain. Fenobar reached his hand up to his sound shoulder to find splinters from the rough wood that had found a new home in his hide. He pulled them out while Stells and the war band stepped warily from their prison, into the corridor, looking toward the upper floor.

As nearly as he could tell in the dim light and shifting shadows, they looked thinner and tired. Their armor had been taken from them, of course, as well as undertunics, and their fur looked matted and unkempt. But their eyes were alight with battle fesen, only thinly held in check. Crests were held at a dangerous tilt and sharpened claws shone palely from the tips of fingers.

They were not just ready to fight, they needed to fight. Fenobar would have to find them an opportunity soon or he would lose them to battle madness.

Stells reached up and took the torch out of the ring, whirling it around his head to bring it back to momentary life. The war band stood grouped around their commander in silence. It was shock which held them still.

"What happened to your crest?" Stells asked, horrified.

"The War God demanded it of me," Fenobar snapped defensively. "It was the only way I could get in here. You just called me 'my Lord' a moment ago. Does a dyed crest make me any less a warrior?" Even as he said it he realized his mistake in asking such a thing and hurried on. "Where is the Axe?"

"It's at the temple. They are using it to drain the power from the Monghanirri as Mad Thenorig was going to do." Stells snarled, his free hand curling into a clawed weapon.

Fenobar felt his heart freeze. "N-Not already! They haven't started already?"

"Peace, my Lord. They were to start the ceremony tonight. They were waiting for the right portents."

"Then we can still be in time!" Fenobar splashed back through the water to the steps, his war band coming along in a murderous phalanx behind him. At the top of the stairs he paused to reconnoiter, with Stells peering over his shoulder. The quiet guardroom had changed. It was full of warriors, whose surcoated backs were wet with rain. The scent of damp fur was added to the generally foul atmosphere.

The Kaymath had their attention focused on the prisoner in the dark cell. A clear, arrogant voice was saying "So . . . this is what Kayrell and the High Priest hold so important in our fight with the Monghanirri! An ugly-looking thing. Come . . . have it out. They are going to sacrifice him in the ceremonies tonight!"

Above Fenobar's head Stells growled, stirring

Fenobar's crest with his hot breath. Fesen scorched the air, and all about him was a subtle stirring, telling Fenobar as clearly as if he'd turned to look that claws and crests were flexing nervously.

A Kaymath warrior grunted heavily, stirring through straw as he chased something around the dark cell. "My Lord, the thing won't hold still!"

"It makes no difference what shape it is in for the ceremony as long as it isn't totally dead," the arrogant voice said. "Hit it!"

There was a shout of surprise and the unmistakable crack of breaking bone. "He's dead, my Lord," someone said in a low, awed voice. "It has broken Kedred's neck." The warriors surged forward, trying to draw their swords, but finding themselves hampered in the confined space. "Stand back! I'll handle this!" the commander ordered.

In a smooth rush, the Fenirri came up out of the stairwell. Fenobar came first, darting into the room with crest erect and battle lust pounding through his veins, bad arm and muscles forgotten. He'd left his sling lying in tatters in the corridor. He reached around almost caressingly and ripped the throat out of the warrior in front of him. He had the Kaymath's sword in his hand before the body hit the floor.

Even as the warriors were turning at the scent of fesen, the Fenirri exploded into the room in an orgy of killing. When they finished, eight Kaymath warriors lay dead on the floor. Two still lived, and they were both inside the cage with the prisoner. One was palecrest and the other the arrogant whitecrest. The Kaymath commander was waiting, sword in hand.

Perhaps it was the shock of seeing what appeared to be a darkcrest coming at him, fesen high, which slowed the whitecrest's first response, for in truth, Fenobar was in no condition to have won. There was a sharp flurry of traded blows, and then the whitecrest was down with a cut throat. Mindful of the other warrior in the cage, Fenobar didn't wait for the whitecrest to die, but whirled around, in time to see a hairless white arm encircle the remaining warrior's neck. Long hairless hands grasped at the jaw and back of the head. There was a sharp snap as the warrior's neck broke. The body was let loose to fall to the straw.

Fenobar found himself face to face with the legendary being. This Demon was a darkcrest, only a bit taller than himself though built as heavy as Stells through the shoulders and chest. The shoulders were wide, but shaped oddly—bulbous, without the smooth sloping of an Imkairan's shoulders.

The hairless upper torso was covered with red scratches. Its only garment seemed to be a very dirty pair of breeches, like the kind the lortel merchants from the far south wore, only not quite as baggy. On his feet were some kind of leather foot protection. This close, the scent of fermented sajawa was overly strong, but Fenobar didn't figure he himself was smelling any sweeter.

From under lank brownish head fur, the Demon was returning Fenobar's scrutiny out of small, narrow eyes set in a flat face. The narrow hands, with their five clawless fingers, were not nearly as long and sinuous as Fenobar had painted them on his shield.

Then Fenobar looked down at the body of the Kaymath warrior with his twisted neck and raised his sword in salute, but the Demon took the movement for menace and stepped quickly backward, hands raised, falling into an unmistakable fighter's crouch. There was no clashing of iron links as he did so. The Demon was free of his chains, and by the look of him, determined to remain that way.

Stells came up beside Fenobar in the doorway, looming large and black. For the first time the sholstan got a good look at what the cage held and choked. "By the Gods, a Demon of Undoing! No wonder the world has gone wrong! It should be killed!" He pushed Fenobar aside, sword out.

"No!" Eyes flashing, Fenobar stared up at Stells, Ranking Palecrest of Fen, and his sword was at the sholstan's black throat. Battle fesen was still high in him and climbing higher as he read contempt in the pale eyes. He had given up too much, gone too far. This is where it ended. He was whitecrest commander or he was dead.

Something of his suicidal determination must have communicated itself to the sholstan, for Stells stepped back.

Breathing heavily, Fenobar caught at his control and sought for reasons to convince Stells. "This is just the sort of situation Tyvai, the God of Chaos, delights in. Would you turn Him against us by killing His servant?"

"You are on terms with Tyvai and His servants, are you now?" Stells' deep voice held a sneer. "I have always relied on the Warrior's God, who is honorable in His dealings with His Own."

"Honorable?" Fenobar nearly screamed. "You call *this* honorable?" and he thrust his twisted left arm in Stells' face. "What right has Shaindar to do this to a cublin, and then turn His face from that cublin? All my life I have had none to aid me—not sire, not warriors, not war band, not House, not Shaindar. Only the Demon of Undoing saw my worth and took me as an ally. That I live, that I am a warrior, I did myself, by being twice as good as the others. And you, you stupid palecrest, can see no further than a crippled arm!"

"You called the Demon into existence and ruined Fen!" Stells roared back.

"I never called on the Demon from the day I left the gates of Bokeem, because I knew what he could do and I did not wish that on Fen. No, not even the day Black Fentaru sold me into the temple did I ask the Demon to act for me!" Every hair on Fenobar's body was standing erect and his crest was shaking in time to his passionate words. But his sword was steady, held only inches from Stells' throat.

"You didn't give it up," Stells accused.

"You would have me dishonor myself?" Fenobar snarled.

"You are already dishonored, you with your right-hand tricks!" Stells snapped back.

"You expect me to use left-hand tricks like you do?" Fenobar yelled, shaking his twisted fingers in front of Stells' face. "I didn't survive Bokeem by being stupid! I'm not weak, either! I got here to save your hide, didn't I? The God and the High Priest put the Axe into *my* care and we *are* going to save it any way it takes, even if it takes a Demon of Undoing!" He paused, gasping slightly, to take a breath.

The Demon broke the silence by clearing his throat. In a deep, burring voice he said, "Look, if you two are arguing over me, I can always leave."

"YOU STAY RIGHT THERE!" Fenobar ordered. Turning back to the sholstan, his tone ominous, he said, "Well?"

Stells was staring at the Demon, mouth agape. "It talks . . ." he said weakly.

"Of course it talks. Did you think it would waggle its ears in code?" Fenobar snarled, admirably hiding his own surprise.

Stells straightened up, took a deep breath. "You seem to have grown up." He pushed Fenobar's sword aside with two fingers.

"Falling off a cliff always has that effect on me," Fenobar agreed, stiffly.

"I'm glad it wasn't dying your crest that did it," Stells replied wryly. "Just how are you going to use the Demon to regain the Axe?"

"You heard the whitecrest say they had come to fetch the Demon to the temple. We dress up as the Kaymath and, taking him with us, we enter the temple. Once there we should have no trouble in rescuing the Axe?"

"As easy as that?" Stells flicked his crest in derision. "In case you have not noticed, we are short by two, the number of guards sent to fetch the Demon to the temple."

Fenobar shrugged. "How close will anyone count when they have such a thing as that to stare at?" He tilted his crest toward the Demon.

"Cublin courage," Stells replied disparagingly. "Yet it might work, considering the nature of the thing." They both turned to look at the Demon.

"I would really prefer not being a sacrifice," the Demon said politely. "No matter how worthy the cause."

"You are not going to be sacrificed," Fenobar said, testily. "We're using you as the key to get inside."

"And what happens when you grab this Axe and leave me behind to discuss the situation with the priests?" the Demon demanded.

"We're not leaving you behind," Fenobar replied impatiently. "You are coming with us."

"Why would the priests want to use a Demon of Undoing for a sacrifice?" Stells asked suddenly, still staring at the alien being.

"I've been asking that question myself," the Demon said, folding his arms and leaning against the wall.

Fenobar stared suspiciously at the Demon. The creature was not acting like a darkcrest. Grimly, Fenobar turned his shoulder to the Demon, putting him in his place, and addressed his remarks to Stells. "As a servant of Tyvai, the Demon would be used to carry the news of the defilement of our clan Spirit to the God of Chaos. Tyvai will then break the bonds which hold the tribe together. With no place for the clan power to go, it would be simple for the Kaymath to shift that power through the Axe and funnel it into their own clan Spirit."

Stells' eyes flicked to Fenobar and back to the Demon. "Why would this servant of Tyvai wish to aid us?"

"Because you are going to take me with you when you leave," the Demon said, speaking for himself.

"You are a darkcrest, yet you talk with a warrior's boldness." Stells' eyes narrowed in distaste.

"These two didn't die of fear." The Demon stirred one of the dead Kaymath warriors with a foot, and with more than a hint of mockery.

A pang of foreboding went through Fenobar. Controlling this Demon might be more difficult than he suspected. He was already on the verge of challenging Stells. "Of course he talks like a warrior. He is a warrior," Fenobar said hastily.

"With *that* head?" Stells asked contemptuously.

"All the Demons are warriors, no matter what color their fur," Fenobar defended staunchily, lying for all he was worth. "Just as all females are . . . female . . . no matter what color their fur. It is a . . . a result of being a servant of Tyvai that they do not hold to the crestcolor like the Imkaira."

Stells was silenced but he looked unconvinced. "We'd better be getting out of here." He turned to see how far Qurngar, Exdem and Peligir had gotten in stripping the dead. The war band had been working silently, in an effort to hear every word.

Qurngar motioned to the armor they'd taken off the dead Kaymath commander. Stells held up the undertunic, examining it critically. "This material is soft but awfully thin. It wouldn't have lasted long if he'd actually done any fighting in it. The armor seems sound enough, but it has too much embossing on it for my taste. It's going to be a little long for you, but . . ." He shrugged as he held it out to Fenobar.

Propping his sword against the cage bars, Fenobar started to struggle out of his darkcrest tunic. To his surprise, Stells pulled off the tunic for him and then proceeded to help him first into the fine undertunic, and then into the whitecrest's armor, as if it were the most natural thing in the world.

The mail was tight across the right shoulder. Stells solved that problem neatly by popping a few of the rivets holding the rings together with the point of a kalnak.

By the time Fenobar was finished dressing, the rest of the Fenirri warriors had found armor to fit them as well as cloaks to cover the telltale bloodstains. By liberally daubing surcoats with filth from the dungeon, they would be able to conceal the scent of fresh blood and their different body smells. The wide noseguards on the helms effectively concealed their faces. It would work, Fenobar thought tensely, if they kept moving and didn't let anyone get a good sniff of them . . .

The Demon had come to the open cell door and was leaning against the bars, closely listening and watching.

Stells dropped the whitecrest's helm over Fenobar's head. It was too big, and the ear guards were forcing his ears into a sideways crink that was going to become very painful, very shortly.

Stells stood back to survey the effect and shook his head. "We're in trouble. It's that brown crest you're sporting." He took the helm off and ruthlessly flattened Fenobar's crest before replacing it. He nodded down at the dead Kaymath commander. "Exdem, shear his crest and stuff it into the crestwell."

"It will not stay," Fenobar objected during this operation. "I will trail whitecrest hairs at every step, until by the time we reach the upper levels, it will be as sparse as a priest's."

The Demon stepped forward, reached out a long, hairless arm, and scooped up a clump of white hairs which had already fallen on Fenobar's shoulder and began twisting them together. A few seconds later he held out the hair with a small braid at one end. Fenobar shrugged and started to walk away. The Demon's hand came down on his shoulder, and with his other hand, plucked the remainder of the crest out of the crestwell.

"What are you doing!" Stells roared. "Put that back!"

The Demon ignored him, working at the long white hairs, braiding the ends together. He held out the fat braid to Fenobar. When Fenobar did not move, the Demon jammed the twist of hair into the top of the helm Fenobar was wearing.

Fenobar swung toward him, his hand going for his sword, while Stells started forward wrathfully, but Fenobar waved him off. "I think he's got something here." Gingerly, he reached up a hand to feel at the loose twist.

The Demon felt it too and grimaced. "That won't hold. Take off your helm."

Unaccustomed to being ordered about by one his

very genes persisted in thinking of as low status, Fenobar was half minded to take offense, and then remembered his hasty words to Stells about the Demon being a warrior. Slowly he did as he was bid and stood uneasily as the Demon ran his fingers through Fenobar's crest.

Paying no attention to the jerking crest under his hands, the Demon began to twist, divide and wrap, and when he as finished, Fenobar's dyed crest was braided flat to his skull and the white twists were woven into it in such a way as to stand almost straight upwards. It was not perfect, by any means . . . but it would pass.

But to have his crest tied down like that . . . Fenobar's crest jerked in dislike and his entire scalp pulled painfully. His ears went down.

Between Stells and the Demon's long, clever fingers, they managed to get the helm on Fenobar's head and the white crest hairs pulled through the crestwell to Stells' critical satisfaction.

They were ready to go. With a cloak around the Demon to disguise the fact that his hands were unbound, they left that fetid level with relief. Boldly, Fenobar led the way up the stairs to the first level. The guardroom there was still empty and, setting his head at an arrogant tilt, Fenobar pushed open the door and strode out into the first level, between the two long cages. The darkcrests were just gathering up the last of the food bowls and piling them onto trays. Fenobar felt a slight shock. Had all that had happened below taken such a short time?

All too aware of the missing guards, Fenobar commenced swearing foully. Turning his head to look back down the empty stairs, he shouted, "If you must fall in the filth and bespatter us all, then stay there where you cannot offend anyone! Do not come next or nigh me until the stench is out of your fur and the memory of your clumsiness is dimmed by time. Say, five or six years!"

He whirled, striking out at his retinue, snarling obscenities at warriors too slow to move out of his way, and paced rapidly down the length of the dungeon level. If any there thought there was something different about the whitecrest commander—that he was a bit short, perhaps—there was no one there who cared to challenge a fesen-high whitecrest. They stood clear, guards and servants alike, turning their eyes aside so as not to attract his attention.

As he reached the guardroom, the warriors leaped to attention, all signs of the dice game removed. Fenobar snarled in passing, "By Shaindar's rump this place is filthy!" Then he and his retinue were through and on the steps up to the kitchens before the Kaymath warriors dared to breathe, much less glance in their direction.

They were nearly to the upper level, just a few steps more to go, when the door opened suddenly and a warrior stepped through. He flashed a startled look at the enraged whitecrest just below him and leaped back into the corridor, flattening himself against the wall as they swept past.

Without pausing, Fenobar led the way past the kitchen, where all was still a blaze of light, heat and commotion. The handle to the outer door was in his good hand. It opened effortlessly. They were out of the building, only to find themselves in a dark, constricted courtyard where on either side narrow, winding steps led up to the courtyard wall. Without slackening his pace, Fenobar strode for the far end, holding his face up to the cold, misting rain and breathing deep draughts of clean air. A gate led into a larger courtyard where guards patrolled the wall above them. An open postern gate led into the city. Within seconds they were striding down a narrow lane between the walls of Male Houses, heading roughly toward the temple.

When they were out of sight of the guards, Fenobar turned into a blind alley. Leaning against the blank side of a House wall he said, "I would never have believed it could be that easy." All eyes turned to the Demon, who shrugged.

Fenobar handed his cloak to Stells and pulled at his surcoat, until that big warrior grasped a handful of the skirt and pulled it over his head. Within moments they had all shed their reeking outer garments. Smelling infinitely better, Fenobar set off at a quick trot, doubling back through the empty streets until they were at a side entrance near the warrior barracks, within the King's compound.

"What are we doing here?" Stells hissed when he realized where they were.

"Myyajmor is in the smithy," Fenobar replied, nodding his head toward a dark building, not far away.

Stells muttered under his breath but didn't try to stop his commander. He knew what Bokeem-won armor meant to the whitecrested kind.

The rain, which had been only a gentle mist, started coming down harder as Fenobar slipped away into the darkness. He reappeared shortly with a cloak-wrapped bundle under his arm and his own sword, once again in the sheath across his back. Thrusting the bundle at the nearest warrior, he turned to the Demon. "Here," Fenobar said, holding out his Kaymath sword and sheath.

The Demon took them from him hesitantly; stood holding the harness a bit helplessly, as if he didn't quite know what to do with it.

"Put it on!" Fenobar ordered, and gusted an annoyed hiss as the Demon somehow became entangled in the straps, trying to comply. He moved to straighten the harness for him, pulling the cloak over all when he was finished.

Qurngar, meanwhile, crest jerking with annoyance at being expected to do a task below his status, was handing Fenobar's armor to Exdem, who promptly handed it off to Gartol, the one among them the least in rank.

Single file they made their way through the silent town, until they found themselves at the plaza in front of the temple. They approached the corner warily, only to jerk back into the dark at the sound of many feet slapping through the puddles. "They are hunting us," Stells hissed.

All eyes went to the Demon.

"They were coming from the Temple," Stells added. Being the tallest, he had the best view.

Fenobar put his head around the corner as yet another troop of warriors trotted past. "Wait here." Tucking both edges of his cloak into his bad hand to conceal the lack of surcoat, he plunged into the street, praying his grip would hold. Catching a warrior by the arm, Fenobar halted him by the simple method of digging claws painfully between the rings of his mail. "What is going on here!"

"The Monghanirri have escaped after killing the King's son, Kaybin. The High Priest is in a rage. He says if the prisoners are not captured in the next two hours, the God's wrath will fall upon all of us." The warrior was plainly frightened.

"How long ago was this?" Fenobar demanded.

The warrior stuttered a little. "Not long, my Lord. They are within the walls yet."

"How many troops are in this hunt?"

The warrior, who was not far out of his cublin years, gulped, and with the rain running off his helm, looked even younger than he was. "There are the temple troops, of course, my Lord. And most of the Second Rank commanders. Please, my Lord, my commander has ordered me. . . ."

"Go. Go!" Fenobar ordered, releasing him without waiting to find out what his commander had ordered. The warrior bowed hastily to him and ran off down the street.

Fenobar returned swiftly to his waiting war band. "They have started the raltmichak but cannot continue it until they have a sacrifice. The warrior I talked with didn't know about the Demon, so by now, the priests must be getting desperate enough to use any warm body they can get their hands on. The entire Second Rank is out looking for us, so we had best be swift if we are to accomplish anything."

Minutes later they were behind the temple, crouched in a growing puddle beside a high, featureless wall. "Give me a hand up," Fenobar whispered.

Silently Stells put his laced hands together for the whitecrest's foot, and hoisted him to the top of the wide wall. Fenobar found himself looking into the temple garden. "This is the place," he said. Then he was dropping lightly onto the short turf on the far side, his feet sinking into the wet ground. He crouched there, motionless, sniffing against the slanting rain. He was nearly nose blind, but that was just as well. If he couldn't smell anyone, neither could temple guards smell them.

The Demon was the next to drop over the wall, the rain covering the sounds he made. One by one the others followed. Exdem's feet had barely touched ground before Fenobar was off, a crouched bit of darkness, heading for the portico that ran the length of the temple. Fenobar stopped his small troop in the deepest of shadows between the pillars and the wall. "Somewhere along here is a door into the living quarters," he told his warriors softly as he moved forward, his good hand sliding along the cool surface until he finally found what he wanted. Warily, he opened the small back door into the priests' living quarters.

There was a hall to his left and one in front of him, partially hidden by the broad steps leading to the second floor, where the High Priest and his ranking priests lived. The corridors were lined with the doors of narrow cubicles where the acolytes slept and were probably as sparsely furnished as those of Fen. A few candles lit the passages. Hesitating on the dim threshold, he sniffed the air. Scents from the cubicles were warm, but those in the hall were cold. So . . . the acolytes slept, and those few awake to do this terrible thing to the clan Spirit of the Fenirri were already in the temple.

Three steps to his right took him to a narrow priest door which opened, as had the one in Fen, onto the interior of the temple. The temple itself was a vast, whispering place of dark and shadow, open on the south side, where it faced the plaza. The God image sat at the far end, dimly lit by candles. In the gloom at His feet came the low, murmuring sounds of chants. A single priest stood upright at the altar placed before the God.

Fenobar padded silently out into the temple. A hand signal formed his Fenirri up in good style to show honor to the God. With the Demon in the center of their small group, they marched smartly up the main aisle.

Halfway to the image, a thin, palecrested acolyte

stepped out from behind a pillar. "Where are you going? No one but priests are allowed before the God tonight. How did you get past the guard?"

"We have brought the Demon," Fenobar said softly.

The Demon raised his head, showing his flat, furless face under the sheltering hood of his cloak.

The acolyte took a step backward, reaching for a nonexistent kalnak. "In praise be Thanked! You have brought it in time!" he managed to gasp in a thin, grating voice. "Sardess was forced to start the raltmichak already. It's difficult enough to have to do a dangerous ritual, without having one of the most important ingredients missing! Fatal!"

"Especially if you're the one forced to make up the lack," a deep, burring voice said from the middle of the war band.

The priest looked startled, eyes going from one to the other of the Fenirri to see who had spoken. "Stay here," he ordered after a moment, and trotted away up the aisle.

CHAPTER SEVEN

Fenobar waited perhaps two seconds and then followed the priest up the aisle, his war band close behind him. "This is not a good place to be trapped," Stells said softly, into his ear. Meaning there were too many empty spaces and too many temple guards who would come running once they realized there was something wrong with the ceremony at the altar.

For the first time Fenobar found some use for the two years he'd spent as a temple guard. The temples of the war god Shaindar were all built along the same lines, as if a single blueprint had been used in their planning. Most of them were nothing more than copies of each other, right down to the secret ways built into the walls. Ways which he, as temple commander, had learned as part of his duty. "We will not be trapped," he muttered to the King's sholstan.

In front of the God Shaindar a whitecrested priest— probably the Ranking Second, since he didn't look old enough to be the High Priest—was standing not at the altar as Fenobar had assumed, but at an ancient, black sacrificial table. The priest was motionless, his hands outstretched over several stone objects on the table, one of which was the Black Axe of Monghan. A low chanting came from his lips. Behind the Ranking Second, seven priests knelt in attitudes of supplication, fervently chorusing the Ranking Second.

As he caught the words the hairs rose all over Fenobar's body. Stells, close behind him, growled a low and appropriate obscenity.

The palecrested acolyte was bending over one of the kneeling priests, whispering into his ear, when he glanced up and saw the Fenirri nearly on top of him. "What are you doing here!" he hissed. "I told you to wait!"

"You wouldn't want the Demon to escape a second time, would you?" Fenobar asked softly, putting his hand back for his sword. There was a concordance of metallic swishes, as the retinue drew with him. In the half second before he struck, Fenobar glanced up into the face of the God and discovered it was a subtly different Shaindar from the brooding, mature figure which ruled in Fen. This Shaindar had the look of a young direhawk, the eagerness of a whitecrest fresh from Bokeem.

Then, like the Axe with which they claimed kinship, the warriors of Fen were leaping forward to deal death, the Demon in the midst of them, his own weapon raised, crying aloud in his strange tongue.

Fenobar's target was the Second Ranking priest. The Kaymath still had his warrior reflexes. He had abandoned his chant and pose as he heard the scuffling behind him and smelled the hot, sweet blood. Snatching up a stone knife, he turned aside Fenobar's first lunge. But Fenobar was young and fast and desperate, and there was no real doubt as to the outcome. However, it took Fenobar, hurt as he was, longer to kill the priest than he would have liked. By the time he finished, his war band had dispatched five of the priests and were standing around watching the Demon and criticizing his technique as he fought off the remaining three priests, barely managing to keep them at bay with a highly inventive style of his own, using, of all things, one of the six-foot candle holders. The Demon might be many things, but he was no sword fighter.

It was not to be expected that the warriors would come to the creature's rescue, for the Demon was not a member of their tightly knit troop. Fenobar jumped forward under the outstretched claws of a priest coming at the Demon from the side. He slammed into the priest with his helm and sword arm, knocked him to the floor, and dispatched him with a single stab to the throat. As Fenobar spun to strike at a second priest, the Demon moved to stand back to back with him. Even as he accepted the alliance, it startled a distant portion of his mind. Unallied whitecrests did not defend each other, and among a war band, only a sholstan would take such a stance. A darkcrest would never have lifted a sword in the first place, and would have kept prudently out of the whole fracas. Perhaps he had been right when he told Stells that crest color meant nothing among the Demon-kin.

Stells' voice rumbled a challenge, and Fenobar looked up from killing the last priest to see a large troop of temple guards coming at a run. He stepped over the bodies of the slain and, tucking his sword under his bad arm, pressed a small block set into the dais upon which the statue of Shaindar rested. A small door opened, and he motioned the retinue into it.

Exdem was closest. He ducked his head to enter,

got a whiff of the air inside, gasped, and leaped back, shield up and sword at the defensive. An elderly whitecrest barreled out of the dark hole, golden knife held for a death stroke. Exdem's leap left Fenobar, unprepared, in front of the door. He caught the movement from the corner of his eye and twisted away from the vicious stroke aimed for his throat. Off balance he went down, throwing himself onto his back, but failed to catch the High Priest on clawed feet. Then his sword was entangled in the High Priest's robes and he was unable to reach the kalnak on his right hip. Fenobar's eyes fixed helplessly on the glimmering edge of the sacrificial knife coming down at his throat.

Above and behind the High Priest, something moved darkly. Shimmering iridescence flashed in a smooth arc as the Axe blade came down and caught the Kaymath just under the shoulder, lifting him sideways up and off Fenobar to sprawl lifelessly under the feet of his God.

The Demon stepped back from the body, breathing heavily, but with the Axe held steady in both hands. For a moment the two of them watched the High Priest twitch in his death throes. Fenobar had never seen such a blow, and judging from the awed look on his face, neither had Stells.

A cry of anguish and fear wailed out of the Kaymath temple commander. He and his war band had been close enough to witness everything and had come to an indecisive halt, not sure what they should do after this sign of the God's displeasure.

"Inside!" Fenobar roared, shoving the Demon, who still had the Axe in his hands, into the narrow passage. The Fenirri warriors scrambled into the dark tunnel. Fenobar slammed his hand down on the catch and dove forward as the heavy stone slammed into place behind him, leaving them in pitch dark, with only the sound of their heavy breathing for company. Fenobar fumbled at the door. He gave an exclamation of satisfaction as something clicked into place. "That will hold them."

"The Demon should not have taken the Axe." Stells' voice came heavily from the darkness beside Fenobar. "He is an outlander."

Fenobar said, "The Demon did the only right thing. You heard the Death Spell laid on the Axe. Do you think either of us could have picked it up and lived? It was a spell directed at the Fenirri. Only an outlander could have touched it without being blasted."

There was an odd, strangled sound from farther up the narrow corridor, where the Demon was standing.

Fenobar continued, "Only powerful blood would give the Spirit back its strength after having a spell like that laid on it. Only the blood of the one responsible for the desecration could wipe away the dishonor."

Stells stirred in the dark. "Is it safe for one of us to carry the Axe *now*?"

Fenobar started to pull at his fake crest. "I don't know," he said slowly. Then, in a more decisive tone, he added, "It is more important to get the Axe out of Kaymath than to worry about who carries it. The Demon is no swordsman. If it comes to another fight, it is better he is carrying it then to hamper you when the additional weight could mean the difference between winning and dying."

"The Demon might do some changing to the Axe," Stells said stubbornly.

Fenobar curbed the impulse to snap at the sholstan, suddenly wildly impatient with the other's lack of knowledge. "Demons deal in ideas—words, not spells. He could talk for weeks at the Axe and not do a blessed thing to it."

"You are certain of this?" Stells sounded doubtful.

"It was so written in the old history sticks and so I have found it to be from experience," Fenobar replied, as patiently as he could, working his way past the warriors, with a nagging feeling he shouldn't have said so much. "We must hurry. The guards know well enough where the passages lead."

The tunnel was not only pitch black, it was also narrow and low. Fenobar kept his head down and forced his weary body into a trot, tapping his sword tip against the wall as insurance against unexpected obstacles. If this temple was built along the same lines as the one in Fen, and so far it had been a near duplicate, there would be a place where the tunnel split in two directions—downward into the subterranean maze that guarded the temple treasury, and upwards through the massive walls to certain spy holes and hidden rooms. From those rooms it would be possible to enter the priests' living quarters. However, if one continued upwards, he would come out, eventually, in a guardroom just under the temple roof.

As he ran, Fenobar kept one ear tilted to the breathing behind him. From the sounds the war band were making, they were all as tired as he was, but in spite of their wounds, they were keeping up. Only the rhythms in the Demon's harsh gasping seemed wrong. He was running just behind Fenobar and the commander sniffed deeply at Demon scent. There was fermented sajawa, blood, muck from the dungeons and some other, fresher odor, with a sharp, unsettling tang to it. He frowned to himself. Why would the Demon be afraid? And what might a frightened Demon of Undoing be capable of?

A sudden emptiness under his sword tip told Fenobar when he reached the tunnel branching. Without hesitation he took the right-hand passage. Five paces, ten, and his sword rang on stone steps. "Now we go up!" he called to his warriors. Five turnings in the spiral staircase brought them to the first passage leading away from the steps, but Fenobar ignored it, taking them up past three more such openings, until finally, gasping for breath on a tiny landing under the temple roof, he slipped his sword under his bad arm and cautiously pushed open a door. The guard-room was empty, long unused, the air lifeless and dust thick underfoot. Through the small, arched glass window, starlight provided the faintest of illumination.

The Demon pushed Fenobar rather roughly to one side as he tumbled out of the passageway, and stood leaning against the wall, the Axe cradled in his arms, breathing in great gulps. Behind him came Pelgir and Gartol, supporting Qurngar, whose damaged leg had given out on the long climb. Exdem was reeling and gasping heavily with fever. Stells came last of all, big and black and nearly invisible until he showed his teeth.

Fenobar was already searching the side walls. "Ah!" It was quiet triumph. "I have found the ladder to the roof." He was about to ask one of the warriors to follow him up, but the Demon was already behind him, one hand reaching for the rungs. Fenobar started upwards with the Demon close on his heels. He worried about being touched with the Axe but could not give the Demon a word of warning in front of the war band, who might interpret the words as a sign of fear.

But he was glad for the nearness of the creature when he came to the top and found his one arm could not budge the trapdoor. The Demon reached past him, adding his strength to Fenobar's. Between the two of them it was only a moment before the door sprang back with a crash.

It had stopped raining, and as Fenobar emerged onto the flat roof, the night breeze was cool against his face, bringing with it heavy, moist scents. The Demon popped promptly onto the roof behind him and stood staring up at the stars as if he could not get his fill of them.

The rest of the war band emerged at a slower pace. One by one they walked or tottered over to the waist-high wall and looked down. Qurngar had to be held upright between his two mates.

"And what are we going to do here?" Stells rumbled sarcastically as he stared down at the ground. "We're going to fly over the walls, perhaps?"

"Something like that," Fenobar replied, noncommittally. They were not far from the front corner of the temple. In Fen, the wall around the city widened where it met the temple walls, and it was possible to drop the ten feet down to it without fear of going over the edge. Fenobar walked over to the low parapet. Once on the guard wall, it was a simple matter to reach the corner guard tower. Once in the tower, escape would be a simple matter of opening a door and walking out.

But his familiarity with the temple had led him into a wrong assumption. Fenobar reached the end of the roof and looked down. The guard wall ended twenty feet from the side of the temple, and the space between was filled by a spear-topped gate. Panic sent him racing the length of the temple for the opposite front corner, but there was a gate there, too.

They were trapped.

Slowly, Fenobar turned to face his war band, who were limping up behind him. He could not see their expressions, but in their scent there was neither anger nor fear, only the sodden smell of weariness.

Fenobar was out of ideas. He sank down where he was on the low parapet, the taste of defeat, like acid, burning his mouth.

The warriors looked down at the gate, and without saying anything, or looking at anyone, settled themselves in a wide semi-circle in front of their commander. Stells didn't say anything either, but his grey crest caught the starlight. It was jerking.

Only the Demon remained on his feet, prowling along the short east side of the temple roof, staring down over the side. When he reached the back side of the temple, he bent over suddenly, staring down into the garden. He turned, beckoning the Fenirri to him excitedly. When they joined the Demon at the parapet it was to search uncomprehendingly in the silent garden for whatever it was that had caught the Demon's attention.

Fenobar looked at the Demon, his head hurting as his crest tried to jerk out his anger. "You expect us to jump, maybe?"

"Not the garden!" the Demon said impatiently. "Look at the wall. They have carved things on it."

"Yes," agreed Fenobar, doubting the creature's sanity that it should be concerned with such things at a time like this. "A lot of buildings have this kind of decoration."

"Not decoration," the Demon contradicted, in a way no warrior would dare to a whitecrest. "Hand and foot holds."

Fenobar's eyes widened. "No!" he said flatly.

"Don't say that so fast," Stells' deep voice murmured admonishingly.

The Demon leaned the Axe against the low parapet, abruptly folded his legs, and began unlacing his leather foot coverings. They extended well up his calves and he had to tug and struggle with them before they came off. His feet, so bared, were long and narrow, with small, clutching toes. He tied the boot laces together and then tore off a strip from the bottom of his cloak, out of which he fashioned a crude harness for the Axe. Boots and Axe went over his shoulders. Then the Demon went over the parapet, where he clung a moment and then gradually disappeared from view.

The warriors exchanged grimly apprehensive glances. Stells threw a leg over the parapet, claws scrabbling for a hold among the incised designs. The others, perforce, had to follow or lose status. Exdem waved aside help, but Pelgir and Gartol went down, one on either side of Qurngar, to give him what support they could. In seconds only Fenobar remained behind.

He faced the direction the guards were sure to come and drew his sword, prepared to make a last defense. The Demon reappeared, sticking his head up over the parapet. "Come on. You can't stand there all night!"

Fenobar sat down on the wall beside the place where the Demon clung. "I can't do it."

"Nonsense. If Qurngar can make it with one leg, you can make it with one arm. Here, let me show you. Put your good hand here . . . and your left foot there, and . . . sheath the sword first, Fenobar."

To ask for help was to lose honor. But he had not asked, Fenobar told himself, so if he took this help (the first ever offered to him without his asking), he had lost nothing. A darkcrest was supposed to serve. He slipped over the edge, pressed against the building, the smell of rain-wet stone in his nose, and sought for his first foot holds.

The scent of fermented sajawa was heavy in the air as the Demon climbed down at his side, the disturbing underlying taint gone now. A heavy, hairless arm came around his waist, pinning him to the wall. Fenobar let go his one-handed hold on the top of the wall, trusting to the Demon's strength until he could find another hand and foot hold. In such a fashion he existed for a timeless interval, until looking down, he was surprised to see the grass only a few feet below him. Thankfully he let go, landing with a jar and a moan he could not bite off in time. No one was waiting for them at the foot of the wall. Stells and the war band had gone ahead.

High above them on the roof a voice was calling, "They are not here, my Lord. They must have gone over the side!"

"That's crazy!" another voice replied. "They couldn't climb down that!"

Without waiting for permission, the Demon grabbed Fenobar around the waist and pitched them both under a low-growing tree. The Demon crouched beside him, the Axe head cutting a curved swatch out of the stars. If his little ears could move, they would have been pointed alertly for danger; almost, Fenobar thought joylessly, as if the creature were protecting a revered and illustrious House Head.

"Check the living quarters. They must have got past us somehow." The temple commander's voice filtered down to them faintly.

"Or they took the lower route, into the temple treasury," another voice offered.

The temple commander's voice was not pleasant. "If they are there, they all die there. They will not find their way out of the maze." The voices drifted away.

A shift of wind brought Pelgir's odor, and a rustle in the bushes warned him as the warrior came to crouch beside them in the dark. "We have tatarra saddled by the priest's gate."

The Fenirri were tired and far from noiseless, but the Demon moved only a little less silently than a rampaging patuz. But he was obviously doing the best he could, so Fenobar bit his teeth together over certain words he would have liked to have said and kept his sword ready. But in spite of the noise, there was no outcry of discovery.

The postern gate was already open. Death smell was in the air and Stells' blade was glistening wetly as he waited for them beside the narrow priest's door. The rest of the war band were mounted and waiting on the other side of the wall. Exdem, his fever rapidly worsening, had been tied to the saddle. Qurngar was holding Stells' tatarra. Pelgir handed the reins of the animal he was holding to Fenobar, while Gartol did the same to the Demon.

The animals fretted at the scent of the Demon, making them difficult to mount. Twice Fenobar reached for the pommel of his saddle, only to have it disappear from under his clutching fingers. It was the Demon who took the headstall in a no-nonsense grip and held the animal until Fenobar could get into the saddle. The Demon was taking an almost proprietary interest in him, Fenobar decided. The question was, was it the service of a darkcrest, or the duty of a sholstan the Demon was showing him?

Stells led the way at a walk. Overcast as it was, it was too dark to see a hand's-breadth in front of their animals. Scent and sound alone would betray them. Then it started to rain again, even more heavily than before. If they didn't break their necks over the low-walled fields, they would get away.

Three hours later, the first lighting of the sky brought things into grey relief, in spite of the low-hanging clouds. The rain had let up and Stells called a halt. They were deep in the mountains and far from any track—as safe as they would ever be, for a time. Stiffly they all dismounted, to collapse gratefully in the thin grass among the rocks.

The Demon settled not far from Fenobar and, pulling the Axe into his lap, sat running his strange hands up and down the haft in a rather nervous gesture.

Stells, sitting slumped with his arms over his knees, eyed that activity with every sign of growing displeasure. "I still don't like the Axe being in an outlander's hands. If the Death Spell is still potent, then what will be will be. It is a warrior's fate to die someday," he said and, getting up, took the Axe away from the Demon.

The troop waited breathlessly for him to be struck by lightning, fried in his own armor. When nothing happened, Stells grunted and sat down again, holding the Axe as he might an infant, running his hands anxiously over the handle and blade.

The thought of reprimanding Stells for taking such a chance ran across Fenobar's mind, only to be dismissed as a sure way to undermine his own authority. He shifted slightly, leaning back against a rock, trying to find a position that was comfortable. All his exuberance at winning freedom was gone, buried under layers of exhaustion. All he wanted to do was sleep. That, of course, was probably the one thing they would not be able to do.

As the light grew brighter, Fenobar noticed a bundle tied on behind Gartol's saddle—his armor, still wrapped in the old brown cloak. His scalp pulled painfully as his crest tried to fluff up in genuine happiness. With a growl, he pulled off his helm and ripped the white twists out of his braided crest. Then his hand was at his own scalp, worrying at the braiding. With a sigh of pure pleasure he finally combed clawed fingers through the long hairs, fluffing them up. "It just occurred to me that with the High Priest and the Ranking Priest dead, they will have to go through the appeasement rituals before they dare start any new attacks against the Monirri. It will take them *weeks!*"

Crests twitched with mirth and all eyes went to the Demon, who lay with his hands behind his head, eyes closed, seemingly oblivious to them all. Stells kept them to wild animal trails, as they searched for a route through the mountains. Their stolen tatarra were fresh and, being mountain bred, made nothing of the steep terrain.

The warriors did not fare as well. Qurngar, his wounded leg swollen from the use it had been put to all that night, bit his teeth together and suffered in silence. Exdem wandered in his mind as his fever grew progressively worse. Fenobar tightened the sling holding his bad arm, knowing his damaged shoulder was swelling under the mail. Every movement sent white-hot pain lancing through his body. He rode hunched over on himself, arm clamped tightly to his chest.

CHAPTER EIGHT

The bright promise of morning soured off as a biting wind brought heavy grey clouds scudding between the mountain walls, to mass above them, cutting off the sky. It was too cold to rain. They were driven out of the heights by needle-sharp gusts of sleet that stung through fur and rang on unprotected mail.

Presently they came down into a low, rolling land. As they descended, the sleet changed to rain, and then faded out gradually until it was a warm mist.

Fenobar forced himself out of the leaden misery that befogged his mind long enough to ask Stells a question. "Where are we?" Flat land looked so strange anymore.

"Near the coast, in Kulmore territory. If we travel north a few days we can cross back through the mountains at the Shulg Pass, and so come into Mone where it borders Kulmore and avoid the Kaymath entirely."

The sholstan's contentment grated across Fenobar's pain-wracked nerves and he wondered if Black Fentaru had ever had a desire to smack his war band First upside the ears. "We have to rest."

"Yes." Stells' crest flicked in agreement. "I see a good spot up ahead."

Lifting a head grown almost too weary to support the heavy burden of his war helm, Fenobar looked where Stells was motioning. It was a good spot, a meadow pocket surrounded on three sides by tree-covered cliffs, with a stream of clear water. By the time they reached it the sun was out, burning off the mist and warming their shivering bodies. They pulled the gear off the tatarra, letting them go free to graze, and collapsed where they stood.

When Fenobar finally awoke it was late afternoon. Except for Stells, the retinue still lay heavily in sleep. The sholstan was seated beside a small, smoke-less fire, dropping hot stones in his clay-smeared helm to heat water, a thing he would never have done with his own armor . . . but he had never hid his disdain for Kaymath workmanship. The Axe was across his shoulders in place of his sword.

Fenobar turned his head painfully to see the place where the Demon had bedded was empty. "Where is he?" he demanded of Stells, nodding toward the Demon's discarded cloak and the mashed place he'd left in the grass.

"Out splashing around in the water," Stells an-swered with disgust. "I knew Demons were other-worldly, but what it's doing is outright unimkairan!"

"Well," said Fenobar reasonably, pushing himself painfully to a seated position, "He is a Demon of Undoing. How would you expect him to act?"

Stells muttered something under his breath and vengefully stirred the contents of his helm with a kalnak. "Did you see the way it swung the Axe at the High Priest . . . sideways? Nothing of Imkairan birth

can move its arms like that." Stells waited, and when
no comment was forthcoming from his young commander went on to say, "Is it fitting to let running
water cleanse the Axe?" He flicked a look at Fenobar.
"I am thinking it would be wise to get the scent of
the Demon off it as soon as possible."

This was a serious question and Fenobar thought it
over carefully, combing through the knowledge he'd
picked up at the temple. "Leave the Axe as it is. The
Demon gave it the blood of its enemy; therefore,
there is a bond between them. It could be that the
Demon's influence plus the blood is all that is keeping the death spell from working on you. When we
get to Mone, the High Priest will know best how to
cleanse it of all dishonor."

Stells grunted, perhaps not satisfied, but convinced.
He bent over his makeshift pot, closing Fenobar out
of his thoughts.

The younger warrior set his teeth against the sharp
ribbon of pain in his shoulder and back and rolled
clumsily to his feet. Following the scent and sound of
water into a grove of tall, old trees he found a wide,
spring-fed pool at the base of the rock wall. The sun
was flooding down through the trees and it was there,
where the glittering rays were the hottest, that he
found the Demon. He was floating on his back in the
very center of the pool, a blissful look on his naked,
flat face. The Demon heard Fenobar and, opening
his eyes, greeted him with a nod, the lips curving
the folds of his face into a non-threatening grimace.

The shadowy Demon of his mind had always been
out of focus and, Fenobar realized, too Imkairan. He
stepped among the mossy boulders, eyes intent on
the Demon, closely studying every movement the
other made. There was a shiver of excitement in his

belly as he took note of the eerie strangeness of the creature he thought he knew so well.

The whitecrest crouched down, trailing his hand in the clear, cold water. He bent to drink and when he looked up, the Demon's strange, smooth shape was gliding lazily toward him, propelled by graceful movements of the arms. One hand grasped a boulder near Fenobar's feet, and the Demon twisted over on his side so he could look up at the whitecrest.

For the first time, Fenobar saw the Demon clearly in daylight. The long, water-spangled body was much lighter than he had first thought and covered with a map of red scratches and pinpricks where claws had broken the thin skin. Fascinated, he put out a hand and stroked a forefinger down the Demon's arm, feeling the resiliency and incredible delicacy of that hide.

His gaze shifted and met the Demon's eyes. There was a moment when the world seemed to go silent and the sky whirled. The flat eyes were not the blue he had always painted them; they were grey. But not the common greenish grey of so many darkcrests or warriors, nor the colorless grey of Stells' eyes . . . they were the dark grey of threatening storm clouds, outlined in black. The eyes of a wild, young direhawk. The eyes of the last image he had painted on the inside of his shield. Shaken, he turned his head away, unable to meet that straightforward look.

"Are you going to swim?" the Demon asked while the water rocked the long, pale body back and forth.

Fenobar cast a wistful look at the pool. The Demon smelled of water and green things, sajawa and the illusive fragrance of crushed moss under his hand. And Fenobar could smell himself—a combination of dried blood, sweat and dungeon filth. His nose wrinkled in distaste as he looked down at the rusting mail, the blood caking his tawny fur. "I have hurt my shoulder and cannot get my armor off by myself," Fenobar said carefully.

He was not yet sure what status this Demon was. He had acted like a palecrest, a darkcrest, and when he killed the priest . . . as a whitecrest. The Demon shifted between status duties with bewildering rapidity and did not even seem to understand how jarring this was on the members of the war band. Not knowing for sure what level the Demon was, Fenobar played it as safe as he could and gave the Demon a reply custom demanded a whitecrest give to one of slightly higher status. If it turned out the Demon was of a lower status, he would not have lost too much honor, and if the Demon was of a higher status, he would have gained honor.

With a surge of those strangely muscled shoulders the Demon heaved himself to his feet and was climbing out on the moss-covered boulders beside the whitecrest, almost before Fenobar had finished. Long fingers lifted off his helm and tugged at his mail skirt. "You have to lift this thing off?" the Demon was asking in his lilting burr.

Once again the Demon was acting out of status, and once again Fenobar was shocked into near speechlessness. He managed to grunt out some simple directions for getting the mail off. Surprisingly, the Demon's touch was gentle, and when he could not help but hurt Fenobar, he moved swiftly. In a very short time Fenobar's Kaymath chain mail lay in a heap on the grassy bank. By that time Fenobar had made up his mind that the Demon was indeed a darkcrest . . . a servant, no matter his fighting abilities. Reeling a bit with the shock of pain, Fenobar nevertheless turned his head to thank the Demon for his help. It was the proper behavior for a warrior to a darkcrest. The Demon was bending over the armor, straightening it, and Fenobar's crest went limp with shock, for the Demon's head fur, now washed clean, was drying in the sunlight and was glinting impossibly golden.

The Demon was the image painted on the inside of his shield. Not sent by his Demon to be a servant to him. The Demon was HIS Demon. For a moment Fenobar was on the edge of collapse. "I asked you for help," he gasped out of a throat so tight with terror that his words were barely intelligible. "I asked you for help, but I never expected you to come to me clothed in flesh. . . ."

But he should have, Fenobar told himself. This was a Demon of Undoing . . . it would do precisely the last thing one expected of him. Stells was right in his accusations. He *had* called the Demon of Undoing into existence. Here was the proof. And once Stells, who had seen the painting on his shield, got a good look at the Demon, he would know it, too. Stells needed a whitecrest to keep up the fiction of them being just a war band. But once they had reached Mone? What then? Would he be denounced and sacrificed to Shaindar?

The Demon, still on one knee beside the mail, was staring up at him in some perplexity. He looked down at an arm, rotating it as if he had never seen such a thing before. "But what else would my bones wear?" And when Fenobar did not answer right away: "You *did* ask me why I was wearing flesh?"

Fenobar managed to flick his crest in assent and, seeing the Demon's deepening bewilderment, tried to make himself clearer. "Why did you come forth from the shadowy places? I did not ask you to manifest yourself to me."

"Huh?" the Demon replied.

Suddenly afraid he was deeply in the wrong somewhere, Fenobar backtracked his assumptions and tried
again, a little less forceably. "ARE you my Demon?"

The Demon slowly rubbed slender fingers over a
prominent chin. "In a manner of speaking, I suppose
I am. I owe you something for getting me out of
Kaymath."

It was a truly ambiguous answer, one worthy of a
Demon, and Fenobar took a deep breath to calm
himself. "Do you know me from a time before
Kaymath?"

"No." A calm no, full of certainty.

"You were not sent by another?"

"No."

"Then why do you walk the earth and trouble the
lives of those you meet?"

The Demon scratched at his golden head fur. "Odd.
I was under the impression the Imkaira I met were
troubling *my* life. Not me theirs."

Fenobar opened his mouth to say something and
closed it again. The second attempt was more suc-
cessful. "*You* are troubled by *us*?" he repeated,
incredulous.

"Since I fell into Imkairan hands my life hasn't
exactly been a stroll through the meadow." Unconsciously, the Demon rubbed at a healing wound on
one arm.

"No, I can see that," Fenobar said a bit faintly.
The Demon had not been sent to him. It was
Fenobar's helping the Demon out of the Kaymath
dungeons which had set a bond between them. Which
had made this Demon truly his. Up to them he had
been no more Demon-ridden than he had ever been.
He uttered a strangled yelp as he realized just how
the Demons had maneuvered him yet again. The

whole thing was truly worthy of the twisted results the Demons delighted in.

It was only later, as he lay floating full length in the waist-deep water under the trees that he realized the Demon had admitted to being subject to the power of Undoing every bit as thoroughly as any Imkairan. Could it be so? Nevertheless, sent to him or not, he, Fenobar, would still be held responsible for the strange being. Everything rested on how Stells reacted to the Demon and how the Demon conducted himself on the way to Mone. If he proved useful and used his powers to aid rather than hinder, it was possible Stells would let them both go free before they actually entered Mone. There was nothing he could do about it yet, so he thrust the worry aside, giving himself up to the full enjoyment of being clean again. He was being gently rocked in the backwash of the Demon's strokes as the creature swam back and forth across the width of the small pool *enjoying* himself. It seemed beyond reason, somehow.

The Demon came stroking back toward him to grasp a nearby rock, blowing lustily to catch his breath, then hauled himself out. He lay on his back in the sunlight near Fenobar to dry in the sun.

Fenobar turned his head slightly to look up at that golden head a little way above his. "How did you get in a Kaymath dungeon?"

The Demon went very quiet and then rolled over, getting to his elbows. Picking at the moss with his long fingers, he answered in a low voice. "I was with my cousin."

"What is this word, 'cousin'?"

"You would say, 'one of a kinship line'."

"Another Demon?" Fenobar asked, surprised. He

hadn't known Demons had kinship relations with other Demons.

"One of my kind, yes. We were coming down the coast of the Shaking Lands in a small boat, when a storm blew us into the shipping lanes. We were captured and sold in some town—I never knew the name of it. My cousin tried to escape and was killed. I was sold to a trader who brought me into the mountains and sold me to the Kaymath. Then you came."

A clear and reasonable story, Fenobar thought, if you didn't look too closely at the beginning, with that deceptively simple, "We were coming down the coast." From where? To where? For what purpose? Why a boat? What did a Demon need a boat for? Questions crowded his tongue, but he kept them solidly behind his teeth. There would be a time for asking the Demon those questions, but it was not now. There was a deep unhappiness in the other, coupled with a strange evasiveness that warned him off. The Demon had told him the truth so far, but to push further might force the creature to lie, and Fenobar did not want lies between him and his Demon.

It was the Demon's turn to ask a question. "Where are you taking your Clan Spirit?"

"We take it to Mone, the Royal Clan of the Monghanirri. It is north and west of this place."

"What will you do once you have come to Mone?"

Fenobar's crest jerked and he gave a jeering little snort. "It all depends on whether Stells permits us to live."

"Why would he not?"

"Because he thinks I called you, a Demon of Undoing, into existence to bring trouble to the Fenirri."

"Oh."

"Is that all you can say? Oh? I tell you, Demon, our lives—yours and mine—depend on how you behave." He pulled himself up to sit, dripping beside the Demon. "You *must* bend your powers to helping us gain Mone. It is the only way. You must show Stells you honor the clan and the Axe. Prove to him you came to help, not hinder or cause mischief, and he may let us go free."

The Demon shredded moss and dropped the pieces into the water, his head bent, watching intently what he was doing. "Fenobar? I have no power."

"Have no . . . !" Fenobar thought he would choke on the words. "You have power enough to topple kingdoms and destroy whole civilizations."

"But we didn't do it on purpose," the Demon replied, sounding guilty even to Fenobar's unpracticed ears. "When we saw how bad things were going, we turned from your people and kept to our holding."

"You mean, you cannot control your powers?" Fenobar asked hollowly.

"Well . . . something like that," the Demon agreed slowly.

Fenobar slanted his crest at the Demon. His voice was grim. "Do the best you can."

"Why are you so afraid of Stells? Isn't he your left-hand warrior?" the Demon asked, giving the sholstan the old name.

So Fenobar told him how he happened to be riding with the Ranking Palecrest of Fen. "Once the Axe is safely in Mone, and you have convinced Stells you serve Fen and the Monghanirri, you and I will be free to go wherever we chose," Fenobar finished tiredly.

"And Stells?" the Demon asked.

"Stells and the troop will return to the King of Fen."

"That leaves you sort of . . ."

"Exiled," Fenobar finished for him. His tone was flat and unencouraging. Retreating into the arrogance which is the heritage of the whitecrest kind and which had been as much his armor over the years as his mail, he tilted his crest at his discarded, filthy chain mail. "I will not wear that again. Demon, bring me my Fenirri armor which Gartol is carrying."

The Demon had turned his head sharply at Fenobar's change of manner, the two ridiculous little strips of fur over his eyes raising in a marked way. But saying nothing, the creature got up and padded back to the camp, the sunlight reflecting brightly off muscles rippling under the bare hide. Fenobar felt a distant pleasure at the Demon's obedience, knowing he could command such power.

The Demon returned shortly with the bundle. And as he knelt in the grass to unwrap the cloak, he said, "I think your Exdem is in a bad way. His nose is dry, his eyes are seeping, and his breath rattles in his throat."

Fenobar got awkwardly to his feet and waded out of the pool. "He is Stells' warrior, not mine. Stells will have to take care of him." He picked up his Fenirri undertunic and held it out at arm's length. It was stiff and odorous, with a combination of overripe Imkairan and mildew. "Waugh!" he said, turning his head aside.

Even the Demon's odd nose wrinkled with disgust. With two fingers he removed the garment from Fenobar's hold, a gesture that broadly hinted at a fear of catching some skin disease, and, holding it well away from his body, gathered up the rest of their clothing in his other hand. Walking downstream a few yards, he dumped his load into the water, stabbed the garments into place with sticks, and vigorously began rubbing the soaked material together.

Left standing beside his armor, Fenobar watched the Demon's actions in bewilderment. The Demon was doing darkcrest labor again. He rubbed at his eyes, his explanation to Stells that Demons were not bound by crestcolor coming back to haunt him. He had not really believed it . . . but it was true. Finally, he wandered over to sit and watch the Demon at his labor. "Take the Kaymath undertunic for yourself," he said finally, remembering how the Demon had shivered his way out of the mountains, wearing only his torn breeks and a Kaymath cloak. "You will take the Kaymath armor as well."

The Demon grunted an acknowledgement.

His good hand had been rubbing at the twisted bones in his left arm for sometime, before Fenobar was aware of what he was doing. Looking down at that exposed, emaciated limb, he realized he had not minded the Demon seeing it. Nor, for that matter, had the Demon made him at all aware of his deformity. His crest fluffed with an odd kind of pleasure, and at the same time, he yawned widely. His eyes felt heavy, so he slipped down to curl up among the sun-warmed rocks. He had a sudden memory of a corner of the herb garden, just beside the female quarters of the King House in Fen, that had been his favorite napping place as a cublin. His whitecrest brothers had usually taken their naps beside one of Black Fentaru's warriors. Being guarded, they could sleep soundly. He had tried that, but too often he would wake up to find his guardian missing and his whitecrest brothers coming at him with claws out. It had been safer to nap hidden in the garden, even if it was less restful.

*   *   *

His ears twitched in his sleep, monitoring the sounds around him. A shrill bird whistle brought him to immediate wakefulness. He lay still, only his eyes moving. From the slant of the shadows, more than an hour had passed. The clothing was draped over nearby bushes and the Demon was sprawled out in the lowering sunlight near his feet, seemingly sound asleep. Fenobar straightened one leg and nudged the Demon lightly in the ribs with a toe.

The creature turned his shining head toward Fenobar and opened one eye. Not so deeply asleep then, after all, Fenobar thought approvingly, "It's time we were joining the others."

The Demon sat up without a word and stretched long arms at impossible angles over his head before reaching out to feel the breeks hanging on the limb of the tree, near his head. "Dry enough to put on," he said cheerfully, "if you don't mind being a little damp."

The Demon in breeks and Kaymath tunic was a different creature; almost civilized. Once again, acting more like a darkcrest than a warrior, he helped Fenobar into his Fenirri tunic, saying not a word about the padded arm. Then came the moment Fenobar was dreading—getting into the armor. But that, too, was accomplished with a minimum of pain and effort.

The Demon, oddly enough, had never seen chain mail, and Fenobar had to show him how to clean the Kaymath armor with sand and cloth. It took an hour of effort to get it even minimally clean again. It was too tight for the Demon across the shoulders and chest. Fenobar was not going to pop any more rivets in the back, where the Demon would be most vulnerable. Instead, he opened up the row of links under the arms and halfway down the side, until the end result was less a mail shirt than it was a breast-and-back plate held together at the shoulders and bottom.

Fenobar stepped back to study the changes. He wasn't happy with it, knowing how bad a swordsman the Demon was, but it would have to do. Picking up the helm, he dropped it over the Demon's head.

There was a shout of pain and it was quickly snatched off again. Rubbing delicately at the small ears growing on the side of his head, the Demon inspected the Kaymath helm. Having had his own ears bent by the same helm, Fenobar sympathized. When the Demon asked him, a bit desperately, if he *had* to wear the thing, Fenobar said no, and they left it there in the grass when they went back to camp.

CHAPTER NINE

Returning to the malin with the Demon in tow, Fenobar found Stells alone, industriously cleaning his dark fur with a brush made of twigs and dried grasses. Fenobar looked around the empty meadow. "Where are the others?"

Offhandedly, Stells replied, "They have gone to bury Exdem."

"But he wasn't that sick . . ." the Demon started.

Fenobar elbowed him into silence. "The sholstan has the right to determine the fitness of the warriors under his command," he explained quietly, feeling that old fear clutching his stomach. For the sholstan also had the right to judge the fitness of the whitecrest to lead.

Stells put down his brush. "Before we move on, that crest of yours is going to be white again. You seem to have forgotten the color, but the rest of us have not!"

Fenobar stood amazed. It was true. He *had* forgotten.

Stells picked up a large piece of bark, on which

131

had been mixed what appeared to be the yellow fat of prairie birds with white wood ash. To this he added a pinch of this and a pinch of that plus a handful of what looked like yellow petals from the Light-of-the-Sun flowers dotting the meadow. Stells refused to say exactly what he was putting together, but the smell alone was making Fenobar uneasy.

Then Pelgir, Gartol and Qurngar returned to drop armfuls of wild durnbag stalks beside the fire and squatted down, watching intently, as Stells began rubbing the salve-like mixture into an unwilling Fenobar's crest.

"How long is this going to stay on?" Fenobar demanded.

Stells was wrapping his head in a portion of the dead Exdem's tunic. "Until sunset tomorrow. Then we will wash it off with lye made of durnbag stalks. The only hazard will be the second-degree burns. If your crest remains on your head, it will be white."

Fenobar rolled an anguished eye at his Demon, but the creature just shrugged and grinned at him.

At sunup the next morning they broke camp. Fenobar rode behind Stells, his crest still wrapped up and his thoughts gloomy. Stells was carrying the Axe and Fenobar watched the curved double heads bobbing against his back, catching iridescent gleams of sunlight. It would be good to get it into a temple again where it could be properly tended. But he, with the Demon attached to him like a burr in his cresthair, would not be likely to see it there.

The Demon was riding beside Fenobar on his right, whereas an Imkairan would have taken up a position on his left. With most of his body covered by breeks, boots, mail and cloak, he did not look too unlike the rest of them, if one did not look too closely at that flat, naked face, with its crown of shining fur.

They kept to the dense woods of the foothills and headed north, just on the inside of the Kulmore border. That night, having seen neither Kulmore nor Kaymath, they camped beside a tiny stream and risked a small, smokeless fire. Stells immediately set about heating water while Pelgir broke the durnbag stalks into a makeshift pot made out of bark smeared with clay. Qurngar limped away into the dark, his crest showing all too clearly how happy he was that his guard duties kept him from having to take a turn at stirring the resultant, pungent mess.

It took two hours for the durnbag lye to boil down to the right consistency. Stells tested it by dipping a gauntleted finger into the stuff. When he withdrew his finger and the metal was bright and shiny, Fenobar's eyes grew large and alarmed. It was with the utmost reluctance he came at Stells' command to bend over the bubbling liquid. The fumes burned his nose and made his eyes water. He also noticed that Stells was still wearing his gauntlets as he picked up a ladle whittled from a tree limb, and poured the lye over Fenobar's head.

The young commander yelped and tried to jerk away. "My crest is smoking!"

"Nonsense!" Stells growled. "Cublin these days have too much imagination," and held him in place with an iron hand on the back of his neck until he was finished.

Then Pelgir poured a helm full of water over Fenobar's head and the whitecrest was released, gasping for breath, with water running into his eyes. Fenobar happened to be looking as Stells wiped his gauntlets off in the grass. Wherever they touched the vegetation it turned white and died.

Later, pulling his drying crest hair down where he could see it in the firelight, Fenobar had to admit he was no longer a darkcrest. His cresthair was white again but the strands were lifeless and brittle. Nervously, he studied Stells across the fire. "You aren't going to tell anyone I dyed my crest, are you?"

Stells' voice rumbled in the dark. "It was an honorable thing to do. Very courageous." After a moment he added, "But not every detail need be part of a warrior's Honor song."

Fenobar stared at the sholstan, his breath coming hard. "You will make up an Honor song for me?" A commander's Honor song was the pride of his war band. The more heroic deeds catalogued in an Honor song, the higher the prestige of the entire band. It was always the sholstan's duty to make up the verses and the tune for the Honor song. And his first verses and the tune which went with them were to be done by Stells, whose praise of his King was almost as legendary as Black Fentaru himself. Fenobar looked down at his good hand, crest flexing, fluffing and flattening in absurd pleasure.

Just before daybreak, Stells, who had the watch, came running to wake them. The Kaymath were on their trail.

"How many!" Fenobar demanded, as they ran to their mounts.

"I counted five whitecrests with four hands each of warriors," Stells replied, his deep voice shaking a little with rage as he checked the makeshift harness holding the Axe. "They carry both their own banner and that of the Kulmore, giving them King's right to walk this territory." He swore an angry, vicious oath. "Deep in strange territory and no idea of who is allied to whom. Talk about wading hip-deep through ghaido droppings!"

It settled into a race then to see who could gain the Shulg Pass first. But the Kaymath had fresh mounts as well as the help of the Kulmore, to whom the Fenirri dared not go. Through the next five days the Fenirri pushed themselves and their tatarra relentlessly, but it was no good. In the late afternoon of the fifth day, the Demon kicked his animal into the lead and forceably brought Stells' tatarra to a halt. "They are ahead of us, Stells," he said in his burring voice. "A troop is waiting in that clump of trees to ambush us."

"How do you know?" Stells was exhausted and his question came out sounding harsh and challenging.

"I saw them," the Demon said, simply.

Fenobar stood in his stirrups, one hand shading his eyes against the sun's lowering glow. He could barely make out the trees the Demon was talking about. The wind was away from them, so no scent came to their noses. But Fenobar had already noted that the Demon had sharper sight than an Imkairan had. When Stells looked as if he would argue and push on anyway, Fenobar said, "If the Demon says there is an ambush there, then there is one. Do not be a fool, Stells. The Demon wants less of the Kaymath than we do."

Cursing, Stells jerked his tatarra's head to the right, away from the foothills, which were now closed to them. The setting sun threw long shadow streamers over the green grass. The eastern prairie stretched undulating waves toward a dark smudge of black where the sky was fading into the greys of evening. It was an empty land and it seemed to Fenobar that the only beings who moved in the twilight were themselves. With nowhere else to turn, they fled toward the east . . . and the sea.

The following evening, ragged, tired beyond death, hungry and staggering in their tracks, they led equally exhausted tatarra. The bottoms of Fenobar's feet felt raw but he refused to look at them, afraid of what he would see. Somewhere behind them the Kaymath were drawing ever closer. But they had to rest, and as they stumbled to a halt below the crown of a low hill, they saw the mellow glow of lamplight in the distance. A town.

Not far from him, Stells stood with one arm over his mount's withers, wide shoulders slumped with a weariness to match Fenobar's. Pelgir, Gartol and Qurngar were silent humps on the ground where they had thrown themselves. The Demon, standing not far away, was staring at the horizon from under a sheltering hand, looking as drained as the rest of them.

The wind brought a new medley of scents, compounded of damp, of fishy smells, of salt, all borne on a clean, wild wind. "Is that the sea I smell?" Fenobar asked suddenly. He had never seen the sea.

"Yes," the Demon said.

Fenobar sniffed deeply, pulling the wind to the bottom of his lungs, savoring it as he would a rare meat.

"The Kaymath are in sight," Qurngar reported tonelessly. Carefully, none of them looked at the Demon.

The news came as no surprise. Fenobar straightened his shoulders. "We can't run any farther. We will go to that town and ask for sanctuary right. Demon, put on your cloak and hide that head of yours or they will never let us near their gates." He half expected to hear a protest from Stells.

But that canny warrior merely nodded. "If we had any other choice. . . ." He let the words and the thought trail off. They were out of any other choices and they knew it. No warrior willingly threw himself on the mercy of a strange tribe . . . and if it were not for the Axe, they would stand and fight to the death. "If they will not give us aid, at least their walls will give us someplace to put our backs."

Fenobar forced his broken, brittle crest up in an attempt at humor, trying to give his warriors hope, as the best commanders did in situations like this. At least, so he had been told. "We are Fenirri. You and the war band are the best of the Fenirri. When the outlander crestkin come outside their walls to look at us, we will steal their mounts and escape!"

"Your youthfulness is appalling," Stells muttered, as he slogged forward down the slight hill, leading his stumbling mount. A little while later he said, "A boat would be better."

"What, Stells?" Fenobar asked, coming along beside him.

"If you must steal something, steal a boat," the sholstan repeated. "This is the sea, you know. They use that kind of transportation here."

Fenobar ignored the sarcasm, chewing over Stells' idea as he walked beside him.

As they came closer to the sea town, Fenobar could see how it sat on a spit of rock around which the waves crashed and rumbled at the base of the cliffs. The walls of the town consisted of only one massive fortification at the narrowest neck of the peninsula. The wall was lined with armored figures, and the great double doors remained open. Fenobar thought this was a good sign, but Stells refused to take heart.

"The Kaymath are getting nearer," that old warrior snapped after a look behind him. "And the outlanders can always close their gates."

The sun was only a red line on the western horizon against which the Kaymath moved, while they themselves stumbled forward into a dusky reddish afterglow, their shadows wavering out over the grass ahead of them. Then the sun slipped below the horizon. Stells looked behind him again. "Get into the saddle," he ordered. "The Kaymath are closing in."

The town grew closer, but not as quickly as the Kaymath. Desperately they pushed their animals to a faster pace, knowing it would be useless. Their tatarra were at the end of their strength, as were the Fenirri. Fenobar turned his head, hearing the rhythmic beat of galloping hooves, and the shrill, excited cries of warriors who see their prey within reach of grasping claws. His tatarra's breath was coming in deep sobbing gasps, and the muscles quivered under his knees and hand as he urged the stallion forward with voice alone. The beast was stumbling now at every step. Willingly, the stallion had given everything he could. There was nothing left. Fenobar slipped out of the saddle, patted the tatarra on the neck in mute apology, and left the animal standing spraddle-legged, head hanging. Sword out, and shield on his arm, he forced himself into a wild, staggering run for the still-distant gate.

Stells' animal went down. The big sholstan leaped clear as the tatarra slowly rolled over to one side, uttered a hoarse cry, and died. Stells lurched into step beside Fenobar, the Axe bouncing heavy and dark across his shoulders at every step, but he had his sword out. Even now Stells was still formidable.

Ahead of them the Demon's animal went to its knees. The Demon leaped from the saddle and pulled the tatarra back to its feet, but it was clearly unable to go another step. There was the swirl of a grey cloak as the Demon came up on Fenobar's other side. His sword, too, was drawn.

Two more animals gave out. Pelgir and Gartol

were also afoot now, some paces ahead. Qurngar, unable to run very far with his bad leg, was still trying to nurse some speed out of his foundered tatarra and falling ever farther behind the rest of them.

Fenobar coolly estimated distances and knew the Kaymath would catch them well before any of them could reach the dubious sanctuary of outland walls. An animal cry of mortal agony sounded behind them as Qurngar's tatarra fell headlong and lay still. The Demon turned, running back for Qurngar. Fenobar stopped, too, to see the Demon pick up the fallen warrior, pull Qurngar's arm over his shoulder, and drag him onwards at a speed none of the rest of them could manage. The Demon and Qurngar caught up with them. The war band had consolidated into a tight little knot of warriors, but compared to the oncoming Kaymath, they moved at the speed of a frightened snail . . . which was to say, no speed at all.

The town walls were a field away.

Three-quarters of a field away.

The thudding of Kaymath hooves behind them sounded closer. Closer. The gates were still open in the outland town . . .

They were only half a field away.

The Kaymath surrounded them, yelping shrill war cries and waving unsheathed blades.

The walls were forever away.

Fenobar shouted a command and turned where he stood, sword up, shield on his shoulder. At his left side, Stells was pressed against him, on the right was Gartol. Qurngar and Pelgir completed the circle of bristling swords and overlapping shields with the Demon, who was the weakest in sword play, in the center. Then the Kaymath were upon them, a confusion of flashing swords and trampling hooves as the tatarra pressed against them, shifting shapes and shadows in the gathering dusk.

Fenobar felt a wave of despair. They were holding their own, but only barely. They could not last much longer. It angered him to see the laughter in the jerking crests, the jeering, which they did not deserve, in the faces behind the Kaymath helms.

"You are going to die!" The Kaymath commander shouted triumphantly.

Fenobar and Stells could not spare the breath to answer him. Then the Axe was taken from Stells' back and the Demon was pushing his way into the circle beside Fenobar, Axe in both hands, fearlessly confronting the Kaymath whitecrests. The Demon laughed his burring Demon laugh, and swung the Axe in a great, impossible overhand arc.

The Kaymath reined back barely clear of that wicked blade, shocked.

"Stay with me!" the Demon shouted, and took a pace backwards, taking the circle with him. Slowly, packed tightly together, the Fenirri moved toward the gate, while the Axe whistled over their heads, singing its ancient song of death.

Fenobar thrust and blocked until his body was shaking with weariness and he could barley lift his weapon, but still the Axe sang its fierce song above their heads, and still the Demon took them step by step toward the outland walls. And then the gate towers were beside them and the gates were being opened to permit their entry. The Kaymath faced drawn bows from the walls and held back, as the Fenirri disappeared inside.

Fenobar watched the gates swing shut, hiding furious Kaymath from sight, and dared to sag against the wall beside him, sobbing for breath. Beside him the

rest of the Fenirri did the same. Swords sank tip
first to the ground. The Demon simply sank down
where he was, bright head cowled under the cloak
hood, held upright only by his clutch on the Axe.
His breath came in great gasps and the air was filled
with the scent of fermented sajawa.

Truly the Demon was a great warrior, even if he
did sometimes act like a darkcrest. The Demon had
earned honor this day and Fenobar must make up a
song about it. Sometime . . . when he wasn't too
exhausted to move.

The town gate was built like the entrance to Fen,
and they were caught in a small chamber between
double gates. He looked up at warriors standing
above them on the crenellated walkways, seeing them
clearly only when they moved against the stars, and
only then did he realize it was full dark.

With a grinding of gears, the gate behind them
was drawn upwards. They pulled themselves away
from the wall, grouping around Fenobar as they
faced the troop of mounted warriors waiting them.
The plaza was well lit, with torches in the hands of
darkcrest and palecrest alike. A great silent crowd of
them formed a crescent of light behind the King and
his war band.

The King's unadorned emblem of his Clan was of a
leaping silver fish on a field of red. His crest flowed
from the top of a fish-shaped helm, and the fur on his
hands and arms looked earth brown in the torch
light.

Fenobar pulled himself up to his full height and
tried to keep his shoulders back. Stells spoke in his
ear. "This is Olkne-by-the-Sea, one of the more prosperous of the Kulmore clans, and one with which we
did not have a treaty. Talk about fighting like a fiend
to gain entry to a pumnor's den! But what can you
expect when you will keep that Demon with us?"

"What do you want from the Olknirri?" the Olkne King demanded.

The answer to that should have been "sanctuary." They were too far gone for any more fighting. But three days of sanctuary would gain them nothing. During that time the Olknirri could take the Axe from them as easily as the Kaymath could later. Swaying on his feet, Fenobar looked as boldly as he could into the King's face. "I want a boat. In return, I and my war band will leave Olkne in peace." Had he overdone the arrogance? He swayed again, and would have fallen except that the Demon moved up to his side, unobtrusively steadying him against his bulk.

"Big talk for one hardly able to stand." The King sounded amused. "Cublin courage. Why are the Kaymath so eager to have your hides?"

Fenobar shrugged. "They war with our tribe and are angered that we escaped from them."

"They have followed you a long way for such a light thing . . ." The Olkne King raised his crest interrogatively.

"In the process of escaping we, er, killed a royal prince and the High Priest and his Second."

"Reason enough to chase you over half the continent," the Olkne King agreed. "Of what Clan are you?"

"Clan Fen of the Monghanirri," Fenobar replied, as proudly as he could.

"And the Clan Spirit is?"

"The Black Axe of Monghan, my Lord," Fenobar said.

The King stroked his chin as he stared at the bloodied Axe in the Demon's muffled hands. He called up to a warrior on the wall. "Sthenek! What do the Kaymath claim we hold here?"

"Outlaws, my Lord," that warrior answered promptly. "They say these six have stolen things of religious importance from their temple and murdered the High Priest. They demand their return."

"They name them as being their own tribe and Clan?" the Olkne King asked.

Sthenek conferred over the battlements with the still raging Kaymath. "Yes, my Lord," he reported.

The King continued to stroke his chin. "You wear Kaymath armor, yet you say you are not Kaymath. How can this be?"

"We stole the armor when we were escaping," Fenobar answered bluntly.

"One does tend to wonder what else you may have stolen. Your honor will not be violated if I question you?" It was delicately put.

As if he were in any condition to protest such a dishonor! Fenobar's wryest twist of ear accompanied his reply. "Speak, my Lord."

"Who is the sholstan of the King of Fen?"

"It is Stells, of the House of the Black Hand—the same House as that of Black Fentaru."

"And what does this Stells look like?"

"Tired," Stells replied for himself impatiently. "And dirty and hungry." He swept off his helm and stared up at the King out of red-rimmed, bleary eyes. "We met ten years ago at the trade council. You are Olkbenor. Then you were Second Son to your sire, Olsank. I congratulate you on your rise in rank."

"Thank you," Olkbenor murmured. The light ran across the incised scales on his helm. "So you are indeed what you say. Yet, why should I let you depart from my city when you have just come, and at such cost to yourselves?"

"Because of me." The words were quietly spoken, but nothing could conceal the otherworldly quality of that burring voice. The Demon pushed the concealing cowl back from his face.

Olkbenor pulled his tatarra back so abruptly the war mount screamed and pawed the air with iron shod cloven feet. The warriors with him all fell back a pace, except for the warrior on his left, who held his position with grim determination. "Demon of Undoing, servant of the God of Chaos! The Kaymath want *you*?"

"I'm one of those 'religious' items they said the Fenirri stole."

Olkbenor's face grew stony as he stared down at the tired Fenirri. His eyes flicked from Stells to the Demon to Fenobar and back again. Then his crest flicked in humor. "The Kaymath have been pushing against our southern border for eight years now, all the while their king mouths honeyed words to me of old laws and inviolate traditions. If I let you go, the Kaymath would be disadvantaged. They would seek to hide the breadth of their loss and all the time knowing I knew, but not how much I know." Once again his eyes settled on the Axe in the Demon's hands. "It is pleasant to be able to twist their ears in so decided a fashion. You shall have your boat. And Demon, see you leave none of your unchancyness behind you!"

The Demon bent at the waist in a stately gesture, which reassured no one.

Olkbenor turned to his sholstan. "See that they reach the harbor and give them my personal sloop."

Six warriors dismounted and handed over their animals to the tired Fenirri. Fenobar could barely pull himself into the saddle. He fell in behind the King's sholstan and followed him through the dark, cobbled streets, lined with the blind walls of the male circle. Where those walls were pierced by streets, lights shone at their far ends . . . the windows of the female circle. Occasionally came the high, thin call of a cublin as they chased each other in wild games in those safeguarded courts.

The road passed through a short wall, dipped steeply downward, and from somewhere in front of them came the sharp, wild perfume of the ocean. Mingled with it was the low, continuous rolling roar which Fenobar realized suddenly was the sound of the sea. Starshine lit their way down the road, while the cliff beside them grew ever higher. Soon, to his right, he could make out the flat tops of warehouses lining the cliff foot. Long walkways made of planks extended out into the water. Tied to these walkways were boats, a forest of masts rising up against the bright stars. The silence was broken by the subtle sounds of lapping water and the creak of wood as the fleet rocked slightly at their moorings.

Fenobar looked at the vessels and his heart went cold. None of the Fenirri knew anything of ships. By the Gods, what had he gotten them into?

CHAPTER TEN

They dismounted. Fenobar stared in dismay at the towering masts, the intricate web of lines running every which way. While he was preoccupied, the Olkne sholstan grabbed the reins from his hand, as if, Fenobar thought resentfully, they thought the Fenirri would try to take the animals with them. The Olkne pointed down the plank walkway in front of them. "The sloop on the left, halfway down," he said briefly and reined his animal around.

"What's a sloop?" Fenobar demanded.

But the Olknirri, leading the spare mounts, put heels to his mount and galloped away among the jumble of sheds and stockpiled crates without answering. "Which ship?" Fenobar's bewildered gaze bounced back and forth from one side of the narrow wharf to the other, where the unfamiliar outlines of ships, masts and tangled rigging seemed as tightly packed as wharful seeds in the pod.

"Come." The Demon started down the long length of slippery, dew-wet wood, the Axe riding over his shoulder as if it belonged there. Not knowing what else to do, Fenobar followed.

High on the cliff above them, the uncertain hoof-beats of animals forced too quickly down a steep slope sounded sharp and clear. The Kaymath were again on their trail. A savage yelping broke from them as they sighted their quarry standing hesitantly at the head of the wharf.

Stells' resigned voice carried easily. "Well, that didn't take long." He unsheathed his sword and stood foresquare across the head of the narrow wharf, the rest of the war band taking their positions behind him. "Lord, take the Axe and the Demon and go."

"I am the whitecrest. I do not leave my war band!" Fenobar snarled, turning back. Black defeat, made all the more bitter by the hope they had had, sent bile up his throat.

"It is I who abandon you," Stells replied imperturbably over his shoulder. "I do not climb into one of those wooden death traps to die with water in my lungs."

"You are the one who said to get a boat!" Fenobar yelled, outraged at this obstinacy. "We leave together or we die together!"

"Use your head, Lord. The war band and I are in no danger from the Kaymath once you are gone. It is the Axe and the Demon they want. The Axe was given in your care and the Demon . . . is yours as well. Shaindar guide your sword hand, Lord." Stells turned to face the oncoming Kaymath.

The Kaymath thundered toward them. Starlight picked out helms, reflected off bared, gleaming teeth, and glittered along the sharp edges of drawn swords.

Stells raised his voice to be heard over the baying. "Demon, take him and the Axe. See they both get to Mone." Stells stood with legs braced, daring the Kaymath to come at him. The war band, too used to Stells' leadership over the years to listen now to a young whitecrest, were raising fesen.

*   *   *

Fenobar took a step toward them, determined to stay with his warriors, as was his duty. A large, muscular arm came around his waist, picked him up bodily, and within five steps dumped him unceremoniously into the bottom of a small sailboat, hidden between two larger craft.

He landed on his bad side, and struggled frantically to right himself, but the shield on that arm caught under a seat and the ribs of the small craft held him in place. With every movement the little boat bobbed and shifted treacherously. The Axe was handed down to him and he grabbed it awkwardly, more out of instinct than conscious thought. A coil of rope landed on top of him, followed immediately by a heavy jolt and violent rocking as the Demon jumped down beside him.

Stepping over Fenobar, the Demon pushed overhand against the fishing vessel beside them. To Fenobar it seemed for a dizzy moment as if the other boat was slipping past them. He snapped at the straps holding his arm to the shield, bit deeply and tore them off. Enraged, he sat up, throwing the damaged shield overboard. It landed flatly with a solid ploosh, rode the waves for a moment and then tipped, sliding straight to the bottom of the harbor, but Fenobar wasn't looking. He was still trying to get his feet under him, but he was tangled up in the rope. He stripped it off him, then stood up, and the boat tilted underfoot. He was about to follow the shield overboard and probably to the same fate when the Demon's long fingers closed on his belt and hauled him back.

"Sit!" the Demon ordered, glaring at him, and to his humiliation, Fenobar sat. He told himself it was because there was fifteen feet of water between himself and the wharf and he didn't know how to swim.

They were past the larger ships now and a wave rocked the little boat. Fenobar gulped and his good hand grasped the gunwale beside him, sinking all four claws deep into the wood. The Demon was searching under the seat by Fenobar's feet and pulled out two oars. He sat down, fitted the rings on the oars into slots in the sides of the boat, and pulled strongly on one. The little boat slowly turned around. When Fenobar could see the wharf, the Demon bent to both oars. With powerful strokes the Demon sent the little boat shooting through the harbor toward the breakwater and the freedom of the open sea.

Anxiously Fenobar strained his eyes to see how the small knot of warriors were faring against the Kaymath. He could still hear the clash and clatter of fighting and he could just make out Stells' form, still on his feet. Then a ship came between them. "We must go north once we are out of the harbor," Fenobar ordered tensely. "Our tribe is allied with the Selnorri up the coast."

"How well can you row, my Lord?" the Demon asked.

"A whitecrest does not do the work of a servant," Fenobar replied haughtily. No one was going to make him admit there was something he could not do.

"Well, my Lord, once we get past the breakwater we will be in the Straits of Tyvai, and the Trulden current goes south at the rate of six miles per minute. If you don't know what that means, then just let me say, it's faster than I can row at the best of times—and right now, I've done about all I can do." For the first time the Demon sounded exhausted.

"Once we get beyond the breakwater, I'm putting up the sail, and where we go depends on the winds and the currents."

Abashed, Fenobar remained silent. The Demon had fought harder than any of them this night. They were beyond the protection of the breakwater now and the waves under their prow grew suddenly choppy. They hit the boat with powerful blows that had no rhythm. The Demon's steady rowing never faltered, and in a few minutes they were beyond the worst of the turbulence. Cold drops sprinkled Fenobar unexpectedly and he lifted his head to see the Demon bringing the oars aboard, stowing them under the seat. Then in a half crouch the creature moved up beside the bare mast, working incomprehensibly. The Demon pulled strongly on a rope and the long bundle at his feet expanded, climbing up the mast and out along the cross pole, cutting a tight triangle out of the stars. With the sail between them, all Fenobar could see of the Demon was his feet.

On the other side of the sail the Demon made a satisfied sound and worked his way back to the square end of the boat with a rope in his hand. By sliding down a little and ducking his head, Fenobar could see the Demon settle down on a bench with the sail rope in one hand and a stick under the other.

Fenobar's crest flicked. He was supposed to be in command, not the Demon. With the Axe in his good hand he slowly worked his way past the sail to the bench where the Demon sat. He settled down beside the Demon without a word. In truth, he was too tired to speak. They were going with the wind and the current, so the Demon said, and those were both in the hands of Tyvai, the God of Chaos. Was it his fault or the Demon's that they were now under the control of the God of Chaos? Fenobar sighed, pulling the Axe to himself for comfort.

The Demon paid out line and the boom swung

around. He was fully preoccupied with his work and paid no heed to Fenobar. The sail filled, billowed outward, and the small craft picked up speed, slanting slightly to one side. The waves ceased their slap, slap, jerk against the hull. The little craft rode smoothly, lifting and then falling . . . lifting . . . and then falling. . . . Fenobar felt his stomach lurch. He eased off the bench and curled up on the deck, hugging the Axe to him, his lips tightly held over clenched teeth.

It seemed hours before he finally fell into an uneasy doze. When he woke the sun was to handwidths above the horizon and he was parched with thirst. The Demon was sound asleep, stretched out on the deck, with the mast line tied down and the stick lashed into place.

Pushing himself up against the uncomfortable curve of the hull, Fenobar scanned the horizon for sign of another sail and sighed thankfully when he saw none.

To the west was a flat stretch of coastline. To the east, the surging water was black and dotted with low, dark islands. Behind them were jagged silhouettes of distant mountains. He squinted in that direction, trying to see those islands more clearly.

The Demon stirred, sat up. "Those are the outlying islands of the Smoking Lands, which you in the west call Namura." The Demon's voice held an odd note of longing.

"You come from those islands, don't you?" Fenobar asked.

"Farther north, but yes, that is home. I have been gone a long time . . . They will think me dead by now." The Demon scrubbed at his face with one hand where, oddly enough, water was spilling from his eyes. "My parents . . . my brothers . . . Carmalita."

Parents? Brothers? There was something too intimate about those words and the images they called up—images Fenobar had never associated with a Demon. Embarrassed, he said, "For having such a bad reputation, these straits don't seem so bad."

"I have kept us to the quieter waters along the coast," the Demon replied. "Farther out, where the Trulden current flows freely, is a lot different."

"If you wish to go home so badly, why have you not set a course for those islands?" Fenobar asked. He was curious.

"The Trulden is not something I would willingly take on at this season with a sailboat and no experienced help," the Demon replied. "It's dangerous at the best of times . . . but now, when the current is changing, it would be death. Even the fisherfolk do not go out in the Straits of Tyvai at this time of year."

"We must go ashore soon," Fenobar said, rubbing at his bad hand. "The Chalig are to the south, and should we find ourselves in their lands . . ."

"We might not have any choice, my Lord. There are not many places to land along this coast, even for a sailboat. It is for the most part sheer cliff with rubble at the base. I know of only one good harborage and it is north of us."

When Fenobar turned to argue he looked at the Demon—really looked at him for the first time. The Demon was a bad sight. His light brown skin was grey. The wild direhawk eyes were puffy and laced with red. Even the bright hair was dulled.

Fenobar wondered if he himself appeared any better. "Nevertheless, we must try to land soon." He was studying the nearer shore now and it was as the Demon had said—all cliffs, with piles of rock at their bases, not a strip of beach to be seen anywhere. He quailed at the thought of trying to land among sharp-edged, jutting rocks. "Do we have any water?"

The Demon shook his head. "But we do have hooks, a line, and even some bait!" He opened a small reed basket attached to the side of the boat beside him and pulled out the items he mentioned, dropping them into Fenobar's lap.

The bait was in a tightly sealed tin and the smell, when Fenobar opened it—the smell was extraordinary. Holding it away from his noise, he asked, "Do fish really eat this stuff?"

The Demon took his place on the seat, taking the rope loop off the stick. He tucked it under his arm and pulled on the sail cord in an authoritative manner. The little boat skipped, and turned slightly away from shore. It was not the commander's place to do darkcrest labor, but even he could see the Demon could not both fish and work the boat. Not unhappily, because he'd never fished before and he'd always thought it looked like it would be fun, he inexpertly baited a hook and tossed it overboard on a line, to trail behind them. Daring greatly, for his balance in this new world was not at all good, he knelt to lean over the side, watching to see what would take his hook. Finally, bored when nothing happened, he turned around and sat down.

The Demon said casually, "Hold this, will you?" and placed Fenobar's hand on the stick he'd been holding and moved to the mast.

The stick felt alive in Fenobar's grip, difficult to hold steady. "What is this?"

"That? Oh, that's the rudder. It helps keep the boat going in the direction we want it to go." The Demon's voice was muffled as he knelt on the deck, pulling his mail shirt over his head. It fell with a metallic chiming onto the deck. "Ahhh . . ." The Demon raised his arms over his head and stretched. "It feels good to have that off! I don't know how you bear it, wearing your armor day and night!"

Fenobar scowled. "A warrior does not remove his armor when he is in the field."

There was a crooked lift to the Demon's lips which Fenobar remembered the books said was a sign of Demon humor. "You are next," the Demon said.

Fenobar stiffened. "I said—" he started in a dangerous voice.

"Common sense, Wrong-Hand. If you fall overboard with all that steel on you, you'll go straight to the bottom."

Sullen and uncertain, Fenobar slipped the rope over the end of the rudder and allowed the Demon to help him off with his mail. The Demon kept his linen undertunic on, but Fenobar used his to wrap up their swords against the salt sea air, which ate through metal faster than a hungry warrior could turn a leg of ghaido into bare bone. He was left with a leather belt into which he had shoved his kalnak and hung the bag containing his firestarter. He sat down, clutching his arm where freshly awakened pain jangled up and down with every movement, feeling naked and uncomfortable under the open sky without his armor.

For a long time he stared at the two bundles of mail lying at the foot of the mast, wrapped in their cloaks. From this angle, he could see that the front of the boat, under the seat, was enclosed. There was a door there, with a simple latch. "What's that?" he asked the Demon.

"The prow storage locker, most like."

Fenobar half crawled, half crouched his way under the sail the few steps to the prow and pulled open the little door. The dark cubbyhole smelled of sun heat, stale air and old fish. Inside was a spare sail, several coils of rope and an extra oar. There was plenty of room to add two bundles of armor, a pair of swords and the Axe of Monghan. In a slightly happier frame of mind he settled down to fishing.

A sharp jerk on the line caused him to give an excited yelp. Gleefully he reeled in a large fish, all silver scales and yellow eyes. Scrupulously he cut it lengthwise and shared it with the Demon. It was a bony morsel, but neither of them cared about that. It slaked their hunger and thirst and that was all that mattered. But while Fenobar ate his half with relish, the Demon seemed to be forcing his share down.

He finished first and was yawning widely, his jaw spread as wide as it would go, and in the act caught sight of the slender, long-prowed ship over the Demon's shoulder. "Ware!" he cried, pointing. "She flies the Olknirri fish and the Kaymath war pike."

The Demon twisted around. "It's between us and shore and coming fast. It is your choice, Wrong-Hand. We cannot outrun her in a straight race. We have a chance if we try to cut across the straits to the islands. It is death either way."

"A more sure death and dishonor if the Kaymath take us." Fenobar's crest jerked in laughter, but fesen lit his eyes. "So let us throw ourselves into the arms of Tyvai, the God of Chaos. Let his power and yours battle it out and see what becomes of us!"

"I don't *have* any power," the Demon muttered under his breath as he swung the rudder hard over, and the little boat nearly laid on her side, sail flapping momentarily before it caught the wind again. "When we hit the Trulden current it's going to be bad."

"Will we sink?"

"Not if I can help it! More like we'll smash against a rock someplace."

Once more Fenobar crawled to the storage locker. Braced against the plunge and wallow of their little craft he pulled out the extra sail and, cutting off several large hunks, wrapped the Axe and the armor, binding them securely with rope. The armor he put back into the storage locker. But he tied the Axe to the mast.

The larger ship gained, until he could see the Kaymath commander standing beside the ship's captain in the prow, pointing at them. But the Trulden current was nearer, and before the two-masted ship could catch up with them, the Demon edged their little craft into the mess of conflicting cross-currents, where the waves met each other at right angles and broke apart in clashing spray. They left blue water, entered grey . . . but beyond the lashing, maddened water, there was a wide stretch where the seas were a glassy dark green. The water changed so abruptly it was as if some God had taken a line and drawn it upon the ocean. Here it was angry . . . here it was not.

"Please let us reach that smooth water," Fenobar prayed—to whom, he did not know. But his desire was a fervent one as they were rocked and battered by lashing waves coming at them, seemingly from every direction. Never had their little boat seemed so frail as every blow communicated itself to Fenobar, who was crouched on the bottom, clutching tightly to wooden ribs. Their forward movement almost ceased. The Demon swore quietly, nursing the winds and the sail. Behind them, the long, narrow ship crept closer, until Fenobar thought he could see teeth gleaming in a triumphant snarl, below a whitecrested helmet.

Fenobar, jammed into a corner beside the stern, endured the jerking, the bounding and bouncing, with set teeth. He was rapidly becoming nauseated and fought to keep the raw fish down where it belonged. Time seemed to last forever and then he heard a wailing, wordless protest and looked up to see the sloop at right angles to them, turning away from that churning zone of false safety. Fenobar squinted past the sail to see they were nearly to the line of quiet water. They reached it and Fenobar sighed aloud as there came a cessation of what he had already endured, a sense of smoothness under the hull.

The water around them was a dark, glossy green. He had time to notice how the Demon was braced in his seat, lips pulled back over flat white teeth. The front of their little boat lifted over a green swell and slid down, and down, and down, until she was almost standing on her nose. Then she started up a mountainous green slope and came up . . . and up . . . and up . . . until Fenobar felt he was upside down, pressed back into his corner. The green waters rose all round and above them and he remembered again that Tyvai was the God of Chaos. There was an instant flash of blue sky and then they were sliding down again. On the edge of his hearing he thought he heard the thunderous laughter of a God.

There was terrible pain in his left hand. He glanced down rather casually because after all, how important could a little pain be, compared to a green wall sliding past his head as the little craft fought its way upward again. He had sunk the malformed claws of his left hand into the edge of the boat. His other hand had a death grip on the seat where the Demon was sitting. His eyes traveled up the length of the Demon's body. The creature was smiling, his head thrown back, braced against the tiller. A sharp breeze was blowing the grain-colored head fur away from his face, where the eyes blazed with all the wildness of a direhawk. The thought occurred to Fenobar that the

Demon was an elemental of the sea and wind, falsely clothed in flesh.

"We are going to fall over," Fenobar said calmly.

"Capsize, you mean? Not us." The Demon dared to laugh. "She's a fine little boat, light and easy to handle. She's a wave dancer, she is."

"I see," Fenobar replied, still in that state of numb calm.

"At the next crest, see if you can spot the sloop," the Demon ordered.

I am a whitecrest. I can move my head. No Demon is going to show more courage than I do, Fenobar told himself. He looked at the sun. They were sailing almost straight south. "She is sailing parallel to us."

"Not coming after us, are they? Very smart. Even if she could survive these seas, she'd never get free of the Trulden current—not until she was carried clear to the South Sea."

"But *we're* in the Trulden current!" Fenobar shouted, his nerve perilously close to the breaking point.

"Yes! Isn't it grand? I never thought it would be so much fun!"

Fenobar wondered if he could free his good hand long enough to sink the claws into the Demon's knee. "How are we going to get out?"

Deftly the Demon trimmed the sail before he answered. "We have to go with the waves or we'll broach in the trough between them. But we can surf the downward slope at an angle, which should throw us up among the islands of the Smoking Lands before we reach the South Sea."

"But you're enjoying yourself!" Fenobar screamed, outraged.

The Demon opened his mouth wide and made a full and hearty sound the like of which Fenobar had never heard before. "God, yes! I've wanted to surf the Trulden for years. This is what flying must be like!"

Over the next few hours, their little craft edged closer to the line of black islands. These seemed to be mostly low, treeless mounds, but among them, especially inland on the island of Namura itself, single cone-shaped mountains rose like teeth. Some of them had wisps of vapor trailing from their summits, the "smoke" for which the Smoking Lands were named. The Olknirri sloop paralleled their path on the far side of the Trulden current at an ever-increasing distance, but still effectively hemming them in.

Fenobar saw little of this. He spent the time braced stiffly in his corner, afraid to move, head down, eyes shut, unable to bear the sight of that glassy green surface looming constantly above them. He only hoped the Demon believed he was sleeping. Perhaps he did sleep, because he came out of some grey twilight of consciousness to the steady sound of a voice. The Demon was staring off to their left, cursing low and monotonously in his own tongue.

When he saw Fenobar's eyes open he pointed with his chin. "Look there, my Lord. More trouble."

Fenobar pushed himself up so he could see over the side. As they came to the top of a swell and hung there for what seemed minutes, he could see a line of mist approaching like a wall into another world, blotting out everything behind and above it. The Demon worked the sail and fought the little boat toward the land in full earnest.

"What is that?" Fenobar asked.

"The Mist of Tyvai. Once it closes around you, you can't see past the end of the boat. Pray we gain the shore while we can still see what we're crashing into."

"Crashing . . . ???" Fenobar closed his eyes. "I knew I should not have even so much as thought that our luck had changed." Opening his eyes again he said quite composedly, "I think you should know I cannot swim."

The Demon groaned. "And there isn't a life preserver on board. Okay, this is what you do. Tie all the oars together, and when you go into the water, hang onto them."

The oars looked very slender and insubstantial as Fenobar wrapped the last of the line he'd found in the forward storage locker around them. He left a sliding loop big enough to go around his shoulders and returned to his place on the deck beside the Demon, holding his makeshift life preserver to the deck with his feet. He sat chewing on his claws, worrying about the Axe tied to the mast.

Meanwhile, they fought closer to the shore, while the mountainous waves shrugged them off again and again. The fog caught up to them and the air turned grey, darkened, and swirled softly around them. The wind died and the sail flapped loosely. The Demon swore some demonish oath. Chewing furiously at his under lip, the Demon peered into the fog, his hand tense on the tiller. The little boat didn't seem to be moving at all, just bobbing up and down in the water.

A gust of wind tattered the curtain of fog for a moment. A black rock slid past them. They heard it then, a booming as water smashed against a shoreline, the sudden change in the feel of the waves. The sail belled suddenly and the Demon worked desperately to catch the uncertain wind. The water turned suddenly choppy, flinging them from one side to the other. The Demon hung desperately onto the tiller, his feet braced, eyes narrowed, trying to steer by

sound alone. There was no laughter in the Demon
now. Water sprayed up over the sides of the boat
and sloshed around their feet. Somewhere in that
impenetrable grey wall enclosing them was a too-
near shoreline.

"We're inside the first line of islands," the Demon
told Fenobar. His face was running with water dripping down from his hair as the fog condensed on
them both.

Something ground along the side and bottom of
the craft. The Demon yelled to hold on and Fenobar
let go the side of the boat to clutch his bundle of
oars, slipping the line around his shoulder, tighten-
ing the stubborn rope with wet, desperate fingers.
The sailboat lurched, tipped, and spray leaped over
the rail, followed closely by a wave, then another,
crashing down on Fenobar. He fought for breath as
the water poured over his face, got a hazy half glimpse
of the Demon, still clutching the tiller. Water streamed
from his body, and his lips were pulled back in a
white snarl. The boat heeled sharply over as something struck the bottom.

A black shape loomed up beside them, shiny and
wet. He shouted once. The boat lifted, slammed
mightly onto the rock, and Fenobar was pitched
overboard, clutching his bundle of oars.

CHAPTER ELEVEN

Frantically, Fenobar fought to keep his head above water, clutching the oars to him desperately. Water roared over his head, filling his mouth as he tried to get a breath. Strangling, coughing, only his Bokeem training kept him from giving way totally to panic. What had become of the Demon he did not know. He was pushed and tugged by ferocious currents, swirled around insanely, and finally smashed against a rock. Dimly he heard the oars cracking as he rebounded from the obstacle and was swept around it. His feet dragged across something which tore at the flesh and he was lifted high to smash down onto another rock, and stuck fast as his bundle of oars jammed between two boulders. Dazed, he clung to them, knowing it was sure death to let go.

His good arm was losing strength and he knew he could not hold on much longer against the incessant battering and tugging of wave and undertow. His bad arm hung uselessly. Foam and grit-filled water poured over the rocks into his face. His hold started to slip. He lifted his head and voiced his despair in a

163

howl which ended prematurely in a gurgle and choke as a wave hit his face. He had lost the Axe. He had failed his Clan. His sire was right. He was weak and unfit to be a warrior, no mater how many tricks he had invented to survive. Lost! All lost! He managed to suck in a mouthful of air and threw his head back for another howl. Three-quarters drowned he heard, somewhere above and behind him, a deep, burring voice shouting. "Hang on, my Lord, I'm almost there!" A strong, five-fingered hand closed around his wrist and pulled Fenobar upwards, but only a foot or so.

"The rope," Fenobar managed to gasp out. "My kalnak. At my back."

Still hanging onto Fenobar's arm, the Demon plucked the kalnak from Fenobar's belt and in a quick movement slashed the rope, freeing Fenobar from the oars. In another moment, he had pulled Fenobar from the deadly waters.

Gasping, Fenobar knelt on the slippery wet rock, supported by the Demon. "The Axe! We must find the Axe!"

"The Axe is with the boat, and the boat is securely wedged. There will be no getting to it until the mist lifts. If you try for it now, you will die, and what good will you be to the Axe if you are dead?" the Demon replied with strong common sense. He put an arm around Fenobar's shoulders. "In the meantime, let's find some solid land not so close to the sea." Unsteadily, they made their way to a broad stretch of barren black bedrock and collapsed in the lee side of a humped ridge, out of the wind.

Fenobar woke with the scent of sajawa hot in his nostrils, overlaid with the distinctive smell of seaweed. His back was warm, the rest of him was chilled. He looked over his shoulder, ignoring the pain the movement caused him. He was lying against the

Demon, who was curled in on himself, looking strangely vulnerable.

The soft grey Mist of Tyvai was all about, and only where they lay did there seem to be a little island of solidity. Stiffly, Fenobar sat up, hurting in every joint and muscle. Gently, he touched the heavy shoulder next to him. "We cannot stay here," he croaked. "It will be full dark soon. We will need a fire, and shelter . . . Demon?"

For once the Demon did not answer. Fenobar stopped trying to wake the other and slowly gained his feet, wincing at every movement. Clouds of white and black sea birds soared dimly through the mist around them. Several were standing not far away, eyeing the two intruders impudently, their blue feet a splash of color in an otherwise monochrome scene. Fenobar found himself drooling. But first, he told himself sternly, they had to find shelter.

They seemed to be on a flat shelf of rock below a cliff. There didn't seem to be any place to go but up. After a little search he found a way to the top of the cliff. He had thought the island as barren as the rock shelf on which they had rested, but the top of the cliff contained a meadow about half the size of a training field. Behind the meadow the land rose to form a single black mountain. The thin soil supported an amazing variety of grass, flowers, shrubs and even some small trees. At the back of the meadow where the mountain rose steepest, he found a tumble of rocks that had fallen in such a way as to form a wide, shallow cave. He stuck his head inside to check it out and found nothing but wind-blown debris. It was getting dark as he went back to get the Demon and the air was turning cool, striking through his still-wet fur. He shivered as he came down the last few feet to the rock shingle.

The Demon was awake, sitting with his knees drawn up, where Fenobar had left him, looking forlorn and abandoned. Against the dark rock, the Demon was a glimmer of white, his pale head almost luminescent. He looked around at Fenobar's approach. As Fenobar drew closer he realized the Demon was shivering convulsively.

"I have found a place, there, above the cliff," Fenobar said. The Demon uncurled as stiffly and as painfully as Fenobar had upon awakening. He said nothing. Perhaps he couldn't, his teeth were rattling in his head so hard. Fenobar had never seen anyone's face shake like that and he wanted to ask about it, but figured collecting driftwood for a fire was more important than making idle conversation.

Fenobar still had his firestarter in a small bag at his belt, and with this he coaxed into life a small flame, fed it wood until it blazed into a hot fire. The heat reflected off the back of the shelter, warming the space quite nicely. They crouched over the flame, and after a time, the Demon stopped shivering. Sweeping together the sand and dried leaves on the cave floor, he fell asleep on top of them.

Fenobar, on the other hand, was wide awake, having reached that point of exhaustion where he was too tired to sleep. He sat staring out at the mist-filled darkness, running his hand through his crest, trying to work out the tangles. He stopped when he noticed broken white hairs showering into his lap.

The Demon stirred in his sleep. There was something curiously secure in the dark, the fire . . . their aloneness. It was the feeling he had sought from his Sire's warriors as a cublin and never found. He had never dared to go to his sire, as his brothers had occasionally done. There had never been any protection for him there . . . and little anywhere else.

Guiltily . . . moved by old, unfulfilled need, he lay down beside the Demon and snuggled up so that his back was against the other. The Demon shifted in his sleep, rolled over and wrapped a heavy arm around Fenobar's middle, pulling him close, burrowing his face into his neck. The creature's warm breath stirred the honey-colored fur on Fenobar's shoulder. In spite of himself his crest fluffed up in response to a keen inner delight.

There was a grunt of surprise near his ear. Warmth was withdrawn as the Demon sat up. Fenobar opened his eyes to morning, the sun shining gloriously and hotly down on them. He yawned and turned half over to look at the Demon.

The other was rubbing at his eyes with the heels of his hands. "I'm sorry. I seem to have spent most of the night hugging you."

Fenobar shrugged, trying to keep his ears from flattening with knowledge of his own wrongdoing. "How else were we going to keep warm?"

The Demon turned red, raw-looking eyes in his direction. "We need to find water. We can't live on fish juice."

Now that the word was spoken, Fenobar realized his mouth and throat were aflame with thirst. He scrambled out of their shelter at the Demon's heels. Hands on hips, the Demon was looking around at the lush, green plateau. "We're in luck at last. These plants are the kind that need a lot of water. Therefore . . ." He tilted his head back to study the rocks and the mountain looming starkly above them. "It should rain a lot. If it rains a lot, there should be places where the water collects . . . or even springs."

They spread out and started looking. It was Fenobar who found the deep basin a short distance up the mountain flank, half filled with scummy water. At his excited hail the Demon came running, to drop belly-down beside where Fenobar was already drinking in long, thirsty gulps. Finally satiated, they wiped their faces and sprawled back among the rocks surrounding the pond. Squinting up at the bright sky the Demon said, "There must be some way of saving this. Perhaps if we put branches over it . . ."

Remembering how the mist had condensed on their fur, Fenobar said, "The mist comes in at night. Is there some way we can collect water from that . . . ?"

"Yessss." It was a long, drawn-out sound, almost a hiss. The Demon's eyes looked a bit unfocused. "If we hung up seaweed, the water would collect to the leaves and drip off . . . into what? Seashells, if we can find ones large enough. Or I could carve bowls out of the rock."

From where they were they could see the Mists of Tyvai had receded back out into the straits, retreating in the face of the offshore wind, and were hanging, an impenetrable barrier, just even with the outer islands. But here and there it was sending in form-less tendrils between the small black islands, as if it were reaching for them.

The inner circle of islands were nothing more than a line of low, humped rocks. Between two of them, washed up like a dead bird, lay the tangled, shattered remains of the sailboat.

"You sound as if we're going to be here for a long time," Fenobar said slowly, his eyes glued to the wreckage.

"I'll tell you the truth, Wrong-Hand. Things don't look real good for us."

"Of course they don't," Fenobar said sourly. "If things were good, you wouldn't be doing your job. What happened? Did they give you to me just to make my life interesting? One day the Gods got together and said, 'Look! Fenobar Wrong-Hand is finally about to make something of his life. Let's give him a Demon and see how long it takes to destroy him.'" He picked up a rock and threw it viciously into the water.

The Demon opened his mouth to protest, but Fenobar cut him off. "I don't blame you for that . . . it's your nature, after all. And if it's any consolation, you have succeeded. You can return to your masters, your duty fulfilled." His voice choked. "I have lost the Axe."

The Demon put a long-fingered hand above his eyes and peered in the direction of the wreck.

"It has no mast. The Axe is gone." Fenobar wanted to howl.

The Demon stood up. "That we won't know until we go look. Come!" He started back down the mountain, carelessly sliding down the slope.

Fenobar stared after him, mouth open. Then rising hope sent him trotting after the other. His more cautious descent gave the Demon a chance to get ahead of him, and when he reached the little meadow, the Demon was already taking the path down to the shore.

By the time Fenobar caught up with him, the Demon was far down the rock bed which served as a beach. He came to a stop opposite the wreck of the sailboat, hands on hips, staring out to sea. To Fenobar, the wreck looked a terribly long way from shore, and he didn't like the look of the foam-topped waves. Without saying a word the Demon removed his tunic and boots. Dropping them onto the black rocks, he waded into the water.

Fenobar suddenly splashed after him. "Wait! You will need a knife." He pulled the kalnak from his belt and pressed the handle into the Demon's palm. "Your challenges be won!"

The crestless head nodded a salute and acknowledgement, put the wide blade between his teeth, and dove into the surf.

Fenobar watched the Demon swimming strongly, his body a pale blot among the green waves. His bad hand suddenly cramped, and started to twitch. He rubbed at it unconsciously, suddenly panicking when he could not find the bright Demon head among the curly-topped combers. His bad hand shook worse than ever.

It seemed an incredibly long time before Fenobar saw a form, starkly white against the black rock, climb out beside the ruined sailboat. The Demon waved both arms over his head at Fenobar, and Fenobar waved as vigorously back, swinging his one sound arm until the pulled muscles in his back protested.

The Demon worked his way cautiously to the wreck, plunged into the water beside it, and disappeared. Fenobar held his breath. The Demon did not come up . . . and did not come up . . . Just when he was frantic enough to start wading into the water, the Demon surfaced with a great splashing. A yell, wordless but exuberant, echoed across the water, as the mast bobbed to the surface, trailing slashed bits of rope but with a white thickness attached to it a third of the way from one end. The Axe. Fenobar's knees gave way and he sat limply down on the rock shelf.

But the Demon was not through. Again and again

he dove, while Fenobar strained to see what he was doing. Finally the Demon was returning, pushing the mast. There were not one, but three bundles tied to the wood. Splashing into the surf to meet him, Fenobar added his strength to that of the Demon's to drag the mast onto the beach. Once safely ashore, he slashed at the lines holding the Axe and pulled open the bundle. Water, tinted pink, ran from the inside of the wrapping, as he pulled the Spirit forth. Gently running his hand over the haft, he turned the double blade in the sunlight, watching the dark rainbows play in the scalloped edges.

He hardly noticed as the Demon plunged again into the waves and only looked up to catch a glimpse of that sun-bright head beside the wreck again. He cradled the Axe to him with his one good arm, asking for protection for the Demon. The waves seemed to be washing higher over the rocks, and the force of them was shifting the sailboat. The Demon did not seem to notice. He was crouched above the broken boat, and finally pulled the sail loose, plus a quantity of rope. He was just in time. When the next large wave swept over the rock it took the wreck with it. The remains bobbed once and then sank.

This time when Fenobar helped the Demon get his booty ashore, the other stumbled and sank down tiredly.

"You didn't need to go back!" Fenobar said angrily.

"Sails are very useful things," the Demon gasped. "And so are hooks and fishing line."

At the mention of fishing line their thoughts turned simultaneously to food. They exchanged a long look and turned as one being to look at a pair of too confident sea birds which strutted not far away. Fenobar was the first to move, and proved faster than the Demon. They cooked and ate them right there.

When they got back to camp, the first thing Fenobar did was to prepare a place of honor for the Axe against the back wall of their cave. Giving it a last, respectful salute, he picked up his bundled armor and took it out into the sunlight to clean.

The Demon had spread the salvaged sail material to dry on the grass. On one section of canvas was a large pile of red seaweed. From this the Demon was carefully cutting sections about three feet long and draping them over a length of salvaged rope which he had tied between two small trees.

"Very nice," Fenobar said, ears flicking. "Very decorative. Just what the place needs for that homey touch."

A little stiffly the Demon replied, "I'm drying this for eating."

"I'd rather gag on a fruit pit," Fenobar muttered.

Finishing with the seaweed, the Demon then spread the sail over the top of their shelter, carefully making sure it formed a deep hollow in the center. "There," he said, adding a last rock to hold the material in place. "When it rains, we'll have our own reservoir."

Fenobar, bent over his armor, let his ears fold back to his skull. Putting down the sand-covered rag he was using, he looked up at the Demon from under the fall of whitecrest. "We must talk."

Giving him a curious glance, the Demon sat down near him and unfolded his own armor. He spread it across his lap, picked up a rag Fenobar had laid ready, and busied himself. When Fenobar still had said nothing, the Demon gave him a sideways look out of those direhawk eyes. "Well?"

Fenobar was not finding it an easy task to put his

thoughts and feelings into words. Matters touched on things he would rather not speak about, but it had become necessary. To waste any more time getting to it was rank cowardice. They might call him wrong-handed and a skirter of honor, but they would never be able to call him craven. Crest held at an uncompromising angle, his suddenly austere eyes sought the Demon's face. "When I first saw you, I said to myself, 'This is a gift from my Demon. He with whom I am allied.' You were a darkcrest, I thought, sent to serve me in the way of a darkcrest. But you change constantly, shifting from darkcrest to whitecrest to palecrest and back again. There is no holding you to one thing or another. You are my responsibility, for I set you free into the world. But which of us is higher in rank?"

The Demon tugged on one round, absurd ear. "I had not thought of status."

The Demon had not thought of rank. Fenobar felt his mind skittering away from the words, unable to take them in. Position was all a warrior ever thought about. Even darkcrests jostled among themselves for standings. Fenobar had a sudden urge to yank at his crest and beat his head on the ground. Instead, he held himself rigidly unmoving. He was a whitecrest, by all the gods, and he was not going to lose control.

He had fashioned a sling for himself earlier to take the weight off his shoulder, and now, hidden behind the material, his bad hand started to twitch. "Once you called me by House name, as a Ranking Ally would. Three times you have used my familiar name, calling me 'Wrong-Hand,' as is proper between unallied whitecrests. More often you have called me 'my Lord,' as if you were one of my war band. Pretending for a moment that you are, or ever could be, such a thing, let me ask you this . . ." He gestured to his twisted arm. "You know I am wrong-handed, that because of this I will never rise very high in status or honor among the clan. But you have repeatedly offered me . . . your hand—help which is usually reserved to the best and highest ranking. Why?"

The Demon's face had taken on a reddish glow and he kept his eyes firmly on his hands as he worked the sand-laden cloth over the same section of mail, even though the rings were already burnished. "At first it was because you took me out of that evil place . . . that cell in Kaymath. And you stood up to Stells when he wanted to kill me. Later . . . I did it because I like you."

"What is this word 'like'?" Fenobar asked, wrinkling his muzzle in confusion.

"I did it because it pleased me to do so."

Again Fenobar was at a loss. One did things out of duty. Or because it was honorable. Or because it was the law. There were the small, secret satisfactions you got from feeling warm and fed and safe. There was the heady, heart-lifting throb of battle madness. But what did any of that have to do with helping one to whom you were not bound? "You risked your life to bring me the Axe. It is no clan spirit of yours. Why did you do it?"

"Because it was important to you."

What kind of a reason was *that?* Fenobar's hand leaped like a wild thing, and at the same time a stabbing pain shot behind his eyes. His right hand grabbed for his left to hold it down and he closed his lids to shut out the sight of the Demon. Licking his lips a bit feverishly he started, "What . . ." and stopped, not knowing what it was he wanted to ask. "Why . . ." He tried again and again ran out of words.

"Perhaps I did not say it right. This is not my own language," the Demon said, peering anxiously at him from under a fall of bright hair. "Perhaps . . . sholstan duty comes closer?"

"No. I don't think so," Fenobar said hoarsely, and gave it up.

"Why does having a bad arm mean you will never rise in rank? I have listened to you and watched you. I haven't seen any reason your arm should stop you from becoming anything you want to become." The Demon spoke calmly, without heat.

Fenobar opened his eyes at that. The Demon was industriously scrubbing away at his armor, bright head bent over his work. The Demon had seen the promise of high rank in him! He himself knew it was there, but no one else had ever seemed to think so. Had the Demon been other than himself, Fenobar would have unhesitatingly (provided he knew the other's rank) have either offered alliance or a place in his war band. He was silent for a long time, and when he spoke again, found himself putting into words the things he'd never been able to say to anyone else, ever.

"There is no place among warriors for a cripple. But I was born cublin to Black Fentaru, King of Fen, and he had named me before my birth. Therefore, I was not killed when they saw how twisted I was. Though Black Fentaru wished to put me aside, he could not, for the Naming has certain duties which go with it. So we were stuck with each other. Yet, I made it part of my honor to be worthy of the name I bore. I succeeded . . . after a fashion. But it was hard . . . you have no idea how hard." Unconsciously he was rubbing fiercely at his bad hand as he spoke.

"They never expected me to come back from Bokeem, where they train whitecrests. They thought

I would die there . . . and I almost did. With the help of my Demon I found a way to survive. But that survival has not been without its price. My bad hand forced me to cast aside tradition, developing my own weapons, which suited my need, learning to mirror all the left-hand moves. I was fast. It was all that saved me in those early years. But I survived and I became cunning as well. I fought differently and the others complained bitterly. They said I skirted dishonor. But it was not the way I fought they disliked. I was *good*. My success was a taunt to their wholeness. But it hurts to know the price of survival is to be not quite respectable in the eyes of your clancrests."

"And to add to your trouble you have a Demon of Undoing following you about?"

"I was bound to be exiled sooner or later. It might just as well be for that reason as any other," Fenobar said wryly, but he could not keep his crest from drooping.

"And a good thing for you, I think," the Demon said judiciously.

"What!" Fenobar was glaring at the other.

"If your clan will not give you room to see what you can do, go somewhere where the folk will. What have you to lose?"

This was the first time the Demon had so blatantly used the disastrous power of his kind and Fenobar gasped. "What kind of change do you think to work on me? Be silent!"

The Demon was startled and turned those grey, direhawk eyes to Fenobar. "But . . ."

"Silence!"

The Demon said no more, but the look in his eyes was that of a wounded cublin. Fenobar had never seen such a look on an adult male before. Warriors fought or were silent . . . they didn't look so . . .

hurt. The books had not mentioned this side of Demon power. Goaded, he snarled, "Oh . . . say it and be done!"

"I wasn't trying to change you. It's just that every situation has a good side and a bad side. You saw the bad side. So I showed you the good side. Those of us you call Demons of Undoing, we have no special powers. . . ." The Demon rubbed at his strange sharp nose with the back of one hand. "I haven't any more supernatural power than you have—really! I'm a very ordinary kind of person. I can't change things, or make them go wrong."

"Demon, I have been with you for two hands of days, and in that time things have done nothing *but* go wrong."

"Like what?"

"The Axe was subject to raltmichak, we were chased to exhaustion by the Kaymath, we had to cross the Straits of Tyvai, we nearly drowned, we smashed the boat in the Mists of Tyvai, and now we are marooned on a tiny island with no way off."

"We saved the Axe from the raltmichak, which was never finished on it. We escaped from the Kaymath, we survived crossing the straits, we didn't drown, and the Mists of Tyvai provide us with water," replied the Demon, ticking the points off with one long finger.

"What about getting off this island?"

"I'm thinking on it."

"Hunh!" Fenobar snorted. His crest could not fluff because of the sticky residue left from the sea salt, but his ears twitched with amusement. In a voice dripping with overmuch sweetness, Fenobar said, "So. It is coincidence you trail change behind you like the Sprite of Spring trails flowers." Purring, he added, "But if you are not a Demon of Undoing, *what* are you?"

His ears twitched wildly as he heard the note of helplessness in the Demon's voice when he answered, "I'm called a human being."

"And you are from?"

The Demon cleared his throat. Not looking at Fenobar, he mumbled something at the mail in his lap.

"What's that?"

"We're from another world."

"Demons are hardly from this one," Fenobar said dryly. "But still you say you're not a Demon."

"Yes."

"Hunh!"

A little wildly, the Demon ran his five-fingered hand through his head fur, which was as stiff and sticky as Fenobar's. It stood up under this attention like a particularly ratty crest. "I'm a very ordinary kind of person!"

"Very ordinary . . . for a Demon," Fenobar agreed.

"For a *human*!" the Demon protested.

"You're still a Demon of Undoing, no matter what you call yourself."

"I call myself Sig," the Demon said, a little desperately.

"Human Being Sig?" Fenobar asked sweetly.

"Sigmund DeGama Cook of the tribe of . . . of . . . United Stars Interstellar Survey. Human being. As you are Imkairan."

"Oh." Fenobar scrubbed at his almost forgotten armor as he thought that over. "How did humans get here?"

"We . . ." Sig gagged on a word and came to a confused stop. "I can't tell you."

"Can't or won't?"

"Won't," the Demon admitted miserably.

"Ah . . . You used some kind of magic ritual which permitted you to fly here, not so?" Fenobar looked slyly up at Sig from under the long hairs of his crest. "Demons use them all the time."

Sig put his head in his hand, surrendering. "All right. I'm a Demon."

"Could you be anything else?" Fenobar murmured. "Let me show you how to clean that leather properly . . . Sig."

CHAPTER TWELVE

"How old are you, Fenobar?"

They were on the beach two weeks later and the question came after a period of silence between them during which the Demon had whacked unceasingly at the prow of the sailboat with his sword. The prow had been cast ashore after a storm and Sig had fallen upon it with cries of delight. He was now making it a part of the raft they were building.

Fenobar was seated nearby, single-handedly twisting seaweed into a rope, and had been thinking, not for the first time, that even though the weapon Sig was using was Kaymath make, it still deserved better than to be used as a wood axe. At least the Demon had never suggested they use his Bokeem sword to do his work. Sig's question caught him by surprise, coming as it did without any advance warning. "I have nineteen summers."

Sig looked up and laughed. "I have nineteen summers, too."

Fenobar was getting used to the strange sound the

other made when he was happy. "So young?" Fenobar asked in surprise. "I thought Demons ageless!"

"Humans are much like Imkaira," Sig said. He was not wearing his tunic and his torso and arms had turned red.

Fenobar thought it interesting that Demons would change their color like that. It had not been mentioned in the old books. "If you are so like Imkaira, then why won't you give me your ranking? How can we continue to live in a state of uncertainty? I don't believe it bothers you at all. *Does* it?"

There. It was out. The matter had rankled with him for the last two weeks but he had kept silent while his shoulder healed. He flexed his bad arm now, experimentally, and was relieved when the movement brought no pain.

"Why . . . no." Sig looked just as surprised as Fenobar had thought he would. The Demon put down the sword and turned to face Fenobar. "Is ranking so important? I thought you had stopped worrying about it."

It was statements like that which jarred Fenobar whenever he was starting to get comfortable with the Demon. There was a hidden sea of differences between them, and every once in a while the Demon swept the veil of familiarity aside and let him see it. Outlander! Outlander! a voice cried inside him. If an Imkairan had asked if ranking was important it would have been taken as a challenge. But Sig had said the words with such an air of innocent earnestness that it must be true that he really did not understand. "Your status is what you *are*. It is an insult not to give your ranking so that others might know what is due you and from you. I do not even know if you are whitecrest or palecrest in your own land." It sounded sullen even to himself.

With a heavy 'thunk,' the sword bit into a plank and Sig left it hanging there. Putting one foot up on what remained of the prow, he leaned both arms on his knee, studying Fenobar. After a moment he said, "We don't figure a person's worth by head color."

Fenobar sighed heavily. "I expected you to say something like that." And then angrily. "But we do! And although I concede you high honor and rank being what you are. I *must* know if you are white or palecrest!"

"Why?"

"Because I cannot challenge you for rank if you are palecrest—it would be dishonor."

"Because you're a whitecrest and that automatically outranks a palecrest?"

"Yes."

"What do you think I am?" Sig asked. "What does your stomach tell you I am?"

Coldly Fenobar said, "My stomach tells me you are close to me in rank and nothing more." That was not quite true. His stomach told him the Demon was a sholstan, for there was none of the tenseness between them that would be there if they were both whitecrests. But neither was there the subservience a lower ranking palecrest would naturally show a whitecrest. Only a sholstan could be an equal to a whitecrest . . . but only if his commander were of equal or higher rank than that whitecrest.

So it would be if the Demon were Imkairan . . . but the Demon being what he was, it might be better to pretend ignorance and see what happened, before committing himself.

But Sig was silent.

"If I am confused as to what you are, it is because you keep changing." Was that aggrieved note really issuing from his throat? Fenobar asked himself, listening to the words with a kind of dim shock. "First I thought you were a darkcrest. Then after a bath you turned out to be palecrest . . . and *now* . . ." He pointed an accusatory finger at Sig's head. "Now you are turning white!"

"What would you like me to be?" The tone was level, mildly interested.

Fenobar scowled at the Demon, his ears flattening. It was a trap. "It is not what I want you to be, it is for you to be what you are." The words came out a near growl.

"But I do not know what rank I hold in your world." It was said oh, so softly. "So. What shall we do about it?"

That was the thing Fenobar liked most about Sig. He never raised fesen. He listened, he thought about what he heard, and tried to find an answer. "I have given it some thought. A warrior determines his personal status and honor by contesting with other warriors. Since I am the only one here, we can start by discovering if you are whitecrest or palecrest. If you are palecrest, you will raise fesen sometime during the fight. A whitecrest would have better control."

"But—" Sig started.

Fenobar, deep in his own thoughts, didn't hear him. "However . . . I don't wish to kill you, and your swordplay is still atrocious, even after ten days of practice. I have given it some thought, and—"

"Are you saying you want to fight me?" Sig asked, disbelievingly.

Fenobar's crest flicked in irritation. "That's what a challenge generally means. Yes."

"Oh." Sig was silent for a long moment, chewing on his lower lip in a manner Fenobar found singularly unattractive. "How about hand to hand fighting . . . no weapons."

Fenobar's crest fluffed and his ears twitched madly. It was too silent for the bubbling laughter inside him, however, and he ventured a very demonlike snort. Holding up his good hand he flexed the claws. "Would you have me pull them out, then?"

"This is a friendly fight. I won't break any of your bones if you won't shred my skin."

"Friendly fight. . . ." Fenobar tasted the alien word. "What's 'friendly' mean?"

"Not serious." Sig had stepped away from the boat and fallen into an unmistakable fighter's crouch.

Taking the same kind of stance, Fenobar pulled in his claws and flicked the crest hair out of his eyes. "Well, I *said* I didn't want to kill you."

"There's a little more to 'friendly' than that!" Sig straightened up, alarmed.

"Like what?" Fenobar remained on guard. He hadn't survived Bokeem by being gullible.

"How about we don't do each other any serious damage."

"You want a *cublin* fight?"

"Yes!"

"That's so . . . immature."

"Humor me."

"Oh, very well," Fenobar said in a bored tone. "But it won't be nearly as interesting."

"I can stand it," Sig replied, resuming his crouch.

"You agree that the outcome holds just as if this were a real fight . . ." It was only half a question.

"I agree," Sig said, and started moving to the right.

Crest fluffed because the Demon was so terribly slow, Fenobar leaped and deliberately struck for the Demon's chest, high, near the throat . . .

But the blow did not land. The Demon jerked up a smooth muscular forearm, knocking the blow aside in a move faster than Fenobar thought possible for the other to make. He was tossed off, onto the rock. He rolled to his feet, eyes alight with sudden interest. Fenobar hurled himself again at the other. Again he was tossed off.

He came in from the side, brought a leg up in a feint and stepped around behind Sig, hand going for the Demon's groin. But a strong, five-fingered grip arrested that movement somehow and a flurry of blows, all obviously pulled to keep from doing any real damage, landed on various parts of his body. His own blows were softened as well, and in the seconds before he was tossed to the ground again, Fenobar figured they could have killed each other four times over in that one exchange alone.

They circled each other, refraining from an immediate bout for the same reason—to rest, to work the pain out of their muscles, and to figure out strategy. The Demon's style was completely different from anything Fenobar had ever seen. He had thought it might be, considering the lack of claws and the way Sig could bring his arm around in a circle. But the reality was fascinating. So was the unfamiliar experience of having a right-handed opponent.

Fenobar realized he was too used to fighting left-handed warriors. This was a serious lack of training he never realized he had. But Sig was making it abundantly clear that whatever Fenobar had in quickness and claw, was more than made up for by Sig's familiarity with a right-handed fighter.

Using his quickness to good advantage, Fenobar ducked under an extended hand, caught that arm, and threw the Demon across his hip, falling with him, riding him down onto the rock. They rolled. His claws were at the Demon's throat.

But instead of yielding, the Demon had his hand

locked around Fenobar's, bent a finger back excruciatingly, and pressed a hard thumb into the inside of
his wrist. Fenobar's hand came loose, surprising him.
He had never let go a right-handed hold before.

They rolled again and this time the Demon was on
top. Fenobar lifted a foot and clawed the other, but
lightly, along the inside of his leg. The Demon stiffened and Fenobar thought exultantly, "He knows he
has lost! I could have laid open the entire thigh . . ."
He looked up to see the Demon staring over his
head at the sea.

"Gods!" Sig was off Fenobar in a flash, hauling the
slighter Imkairan to his feet, thrusting him toward
the cliff. "Run!"

But Fenobar turned around. The surf was filled
with huge, dark bodies bearing sleek, bewhiskered
faces. Dark liquid eyes gazed at them over foot-long
tusks. Fenobar backed up slowly as the first of the
creatures rode in on a breaker, humping itself awkwardly over the rock on broad flippers. It was huge!

A five-fingered hand caught at the loose roll of fur
at Fenobar's neck and yanked him out of the way as
the sea creature lunged at him. Missing its strike it
reared up, overtowering them. A short crest lifted
along its head. The large, bewhiskered face, sporting
teeth as long as a forearm, stared haughtily down at
Fenobar for a moment and then snaked forward to
honk deafeningly into his face.

Fenobar turned and was gone like an arrow, the
Demon not far behind him. Seemingly satisfied with
this retreat, the sea creature promptly lost interest in
them, turning on its fellows, who were sliding in on
the surf, bellowing an unmistakable challenge.

Fenobar's feet didn't slow until he was halfway up
the cliff path. And then it was only to take the time

to glance over his shoulder to see where Sig was. That bright head was only a little way below him. They sat down at the top of the cliff to catch their breath. Below them, the beach was alive with heavy bodies, all roaring at the top of their tremendous voices. The bellowing and honking grew louder with every passing moment. A bull made a lunge and within seconds the beach was seething with conflict.

Sig had contorted himself into his usual cross-legged tangle, elbows on knees. Gloom was settling around him like a palpable force as he watched the animals.

"What are they doing?" Fenobar asked. They had not finished the challenge to his satisfaction, but somehow this did not seem the time to revive it.

"Staking out territory, so when the females arrive to have their pups they can mate with them." Dejectedly the Demon tossed a small pebble over the edge as even more of the huge beasts climbed out onto the rocks and fought for space.

Fenobar had never heard such a dispirited tone in the Demon's voice before. "What are they?"

"Well . . . we call them walruses in our own tongue, but I think you Imkairans call them tyforndor. Tyvai's hearth watchers."

"Sig, I don't like this. They're awfully big, and the raft . . ."

"Exactly," Sig said heavily.

For a long time the raft went unnoticed, and then one large tyforndor took exception to this thing taking up more than its fair share of the property he was claiming, and with a fierce honking, attacked it. Under that immense blubbery tonnage, the raft on which they had worked so hard for so long was reduced in moments to splintery firewood.

Sig groaned and rolled over on his back, throwing one arm over his face, as if he could not bear to see it.

"We'll have to build another one," Fenobar said stoutly.

"Out of what? That beach down there is where the driftwood comes ashore."

"It's not the only place where wood comes in," Fenobar said quietly. "I have seen logs here and there on the sands as we scouted."

"Here and there is right. There are not many of them and they are scattered all over the place. We'll have to drag each one for miles and we don't have the remains of the sailboat to use for decking."

"We'll think of something." It seemed like a good time to turn Sig's attention to something else. "Are we going to have sea bird again for supper?"

"I don't know and I don't care." Sig buried his face in his arms. "I wanted to go home! We're so close!"

Fenobar shifted uneasily. Sig wanted to leave him? He was outlander, certainly, but still. . . . Perhaps it would be wise to have some understanding of all those things that tugged at Sig. Awkwardly, because curiosity about another's clan could be so easily misconstrued. Fenobar asked, "How many other Demons are there in your Clan?"

Listlessly, Sig turned his head on his arms. "There aren't any Demons. Just us humans."

"Well, then . . . tell me about you humans."

"My Great-great-grandparents came here to study Imkairans—to learn your culture and your languages in secret. Then there was a war and the Federated Colonies forgot they were here and just left them. That was a long time ago, but we still wait for them to come back."

"How long ago?" Fenobar's ears pricked with interest. The only thing really clear to him was that there had been a war somewhere.

"My people have been here a hundred and twenty-three years this winter."

"Odd how no one has discovered you," Fenobar said thoughtfully.

"We don't want to be found," Sig sighed. "We're still holding to the first-contact imperative."

"What's that?"

"Not to let you know we're here."

Fenobar wrinkled up his nose, his ears twitching uncontrollably, "But Sig, we *do* know you are here!"

"Por Dios!" Sig buried his head in his arms again. "I don't want to hear!"

Ears still twitching with laughter, and snorting a little, Fenobar asked, "What is your town strength?"

"Six hundred and twelve, if Serena had her baby."

Fenobar was considering the mathematics of it. "That's not very many for a hundred and twenty-three years."

"Well," Sig lifted his head. "If you count the other six towns, there are around five thousand of us."

Fenobar blinked.

"There would be more than that, but we're having a terrible problem with in-breeding. There were only fifteen people in the original group. Certain genetic problems keep cropping up. A lot of the babies die."

Fenobar blinked some more. Babies dying or not, that was one heck of a lot of Demons—twice the growth rate of an Imkairan population. What had Sig said . . . from an original group of only *fifteen?* He couldn't think of anything to say. At the moment, no topic seemed safe.

Silence fell between them. After about an hour Fenobar said, "You left your sword down there."

The Demon shrugged a heavy shoulder and Fenobar's crest began jerking with temper. Without the Kaymath weapon, they would be using his treasured Bokeem sword for a wood axe. When they were angry, Imkairan males fought or remained silent, and Fenobar was whitecrest. Eyes blazing, he snarled. "We have not finished our challenge."

"I don't want to fight." Sig's voice was listless.

Fenobar limbered his fingers, flexing the claws in and out of the sheath. With a finicky, almost delicate touch, he placed his good hand on Sig's shoulder. Sig didn't move and Fenobar clenched his hand. The claws slid into the naked hide. With a satisfying yell the Demon leaped to his feet and turned on Fenobar. This was more like it! Fenobar thought approvingly as he danced out of the way of the Demon's deadly hands.

They fought until they couldn't stand any longer. Slowly they sank to their knees, disheveled, bruised, a bit bloody, gasping for breath.

"Satisfied?" the Demon croaked past a bruised lip where Fenobar had hit him with an elbow.

"You are whitecrest," Fenobar conceded. "You didn't raise fesen at all." He was strangely disappointed, but was too tired to feel it deeply. "Now, we have to find out if you are better or worse a fighter than I am," he panted.

"You mean we're going to have to do this all over again?" The Demon rolled over on his back. "No! You can be the ranking warrior here."

"You can't do that!" Fenobar was truly shocked.

"We can," the Demon said firmly. "Because I can't raise fesen."

"You can't . . . what?"

"Humans do not raise fesen. Ever."

"By Shaindar's falling fur! All this time I thought

you just had great control, and you can't. . . . Not at all?" Fenobar ended, wondering.

Sig shook his head, his eyes weary.

"But if you can't, then . . ." Fenobar stared down at the Demon, his crest limp and his eyes wide with dismay. "We will never know in truth if you are whitecrest or not!"

The Demon turned to look at him and bared flat teeth in a wide, smug grin.

CHAPTER THIRTEEN

A couple of days later they were on the opposite side of the island, where the mountain went nearly straight down into the ocean. Fenobar spotted a tree limb caught among the off-shore wrack. Calling the Demon, he scrambled down to a narrow apron of wave-swept boulders where more than one piece of driftwood was caught in the tumbled rocks. It was a good find. There was wood here that would serve for both the raft and their fire.

Sig worked his way out to the edge, where the waves rumbled and rolled. The foam-swept boulders were covered in a kind of slimy green seaweed that made footing treacherous. Balancing precariously, Sig pulled out the sea-whitened branches one by one and tossed them up to Fenobar. There was one good raft log caught just out of reach. Sig plunged into the sea surge up to his waist among the boulders, grabbed a branch nubbin and pulled. It didn't budge. He pulled again and his feet flipped out from under him just as a big wave rolled in over his head.

Fenobar wasn't too concerned. After all, Sig could

swim. But the wave rolled back and Sig wasn't there. Fenobar's stomach tightened with painful intensity. He found himself scrambling across the slimy boulders yelling Sig's name.

As if in answer to his call, Sig popped up some distance away, close to the sheer cliff face. He was yelling something too and frantically stroked for the rocks where Fenobar waited, dragging himself clear of the curling foam with such recklessness that he tore the nails of one hand and didn't even notice.

Trying hard not to show his relief, Fenobar forced his crest fluffy. "I thought for a moment that Tyvai had called you home." But his voice shook in spite of himself and the joke went lamentably flat.

Sig didn't answer his nonsense. He wrapped white-knuckled hands around his knees, while tremors shook his body.

Fenobar listened to the ragged breathing, the fermented sajawa tang of Demon fear sharp in his nostrils. Warriors were not supposed to feel fear but it was all too familiar to him. There had been times in Bokeem when it had taken all his control to hide a rising terror and then, when free to do so, he had found a small dark corner and shook as Sig was shaking now. The cause behind that fear still had the power to bring him to panicky wakefulness in the dead of night.

It was a secret he hid well from the warrior kind. They were unforgiving of any show of fear. Once that stigma was attached to a warrior he was ruined for what remained of his life. That remainder was generally short. No warrior could accept loss of prestige. They put an end to themselves, usually by cutting their throats with their kalnaks.

Crouching in front of the Demon, hands clasped

loosely together, Fenobar asked, "Sig, what do you fear?"

"The wave shoved me into a cave." Sig's voice was shaky. "I couldn't get out! It was dark and there wasn't any air and I couldn't get out!"

Fenobar remembered the secret way through the Kaymath temple. It had been dark there, too, and narrow. But only the Demon's scent had given away his fear. "That was not what I asked. What do you fear?"

Sig raised his head and controlled his breathing, trying, even now, to consider the question. Perhaps grasping at the necessity of considering. "The dark. The closeness," he said after a moment. He was calmer.

"The dark. The closeness. Those do not kill," Fenobar said wisely. "It is fear which kills."

"It is an old fear," the Demon said. "I have tried to rid myself of it . . ." He turned to look at the log still caught among the rocks. "We need that log." He got up determinedly and started for the water.

Fenobar let him go without a word. If he had a war band, they would have stood around and sneered at Sig's terror and called him a coward. And they would have been wrong, he realized suddenly. For among the warriors he knew none would have done what Sig had just done.

None could have done what he had done at Bokeem. He, too, had gone back and faced that which he feared. And did it day after day, week after week, month after month. Doing what had to be done because there was no other choice. It suddenly occurred to him that there were many kinds of courage, and the kind that sent one back to finish a job despite fear was far from being the least. Fear was not the weakness; Sig had shown that clearly. Giving in to the fear . . . *that* was the weakness.

The secret fear, greatest of all his fears—that he was a coward—slowly ebbed away as he went to help the Demon haul the log onto the rocks. They left the log at a little cove where they had begun to rebuild their raft, a place not likely to be found by the tyforndor. After making another trek to collect the firewood, they both felt they had done enough work for one day.

In the dappled shade of the small tree where they had stretched out to nap, Fenobar heard the Demon get up but did not come fully awake. He hoped the Demon was going to practice, for Sig was lamentably bad with a sword. Fenobar wasn't even sure why it bothered him that Sig was so bad a swordsman, yet could fight the crest off Shaindar with his bare hands.

Resolution hardened. Rolling to his feet, he went to put on his mail. Sword at his back, and the Demon's mail under his arm he went to find Sig. The Demon's whereabouts were no big secret. Sig was in his favorite spot on top of the cliff, watching the tyforndor and munching on dried seaweed leaves as if they were meat chips. The stuff had long since lost its allure for Fenobar. He picked up a leaf and sniffed it contemptuously before putting it back. "How can you eat this stuff?"

The Demon grinned. "Vitamins and minerals. They make you strong and healthy. Puts hair on your chest."

"And elsewhere, I presume, though it doesn't seem to have done all that much for you," Fenobar said, eyeing the Demon's torso critically. It had stopped being red and was turning brown and, in places, rather blotchy as the skin peeled off. He hoped the Demon wasn't coming down with some kind of disease. "We need to make shields tomorrow."

"Oh? You're going to attack the tyforndor?"

"Not just yet. We need to practice."

"Right now?"

"Yes! Yes!!" He dropped Sig's mail beside him.

"What's this?"

"What it looks like! Put it on. We must get to work."

Reluctantly, the Demon pulled on the mail and trailed after Fenobar. "It's too hot for swordwork," he complained, pulling out the wooden sword Fenobar had made for him since his Kaymath weapon was somewhere under several tons of easily agitated tyforndor.

Fenobar took his stance, giving Sig a stern look. "Practice is survival. You can die just as easily on a hot day as a cold one. That is *not* how I told you to hold your weapon." The practice session commenced. After ten minutes of attack and parry, Fenobar angrily stepped back, slammed his helmet onto the ground and announced, "You could not defend yourself from a three-year cublin with a sharp stick!"

Sig ripped his helm off as well and threw it after Fenobar's. "Well, who says I have to!" He was about to walk off their improvised training ground when Fenobar yelled, "Ware!" and came after him.

Fenobar slashed his sword at the Demon, who parried it clumsily. He would have lost an arm if Fenobar had not pulled the blow at the last minute. Running the hilt of his weapon down to the Demon's hand, Fenobar turned it so the hooks caught. He held the Demon easily, swords locked together at the hilt. They would remain that way until Fenobar chose to disengage.

Crest jerking, Fenobar glared up into the Demon's grey eyes. "Who says you have to? I say you have to. I am Ranking Male here. You agreed to it yourself."

He disengaged and leaped back. Sig fell into a

fighter's crouch and Fenobar came after him, swift and deadly, raining blows faster than Sig could counter them.

"There! You have lost an arm!" Fenobar cried. "There! I have cut your chest, and your leg. There! You are dead! I have cut your throat!" At each "there" he touched Sig lightly with the tip of his weapon. Fenobar stood back, breathing a bit heavily. "It was too easy. And . . . I am out of shape. If I could turn you into minced meat, think what would happen to you if you were facing one of the throng who are better than I am. Now. Hold your weapon so. Move!"

A shaken Sig began to pay serious attention to his teacher.

Fenobar thought the Demon was extraordinarily slow in picking up what every cublin knew, but at least he was powerful. There were very few who could parry one of his overhand blows. Fenobar himself learned quickly to step out from under it. If it landed, even on his shielded arm, it numbed the shoulder.

There was great satisfaction in teaching Sig. It was part of the duties of a commander to teach the warriors, to hone their abilities, and this was the first time he had had one to teach. There was also, for the first time, a right-handed opponent, so that he could fight sword to shield, instead of sword to sword. He also made sure the Demon knew how to guard against a left-handed opponent. But even with the sword clutched in his weak and twisted left hand he was still a better swordsman than the Demon.

But he was not the only one to teach. After several days of enduring insults and being whacked black and blue, Sig decided to get even by teaching Fenobar the Demon way of unarmed fighting.

Fenobar snorted his amusement, ears flicking. "That's a contradiction of terms, Sig."

They were sitting in the shade of the little trees as Sig made his proposition. "Not at all." Sig got up. "Let me show you." He dropped his weapon, and took up a position in the training circle.

Intrigued, Fenobar pulled his sword and ran at Sig when the other called him. The Demon was standing relaxed and easy, his hands held in front of him. He shunted Fenobar's weapon aside with one mailed arm and in another second Fenobar was flying through the air to land solidly on his back. Before he could regain his breath, the Demon was upon him, one knee on his chest and his hands touching lightly at temple and throat. "There! I have crushed your head. There! I have crushed your throat. You are dead."

"I knew you wouldn't forgive me that first lesson." Fenobar panted, ears twitching.

Afterwards, there were movements to go through for loosening the muscles, balance and coordination. "I have seen you do these," Fenobar said during the second set. "You dance like this in the early morning. I thought you were doing some religious thing for bringing up the sun." Fenobar felt uneasy doing the movements. They were too much like the Dance of Life he had done as a cublin when he was still young enough to accompany Black Fentaru's wives to the spring rites in the Goddess Garden.

Then there were the lessons themselves. Many he could not do, for his joints could not always move the same way that Sig's did. But he learned what he could of them, and Sig modified others for his use. This was a marvel, for no one else had ever tried to teach around his handicap. He had always had to take what was given and adapt it for himself.

Two hands of days passed. They were resting in the grass under the trees after a long morning of

shield work, and an afternoon of ka-rah-teh. Sig
reached out and idly picked up Fenobar's bad hand,
turning it over and examining it. Fenobar stiffened,
his crest jerking.

"How much strength do you have in this?" Sig
asked.

Fenobar shrugged. "Sometimes some, sometimes
none. It is not dependable."

Gently, Sig worked those twisted bones and withered tendons between his hands, and Fenobar hissed
a warning as he felt the first twinges of pain.

"You should work with this hand to keep it as
flexible as possible. You could do a lot with this if
you could flatten the fingers a little more."

"Why?" Fenobar said with a shrug. "It is good
only for holding a shield on that arm, nothing else."

"I think there is a way you can use this to fight
with," Sig said, rather astonishingly.

Fenobar snarled softly, although he knew it was
not Sig's way to tease him about his one-handedness.

"No, really!" From their wood pile Sig picked up a
log as thick around as his wrist. He lay it across two
rocks and poised his hand above it as if it were not
flesh, but an axe.

Ears twitching at the absurdity of his Demon,
Fenobar watched as Sig took a deep breath, slammed
his hand down and broke the stick in two pieces.
Fenobar jerked upright to stare with awe from the
wood to Sig and back again. "I would learn that," he
said, almost humbly.

To Fenobar's great disappointment, he never managed to break a stick like Sig could. But as Sig
pointed out, how often was he going to be attacked
by a stick? Instead, he showed him the killing in-
fighting blows, where he could use the strength of
his shoulder behind the stiffened hand and arm.
Fenobar practiced until Sig was black and blue.

Time passed. The tyforndor pups were born and thumping happily about the beach between their huge parents. Sig was improving his swordsmanship daily and Fenobar had gone fanatic about learning ka-rah-teh. One afternoon, Sig was showing Fenobar a high, kicking jump when they both went to their knees as the earth moved under them.

Fenobar tried in vain to regain his footing. Sig, knowing better, lay where he'd fallen, looking up at the mountain above them with terrified eyes. The fear-filled cries of the tyforndor rose from the beach. The huge animals thundered for the safety of the sea as the earth shook under them a second time.

Then everything went still. The tyforndor were gone. The earth remained solid and unmoving under them, like it was supposed to be. "They call these the Shaking Lands!" Fenobar commented breathlessly.

"We have to get out of here!" Sig got to his feet, still with his eyes on the tall black mountain. Smoke was streaming from the top. "That's a volcano and it's going to blow."

Fenobar followed Sig's eyes. He did not understand what a "volcano" was, but mountains did not ordinarily smoke and Sig was not one to be afrighted easily. Therefore, when Sig said, "Come on, we have to get out of here!" he followed, asking no questions.

As he was helping Sig pull the canvas sail from the top of the cave, Fenobar found time for one very important question. "Where are we going?"

"Out to sea," was the grim response.

"The new raft isn't finished."

"We're going on what we have." It was an uncompromising statement underlined by a sudden rumble from above. Sig's skin changed color again, looking a bit greenish.

They were both in their mail and it took just a

moment to gather their belongings. Fenobar made a
bundle of their cloaks and slung it over his shoulder
with the Axe, his sword and the two full water bags
they'd made from stomachs of tyforndor. Sig threw
all the extra canvas on top of the folded sail, including
the bags holding their dried tyforndor meat and
seaweed cakes. Wrapping it with what was left of
their salvaged rope, he made an unwieldy back pack
of it all and without a word started around the mountain toward the little beach where they had their
raft.

Fenobar put down his burdens beside the unfin-
ished collection of logs and inspected the whole of it
with a jaundiced eye. The Demon might speak blithely
of taking this thing out onto the water, but it was
only a third the size of the first one, which had not
seemed overly large. Appropriating a large bit of the
extra canvas, he spread it out on the ground and with
reverent hands placed the Axe in the center of it,
wrapping it tightly and securing the folds with rope
he had made for this very purpose. Every protective
charm he knew had been woven into those four-
times-four strands.

The earth rolled under them. Sig, busy lashing a
makeshift mast into place, slipped, losing his hold on
the line. The heavy pole swayed dangerously above
that yellow-white head and Fenobar scrambled to
help support it before it went over. Sig was using
short, pithy Demon words as he yanked on the lines.
Fenobar's own curses were silent. Demons, he was
beginning to realize, had no power of their own.
They were only the focus for the arrows of Chaos
unloosed by the God Tyvai and were all too apt to
get caught in the backlash.

Above them part of the mountain gave way, loos-
ened by the earth tremors. Slabs of rock bounced

down the slope, unleashing great clouds of dust and shooting vicious, sharp-edged splinters in every direction. Fenobar threw the Axe, his sword and the provisions aboard even as Sig was shoving the raft into the water. Ducking the flying rocks, they poled frenetically out of the little bay and when the sea bed dropped away beneath their poles, they rowed. Sig had saved the oars and the oar locks from the sailboat and it was only a matter of seconds to thrust the point of Fenobar's kalnak into a log and drill out a hole for the pins.

At the first safe moment Sig stripped the armor off himself and Fenobar and stuffed it into one of the bags, along with Fenobar's sword. The bundle was lashed to the bottom of the mast along with the Axe.

Sig ran the sail up. The wind filled it and pushed them, albeit sluggishly, over the waves. Then they sat down and stared at each other and the island receding behind their stern. Fenobar was about to say something when he felt the raft speed up, almost as if it had been grasped from below. He looked over the side, not knowing what he expected to see.

"It's part of the Trulden current," Sig said. "It's pretty strong through here."

Fenobar heard only dimly. He was staring in fascinated horror as water lapped up between the logs and over his legs. Slowly, as if he were afraid the water would reach up and get him if he were to move too fast, he pulled himself up onto the armor and sat tucked up there, watching the water sliding past his toes. "We are going to sink," he said calmly.

Sig made a choking noise, quickly cut off. But when Fenobar tore his eyes away from that heaving greenness between the logs to give the Demon a suspicious glance, the other's face was without those wrinkled lines that denoted Demon humor. The Demon's grey eyes were a bit brighter than usual, but it probably meant nothing.

Time passed. Their island had become a dot on the horizon. Water continued to wash over the logs. "It's been a long time. Nothing has happened. We left too soon."

The Demon said firmly. "No." Even as he spoke there was a great gout of smoke from the direction of the island, followed by a deep, heavy rumble on the horizon that built quickly to a roar. Fenobar stared at the boiling mass of steam and smoke, awestruck. A few minutes later, a huge swell of green water sped toward them, lifting them grandly upward, like the leaky mass of twigs they were, letting them slide down behind it, and was gone into the distance ahead of them.

"Not very exciting as far as volcanoes go," Sig said, judiciously, studying the cloud from under a sheltering hand. "But more than enough to cook us if we'd stayed. It's the little, fast ones you have to watch out for."

Instinctively hiding his panic from Sig, Fenobar dipped his crest at him and tried not to sound too humble. "You are the Ranking male here."

"Ah . . . Fen. That's not necessary." Sig turned his eyes away, embarrassed.

"Yes. It is. I am about to be extremely unwell." And with as much dignity as he could manage, Fenobar leaned over the side of the raft. From there it was only a step to curling up on one of the shields, his head pillowed on the armor, moaning to himself. The motion of every wave was transmitted straight to his head and stomach through the wood. It was bad when he had his eyes closed, but worse when he opened them, for then he had to stare down at the waves between the logs directly under his nose.

Three days went by. Both of them were constantly soaked. They had drunk the last of their water and Sig was fishing, but without much luck. They did not know when or even if they would be able to make landfall. The Trulden current was taking them south at a great rate, and Sig had little control over his makeshift sail.

"Will this never end?" Fenobar moaned, words he would have cut his throat before uttering in front of any other male but Sig. He was blearily trying to calculate how much dishonor would accrue to him if he accidentally fell on his sword, when Sig's hand came down on his shoulder and shook him. "Don't *do* that."

Sig was kneeling over him, hand shielding his eyes from the sun, looking south. "We left the straits four hours ago, and if my calculations are right, we're in the middle of the southern shipping lanes."

"Ships?" Fenobar asked shakily, getting to one elbow. "Ships? The western Chalig are a ship-building people. We can't, Sig . . . Talk to Tyvai. Tell Him I'll do anything, but the Axe can't fall into the hands of the Chalig! *Any* clan but the Chalig."

"It's too late to ask," Sig replied, and there was real perturbation in that burring voice. "Tyvai has already made his decision. That's what I was going to tell you. There's a sail coming toward us."

Fenobar got shakily to his knees, crest shading his eyes against the sunlight. It was indeed a ship—a high-decked merchantman with three masts. Above the tallest mast hung a bit of cloth. The wind whipped it out flat even as he stared, revealing a green field crossed by a yellow and white flower. "It's Chalig," he said, resigned. His hand reached out to touch the Axe. "Sig, I must ask something very great of you."

"What?"

Such a prompt answer, with no wariness. Ask and he says, "what." Fenobar's stomach filled with warmth. His eyes met the Demon's. "I . . . must ask you to play the part of a palecrest." He held his breath.

Sig blinked at him, tilted his head to one side, and rubbed at his strange, sharp nose. There was a quiver of laughter in the burring voice. "I don't think it will fool anyone."

Carefully, Fenobar said, "We will be among enemies. You they will sell as you were sold before, unless you can claim a place with a whitecrest. The only way we can remain together is if we tell them you are part of my war band. I will tell them you are my sholstan," he said a bit desperately, as the Demon made no reply.

"But why won't they just take me away from you and sell me anyway?" he asked at last.

"Because you will be . . ." Fenobar stopped, crest tilted slightly to one side as he thought about it. "The only males who are ever seen . . . really seen . . . are whitecrests and outlanders. Once you are part of a war band and wear a House badge, you exist only as part of your commander's honor."

"I would be invisible, you mean . . ." Sig shrugged. "I don't see how it will work, but if you say this is what I should do, I'll try it."

"Spoken not quite like a true warrior, but close enough," Fenobar murmured, gratefully. He leaned back against the mast, closing his eyes against another upwelling of internal misery. "You do not have a sword," he said suddenly. Opening his eyes wide, he looked steadily at Sig. "You must carry the Axe, then."

"You think we'll both become invisible?"

"It can't hurt to try," Fenobar muttered.

There was silence for a while, as they watched the

ship come closer. "It's probably a good thing this Chalig ship showed up when it did," Sig said.

Fenobar's eyes snapped open. But he had learned over the last few weeks. In a calm voice he asked, "Why?"

Sig rubbed at his nose. "You remember the vines I used to tie the logs together? The ones you never liked the idea of using? Well, you were right." He coughed. "They are coming apart."

There was a long, unbroken silence as they watched the merchantman come closer. A shout told them they'd been seen and the ship turned to match their course.

The merchantman was wide of beam and loomed very tall above them as it came alongside. Faces, topped by dark crests, peered down from the railing. A rope ladder was thrown to them, and burdened under the weight of armor and weapons, they swayed precariously upward.

CHAPTER FOURTEEN

Fenobar climbed over the railing, steadied by the ship's crew. As his feet hit the deck he looked up. Standing beside the mast, amidships, were a group of brightly clad females. He felt his crest start to sag and forced it back up before he embarrassed himself by showing his shock. Turning to grab Sig's arm as he came over the side, he muttered in the round ear, "This ship is run by females! This changes everything. They don't think like males. I don't know what they will do."

"Stay calm," Sig murmured in reply.

Acutely conscious that his bad arm was clear to be seen, Fenobar turned anxiously to Sig, running his hand over his crest, feeling the uneven lengths. "What does my crest look like?"

"Motheaten," Sig replied bluntly. "But it's growing in white and thick. Don't let it worry you."

Fenobar gave Sig a raking glance of disbelief. "They will cut us up for tagris meat," he muttered. The Demon was dressed in ragged breeches and even more ragged tunic. Only his boots showed affluence. His eyes rested a second on Sig's head fur, which had grown long, tied back at the nape of his neck with a piece of string. No crest, but it would have to do.

He himself wore nothing but a belt, from which hung his kalnak and the bag containing his strike-a-light and the fish hooks.

He turned around, pulling himself up to his full height, and assumed the cool arrogance of a high-status whitecrest, trying not to notice how every eye stared past him at Sig. He gave the sailors a raking glance, but they, like himself, wore nothing but a belt hung about with tools. They did not need badges on the enclosed world which was a ship at sea.

He swaggered a bit as he walked over to the cluster of females. They wore their badges on the shoulders of their filmy tunics and were all from the same Family of a Chalig clan unknown to him. One, very beautiful with long, reddish fur, wore the House badge of a Captain on the front of her tunic. Ordinarily a male insignia, it looked strange on her. Gently letting his armor down onto the decking, he looked her in the eyes and very deliberately bowed. He didn't think she saw him because just then Sig came up behind him, dropping his armor with a heavy thunk beside his own.

There was a remoteness in the Captain's tone which Fenobar did not think bode well for them when she said, "The lookout insisted he saw a whitecrest and a strange creature. I see he was not wrong." Still looking past Fenobar, she addressed herself directly to Sig. "Why have you come to walk the world again, Demon?"

Fenobar spoke sharply to get her attention. "He is my sholstan."

"So?" Her green eyes focused consideringly on

Fenobar, on his twisted left arm. "One wonders what it sees in you."

"Considerable," Sig interjected in his deep, burring voice, speaking out of turn for a palecrest.

As all eyes jerked once more to Sig, Fenobar reached back one foot and stuck a claw in the Demon's leg above the protecting boot.

"It talks!" The lanky female beside the Captain said aloud what they were all thinking.

"He is my sholstan," Fenobar repeated with an edge to his words, as if to say, "Of course he speaks—what else do you expect of the palecrested kind."

"Your sholstan. Of course," the foremost female, the Captain, said, taking a deep breath. Brusquely she turned to the crew. "Get back to your work. There is no reason to be standing around this way."

Reluctantly, with many a backward look, the darkcrested males went about their business.

Fenobar lightly let go the breath he was holding, and for the first time really looked at the ship's captain as she turned brooding green eyes onto Fenobar, ignoring the Demon standing by his shoulder. She was of medium height and slender. Their eyes were on the same level. Her chestnut fur was long and glossy. There was about her the sleek look of leashed power. His first impression was that she was very beautiful, and it had not lied. Her green eyes went from his ragged crest, rested a moment on his shoulders, then went down to his bad arm.

He had not had to endure such a stare since leaving Bokeem, and his own pale yellow eyes suddenly glittered with anger. It would have been terrible manners to allow his crest to jerk in her presence, but his ears flattened tight to his skull.

The Captain's ears twitched when she saw that. "I

am Keltain, Captain of the *Wave Dancer*, of Clan
Bektar of the Chalig, and Foremost of my sister-
group." She tilted her head slightly to include the
females behind her.

Fenobar looked past her. Of her sisters, one was
slender, almost ethereal, with huge, grey-green eyes.
The second was nearly all white with black splotches
here and there through her coat. Her eyes were
deep yellow, and as he caught a whiff of her scent,
his heart began drubbing in his chest with excitement. It was with difficulty that he turned his attention to the third one—the lanky one who had spoken.
She carried herself like a warrior and her grey coat
was highlighted with silver rosettes.

Fenobar inclined his crest politely, speaking as
only a warrior could who had been raised in the King
House. "Foremost, I am Fenobar, born favorite son
of Fentaru, the malintaz of Fen, of the Monghanirri."
That was no lie. He *had* been born favorite son.
Perhaps that bit about being favorite son would give
her cause to rethink the withered arm.

Her green gaze went past him again. "Can you
control it?" she asked abruptly.

Fenobar flicked his crest, dismissing her alarms.
"He is sholstan."

Keltain snapped her fingers and a dark browncrested
male hurried forward. "Belam will take you to your
quarters. We will speak further after you have rested."
With that she walked off, her sister-group following
without a backward glance.

Eyes wide with wonder, Belam led them to a hot
little cabin in the prow of the ship, just beside the
stairs that led to the darkcrest quarters below decks.
There was a narrow bunk built into each side of the
cabin, with a low table between them. Another darkcrest brought food and tunics of juras cloth from

which the Bektar clan badge had recently been removed. "Would you have one clean your armor, Lord?" Belam murmured as he set the food out on the table.

The only time Fenobar had ever had a servant to clean his mail for him was after he'd become temple commander. However, he accepted graciously for both himself and Sig as if he had never in his life had to do for himself.

Sig stopped the darkcrest on his way out the door. "I would like a couple of pegs placed on the wall where I can hang my Axe." It was, strangely enough, less a command than a request, and Fenobar did not for a moment think Belam would attend to the matter. He didn't say anything, however. Sig would have to learn.

Clean, fed and dressed in clean clothing, they stretched out on the beds and slept like the dead until a discreet knock on their door brought Fenobar wide awake. The darkcrest Belam stood there, eyes respectfully lowered. Keltain wished his presence and that of his sholstan. Would he come?

Fenobar looked over his shoulder as a rustle from the other bed announced that Sig was alert. "They want to see us."

"Only natural," Sig said easily, preparing to accompany him.

The sun was sinking redly toward the horizon, burnishing the white-topped wavelets in russet, as they made their way the length of the ship to the big cabin in the stern. Above them the sails snapped and strained. The wind caught at the lines until they hummed. The wooden deck under his feet was cool and smooth and all around him were the low voices of the darkcrested sailors at work. It was an orderly world and he realized how much he had missed being among his own kind, where the rules were clear and one's duties defined. He sniffed the air as if he could draw into himself the undefinable aroma that said "civilization."

The aft deck cabin was spacious, the red and gold carpet thick and soft. It was a comfortable place to sit. A single lantern hung above the low, black lacquered table. The yellow light softened the colors of the many red and orange pillows scattered about.

Fenobar did not like having the lantern directly above him. He could not see well past the glare and was all too aware of Keltain's sister-group lounging half-seen in the shadows, whispering among themselves. Fenobar set his greeting cup carefully down on the low table in front of him, having scarcely tasted the tamor brew. Keltain, kneeling opposite him, was studying him over her cup with the same satisfaction as one who holds a pandor in a net, and he was suddenly regretting that custom had not allowed him to wear his armor to this meeting, nor permitted him any more weapon than his kalnak.

He was very conscious of Sig behind him, of the strangeness of him in this place. Sig, too, was without his armor, but carried the Axe across his back as if he had done so all his life.

Keltain put down her cup. The ritual greetings were finished. The tamor brew had been poured and drunk. Now came the business.

Black Fentaru had once said, "Don't let the females control the conversation if you wish to come out of it with your crest intact." He had been referring to the annual budget meeting, but it seemed like sound advice. Fenobar's bad hand twitched slightly in time to his words and he thrust it into the shadows under the table. "There is no blood feud between your clan and mine. I claim passage right."

Keltain looked at him from under long lashes. Her simple white tunic of getar silk shimmered as she moved. Deliberately, she raised her cup and took a delicate sip. "We are not in Chalig territory . . . and you are not passing through. How can you, therefore, claim passage right?"

"Is this ship not Chalig?" Fenobar opened his eyes wide in feigned surprise. "Surely it can be said, therefore, that it is Chalig territory? My sholstan and I are on a journey which was well begun before we met your ship and will continue after we have left it. Therefore, we are passing through. I claim nothing of yours, I challenge no one. I claim passage right for myself and my sholstan."

Keltain put the delicate porcelain cup down gently on the highly polished table. "Speaking of your sholstan—Belam tells me neither of you have the bonding mark." Her green eyes went to Sig, and there was that in her manner which seemed to ask which of them was in truth the Ranking male.

Fenobar held out his right wrist and parted the fur with the misshapen claws of his left hand. The triangular brand was clear.

The Captain leaned forward to look at it, her nose wrinkling a bit. "I have never heard of the bonding being on the right arm."

Fenobar shrugged nonchalantly. "He is a Demon, and therefore, he is a right-hand sholstan."

"I see." Keltain's ears flicked. "His brand would therefore also be on the right wrist."

"Of course," Fenobar said haughtily, and hoped Sig had enough sense to keep his right arm out of sight.

Keltain leaned both elbows on the table, laced her hands together, and peered at Fenobar over the top of them. "Because if he were not your sholstan, we would buy him from you in return for your passage."

Take him, she meant, Fenobar thought, and flicked his crest over his eyes so she could not see the red haze of anger there. "But he *is* sholstan," he said softly. "And I still claim passage right."

"So you do," she said. "But I am not so sure our clans are not at war. It is said that Mad Thenorig attacked the Fenirri lands in early spring."

"Yes. And took the males into his war band," Fenobar replied without a tremor. "Any blood feud is therefore forbidden until he releases them."

"Why are you not with Mad Thenorig?" This was said with a sharp look.

Fenobar shrugged again. "I was away from the Clan at the time . . . selling weapons up north. We are good weapon makers, we of the Fenirri."

"We have heard." Keltain's ears were at half mast as she played with her cup. "You have come a long way from your lands, warrior."

"Yes," Fenobar agreed. "And I have, more than once, asked for and received passage right . . ."

"We're back to that again, are we?" She sounded a little sour. "Very well, I give you passage right. However, as you pointed out, this is a ship. Were you indeed passing through our lands, you would have to pay hunting right or bring your own food. Here, I must provide all. Therefore, you must pay a price for food and drink. What say you to that, warrior?"

"It is well within the conventions."

She tapped one delicately pearly claw-tipped finger against her chin, eyes half closed in thought.

That thought was a sham, Fenobar suspected. Keltain had already considered and discussed her actions with her sister-group, or she would not have called them to her like this. He fought down the flutter of tension in his stomach.

Keltain turned slightly to speak to the females behind her. "What do you say, Bril?"

The lanky grey female came forward out of the shadows and knelt beside Keltain. Her dark eyes on Fenobar, she said, "His arm is no new injury and yet he keeps by him a sholstan. And his sholstan looks and speaks as one who has known him a long time, with considerable respect and honor between them. On that evidence alone I say he is probably something special as a warrior."

"Sorlain?" Keltain addressed the white one with the heart-stopping scent.

She remained in the shadows where Fenobar could not get so much as a trailing curl of her scent. "He is strong, and moves easily. He is also very beautiful. He speaks well and argues logically. I accept him."

"You do?" Keltain asked with just a thread of surprise in her voice.

"Mertis has had a seeing." Sorlain lay a claw-tipped hand on the arm of the ethereal female curled up beside her in a gesture of familiarity no male would have tolerated. "Sons by this one will be whitecrest and daughters will rule their Families."

Keltain searched Fenobar's face as if she were trying to see if this "seeing" Mertis had could possibly be true. "The payment for passage we have decided upon is for your presence in Clan Bektar for one year."

Fenobar blinked. "One year? You rate your food and drink rather highly for such plain fare as we have been given."

"Ah, but consider," she said gently. "If we had not picked you up? That is the price. If you do not wish to pay in time, you can always sell us your arms and armor. The weapon smiths of Fen are well known, and Bril has taken a liking to that ancient war axe your sholstan carries."

Fenobar's bad hand betrayed him by quivering. "It is well known that a warrior would prefer to lose his head than his weapons. If I protested the length of time it was because I was surprised. I do not see why you should wish for an outland whitecrest to bide so long within your walls."

"Do you not?" Her ears swiveled in time to the wry note in her voice. "What happened to the fine intellect Bril said you possessed? Our whitecrests are out starving and dying, following Mad Thenorig." She ground the High King's name between pointed teeth and her ears had gone flat. "May all his cublin be brainless whitecrests who bring dishonor upon his Clan, House and line!" Taking a deep breath, she resumed. "He took our Clan Spirit when he challenged our King three years ago. Since then all the whitecrest cublin seek service in other tribes and do not return to Bektar."

"The law says that only a whitecrest may meet with one not of the Clan," Fenobar said slowly.

"You're catching on," she said, dropping her slightly formal manner. "We don't have any whitecrests, so the other Clans won't do business with us. It's been like this for three years. Our ships sit rotting in the harbor and our warehouses are full of dust motes."

"But . . ."

"Why are we out here in a ship? I was fool enough to think the law might be different if we went far enough away." Her lip lifted in a white-toothed snarl at the cup of liquid in her hand. "It wasn't."

"You want me to . . . ?"

"Go with a ship if we get a cargo, sign trade agreements, finalize contracts—stuff like that."

"But . . ."

"Look, we don't expect much from you. All you have to do is act as if you are vaguely aware of what is going on, sign where the cargo master tells you to sign, and keep your mouth shut."

"I think I can manage that . . . just barely," Fenobar said, holding a tight rein on his anger.

"Good!" Her eyes went to Sig again and she chewed at her lip, but said nothing.

Fenobar and Sig were dismissed from the cabin shortly after that. Fenobar stomped down into the ship waist, still angry, and stood in the deepest shadows under the sail, crest jerking. Sig eased up beside him and stood leaning one broad shoulder against the mast, silently watching. Fenobar took a deep breath and his crest slowed. He jerked his chin at Sig and led the way to the side, where they stood shoulder to shoulder, leaning elbows on the railing and staring down at the starlit waves. "I thought telling them you were my sholstan was a good idea."

"It is," the Demon said, mildly.

"I knew they were going to look for proof, but I thought I could tell them some story they would believe."

"You can't?"

"If there is no mark on your wrist tomorrow they will take you and sell you somewhere. They do not need a whitecrest for that." Fenobar's left hand began to cramp and he pulled it off the railing to pinion it between his stomach and the wood.

"What is the difficulty?"

"Sig, once that mark goes on your wrist it means you are no longer a Demon, no longer have the power you have now. You will be only a palecrest warrior, part of my war band. But worse than that, you will have done the Forbidden Thing, in breaking your bond with Tyvai." There. It was out. There was silence in which Fenobar's heart drubbed in his chest and he felt a little sick.

"I never was a Demon," Sig said calmly. "I am a human and have no power to lose. And I never had a bond with the God Tyvai. I will be well satisfied to be your sholstan."

Fenobar's heart slowed. He took a deep breath, feeling a bit lightheaded, and leaned against the secure warmth of Sig's shoulder.

The Demon spoke again, his burring voice unusually serious. "Being of your war band might suit me well enough, but what about you? You cannot walk the world with me forever at your shoulder. My presence would be a weight on your life. How can you attract warriors to you if they have to look at me staring at them over your shoulder? It is too much to ask of them. Long before I become weary of being your sholstan, you will weary of having me beside you."

There was some truth in what the Demon said, Fenobar admitted, but his words had also made clear certain things to Fenobar which he had never before dared to look at. His crest came down, covering his eyes, hiding his pain. "There may come such a time as you speak of," he whispered through a tight throat. "But Sig, I have never asked anyone else to be my war band First. There is no one else I *would* ask to be my First. It is in my heart that it will be a long while before I weary of you."

There was another long silence from the Demon. "A sholstan leads the warriors," he said at last. "I cannot do that for you, even if they would permit it. Not because I will not, but because I would not know the proper way of doing it. Warriors who came from my teaching would be . . . changed. You have told the Captain I was your right-hand sholstan. If you promise to get a left-hand sholstan to lead your war band, I will be your right-hand sholstan for however long you need me."

It was one of the great moments of Fenobar's life. It seemed to him that everything had gone very quiet. With sharp-edged clarity he heard the flapping of the sails overhead, the soft shush of the water passing over the hull, the low voices of the crew talking somewhere, and mainly of the scent and sound of Sig standing beside him. He knew he would never forget this moment as long as he lived, nor, no matter how bitter the future, would it change the singing exultation now rising through him. Sig was his!

He looked over at his sholstan, at the black, curved head of the Axe rising above his shoulder. "Do you think it will be dishonor to wait a year before bringing the Axe to Mone?"

"The Axe is safe from Mad Thenorig, and the God knows you tried hard enough to get it where it belonged. Surely, as long as it is kept safe, it does not matter where it bides?"

Comforted by his sholstan's reasoning, Fenobar pushed away from the railing. "We must get on with the bonding."

In their absence the stuffy little cabin had been enhanced by the addition of a window in the far end and, rather to Fenobar's surprise, three pegs above Sig's bunk where he could hang the Axe. The air was redolent with the scent of freshly cut wood and a small pile of sawdust adorned the floor under the new opening. The newly made storm cover was hinged open and fastened to the wall by a hook.

Fenobar inspected it closely, running his fingertips around the fresh cut. "Hunh! They *must* need a whitecrest. All I said was that the cabin was stuffy."

Sig took off his brown tunic and hung it on a wall peg beside the Axe. "Ah, but it was the *way* you said it—with your crest all limp like you were going to fall over." He picked up something blue folded on his blanket. "Look! Someone made me a new pair of breeches!" He put them on right then, a big grin on his face. "It's a bit cool, having the wind whistle up under the edges of a tunic." He stood looking down at himself with evident satisfaction, wiggling his bare toes against the sanded floor.

"You will need a weapon," Fenobar muttered, and went out to hunt up Belam. He returned shortly with an earthenware jar of hot coals, a small amount of charcoal, and a kalnak. "The bonding should be done with swords," he apologized, kicking the door shut behind him. "But this was the best I could find in the pitiful collection of scrap metal they call a warkip. He put the jar on the table and blew it into a light.

Sig picked up the kalnak, running his thumb along the cutting edge. "It seems very fine to me. We don't have much metal in the valley."

Fenobar removed his tunic of white juras and hung it up, took his sword from the sheath hanging against the wall, and faced Sig with it bare in his hand. The Demon's eye caught the light and glimmered under the light hair as he stood watching him, kalnak still in one hand.

"Place the tip of your knife in the coals," Fenobar said, thrusting his sword into the jar as he did so. "You must say, 'I, Sigmund, accept Fenobar of Fen as commander, to follow, to obey, to help him rise in rank."

Sig repeated it flawlessly, and then it was Fenobar's turn to complete the old formula that he had almost despaired of ever saying to a warrior. "I take you in bond to me, in return for your obedience to provide you with food and shelter and hunting. To take you with me as I rise in rank." He nodded his crest at Sig. "Take out your kalnak."

Sig removed his knife from the coals, the red point glowing brilliantly in the darkness. He lay it on Fenobar's outheld wrist and repeated, "This is the mark of our bond." There was a hiss and a stench of burning hair. Fenobar did not so much as quiver as the hot steel sunk a thin triangular mark into his skin.

He took out his sword and, mindful of how thin Sig's furless hide was, chose a place well into the muscle to lay the point of his blade. "This is the mark of our bond." The smell this time was of burning meat. Sig's arm shook slightly, but there was no sound from his lips.

Fenobar quenched his blade in a cup of leftover wine, then took Sig's kalnak and did the same for it, to keep the temper in the steel. The thing was done, for better or for worse, and there could be no undoing it, no matter what Sig thought.

CHAPTER FIFTEEN

At dawn, darkcrested sailors brought breakfast to their cabin. They placed it on the low table between the beds, and beside each place a clan badge was laid out for their inspection. They bobbed their crests in Fenobar's direction and smoothly left. Fenobar, still a little sleepy, reached a hand out for the square of silk and embroidery, held it up to the light, and sat straight up, throwing off the light blanket. He was at the door in an instant, calling them back. But it was Belam who hurried up, anxious to know what was disturbing him.

"Look at this badge!" Fenobar shook it under his nose.

The browncrest studied it carefully. "Is there something wrong with the workmanship, my Lord?"

"It's a *King's* badge. I'm not entitled to this!"

"But my Lord, the Captain said . . ."

"I do not care what the sister-group has said. I will not have this. I have not become Bektarri. My clan badge will share space with the Bektarri badge, as is proper for an outlander doing service."

"As you will, my Lord," the browncrest said, his ears tilted at an unhappy angle. "I will inform the Captain."

Fenobar turned around, still agitated. Sig was seated on the floor, at the table, pouring out two cups of hot singali brew and sniffing carefully at the tan-colored liquid. "What is this stuff?"

Savoring the aroma as he brought his own cup to his nose, Fenobar replied, "The drink of the civilized world. Gods! How I have missed singali at breakfast." He sipped carefully, his eyes half shut with pleasure.

Sig drank, too, but a bit doubtfully. He picked up the square bit of green fabric on which his own badge had been made. "What is this?"

"The symbol of Clan Bektar. The green square is the sign of the Chaligirri, as the black triangle is the sign of the Monghanirri. On the green background is embroidered the Clan symbol and Spirit. For Bektar it is the flower of the lurmor tree."

The browncrest was back, dipping his crest submissively at them from the doorway. "My Lord, the Lady Keltain has instructed me to present you with the materials needed to draw the badge of your choice." He motioned forward another sailor, who placed on the end of the table, beside the jug of brew, several thin sheets of wood, a bit of finely sharpened charcoal, and ten different pots of colors, plus brushes of the finest tatarra hair.

With another bob of his crest Belam said, "My lords, the sail sewer sends his most profound respects. The two new badges can be ready for your approval this evening."

"Give my thanks to the sail sewer. I shall have the pictures ready in just a short while." Fenobar dismissed the darkcrests as he reached out to break the small loaf of bread to share between himself and Sig. "I will be glad to have it done. It was embarrassing to sit in front of those females last night and know we were not badged. Outlaws are not badged . . ." he brooded for a moment. "Temple guards are not badged."

Pushing aside the rest of his breakfast, Fenobar pulled toward him the wooden sheet, picked up the charcoal, and drew a square. The upper left-hand corner was shaded in by the charcoal . . . a triangle.

Dipping a brush into a pot of green, he painted a square in the lower right-hand corner. Catching Sig's eyes on his work he said, "Crossed lances on green are my mother's Family badge." In the lower left-hand corner he painted a white square. "The Black Hand on white is my sire's badge. The last square he painted red. "This is my personal badge—a black right hand on a field of red, to show that although I am wrong-handed, I am still dangerous." He set it aside to dry. "This will form half of the Bektar badge they will make for me." Pulling a second board to him, he looked expectantly at the Demon. "Now for your badge, Sig." He picked up the charcoal. "What is the symbol for your tribe?"

Sig stared blankly at him a moment. "Uhhh . . . Colonial exploration teams wore a terra patch surrounded by oak leaves."

Fenobar blinked. "What?"

"A blue and white circle on black. Forget the leaves."

This drawn to Sig's liking, Fenobar dipped his brush in water and poised it over the color pots. "Your mother's House sign?"

Sig nibbled on his lower lip a moment and then, picking up the charcoal, drew on the table. It looked like two spirals going around each other. "Put it on a white square."

Fenobar stared at it in perplexity. "What is that?"

"A double helix. My mother is the clan geneticist."

Fenobar stared at his sholstan, but he'd be damned before he'd ask what Sig meant by that. Gritting his teeth slightly, he said, "Now your sire's symbol . . ." He drew another square in the lower left-hand corner.

Sig thought a moment and then finally drew a crooked line. "Put it on a brown background."

"And what is that?" Fenobar asked suspiciously.

"A plow."

"It's the strangest plow I've ever seen. Why a plow?"

"Because my sire is a farmer."

"A *Dark*crest?"

"No. A farmer."

They exchanged long looks.

"Darkcrest." Fenobar was derisive. "They cannot fight and therefore have no honor."

Sig tugged at one ear, and his eyes twinkled. "He taught me all that ka-rah-teh I showed you."

Fenobar was silenced. He leaned over and drew the strange-looking plow into Sig's sire's corner. "Hunh!" Fenobar looked down at Sig's badge and shook his head. "They won't know what to make of this, that's for sure." Picking up another brush, he drew another square beside Sig's badge and painted his personal badge in the center. "Because I am your commander." Then he crossed his badge with a sword. "To show you are in my war band."

Dressing in his cleaned undertunic with its padded arm and his brightly polished armor, with his sword hanging as a familiar weight at his shoulder, Fenobar went to look for Keltain. Before he went out the door he remarked rather pointedly to Sig, who was still looking at the badge drawings, "A warrior wears his mail and weapons at all times." He got a grunt for a reply, but went away satisfied.

Keltain, wrapped in her cloak against the morning chill, was in the stern, talking to her darkcrested pilot, who was keeping a sharp eye on the two sailors working the rudder sweep. She turned at his approach. "So. I understand you were displeased to wear the badge of a King of Bektar?"

Here lay danger. Fenobar said carefully, "Not at all, Foremost. It is just that such a position has an air of . . . permanency . . . and I will be gone after a year."

"I thought to show you honor," Keltain said, not quite looking at him.

It came to Fenobar that she was hurt at his refusal. Haltingly, he said, "It was honor. But honor must be earned."

These words produced a sideways, speculative look from her green eyes and an ambiguous ear twitch. She pointed her chin at his arm. "I have been told that you and your . . . sholstan . . . acquired new scars during the night."

He did not know what to say and so said nothing. The pause lengthened, grew awkward. In desperation he blundered on to say what had been in his mind when he came looking for her. "So, I would see your cargo manifests, ports of call entries, and all other information pertaining to the selling and buying of cargo."

Her ears went back and, eyes slitted, she hissed, "You take much on yourself, whitecrest."

Fenobar kept his head up, crest relaxed. "This is what you desired of me, after all, it is not? I would

like to begin paying my debt as soon as possible.
Please send your cargo master to me with the necessary documents. I will be at my cabin." He bowed,
turned to go and paused, looking back over his shoulder. "I have been told we will be coming into the
harbor of Shundor to take on water. It would be a
shame to pay harbor fees for so slight a stay. We
might as well make the most of the opportunity to
sell your cargo."

Her face had relaxed and she was studying him.
"Do you think you can do that?"

Fenobar shrugged. There seemed to be no point
in telling her he'd been able to hold his own in
bartering since his fifth year. "I am of my sire's true
blood. The greater part of Black Fentaru's personal
honor came from the amount of revenue he brought
into the clan."

Her ears came up and her green eyes held more
warmth than they had since he and Sig had climbed
over the rail onto her ship. "The records will be
given to you."

He tilted his ears at her in respect and walked
sedately away.

Sig was not anywhere around when he returned to
the cabin, but a sailor was quick to obey his commands and brought the table from the cabin, out
onto the deck, for him to sit at. In due course Belam
arrived, carrying a large basket of color-coded book
sticks. Accompanying them was Keltain herself. "You
need to know the codes," she explained briefly, settling herself on a pillow the browncrested servant
brought for her.

Keltain reached into the basket and pulled out a
bundle of yellow sticks. "These are the records of our
ports of call for this trip." She watched in silence as

Fenobar ran his fingers across the incised information. He frowned, and when he put them down, she handed him green-tagged ones. "This is the cargo manifest."

He ran his fingers over them. "Three eld dried suggoleth fish cakes. I have heard of these—in Fen they are a delicacy. Sixteen bolts getar silk, various colors. Twenty-three bolts wool of the ghaido, various small amounts spices and perfumes. Ten ektorn . . . What are ektorn?"

Keltain's ears drooped, embarrassed. "They are a kind of whistle . . ." She shrugged. "We make them in our clan. They are very popular among the cublin."

After explaining what the other sticks contained, Keltain left him. Fenobar sat puzzling over the various port laws of the different clans, and going over and over the sticks that bore the notes of fifty years of trading experience with clan Shundor.

Heavy feet on the steps announced Sig before his bright head emerged from the deck well. The Demon looked contented, as if he'd spent a profitable hour. He sat down on a coil of rope near where Fenobar was working, pulling the Axe off his shoulder and setting it down beside his knee. "What is it you are doing?"

"I am reading the cargo master's notes."

"Those are books?" The Demon got up and ran one through his fingers. "You read by touch!"

"Well, you can't read with your eyes!" Fenobar snapped.

"We do," the Demon said softly.

"It figures." Fenobar ran his hand though his crest, a gesture he'd picked up from the Demon, and his ears described a worried arc. "I cannot seem to make sense of this information," he confessed.

"I know even less than you do," Sig replied. "Why don't you ask the cargo master for help?" He saw the browncrest standing a little ways away and called gaily, in a way no true warrior would, "Ah, Belam! Come on over here. We need your expert opinion."

"Sig, silence!" Fenobar hissed, exasperated. "NO whitecrest admits in public he needs help . . . and certainly not from a darkcrest."

Sig opened his eyes wide. "If you want information, you seek it from whatever source has it."

"No. I do not ask . . ."

"I am pledged to raise your rank. If you fail, you will be less than dust. If you succeed . . . ??" Sig raised his voice a little as the browncrest came closer. "Belam, Fenobar has some questions for you."

Fenobar took a deep breath. Sig was sholstan. Sig was doing this for ranking. It was unorthodox, and obviously no bond mark was going to change the Demon. Sig was also right in that he needed help. But what could he possibly learn from a darkcrest? He forced his crest to be still as Belam came rather timidly to where they were sitting. *He* hadn't missed Fenobar's jerking crest.

To Fenobar's embarrassment, Belam could not only understand the reports, he could explain them so that Fenobar understood them. It wasn't long before the browncrest was kneeling beside him on the deck, running a claw down the book sticks and talking at length about docking masters, port fees, and merchant row, where the incoming cargos were sold. Fenobar had forgotten his embarrassment and was talking to him as easily as if to a member of his war band.

Sig sat on his coil of rope, listening and whittling at a piece of wood with his kalnak, an occupation which, if Fenobar had been aware of it, would have earned him a sharp reprimand. One did not use his kalnak for idle amusement.

It was a thoroughly instructive morning, and Fenobar dismissed Belam at last with a feeling of accomplishment. "I think I'm going to be able to do it!" he confided to Sig. He looked closer at what Sig had been working on. "Why, you've carved a tyforndor!"

Sig grinned and put the small wooden carving into Fenobar's hand, as he slipped his kalnak into the sheath at his belt.

Fenobar stood running his fingers over the figure as Sig carried the table back into the cabin. When one reached adulthood, one did not receive gifts. It was a thing for cublins. From one's dam, balls and hoops for coordination. From sires, a wooden sword or shield.

He had made his own ball and hoop, carved his own sword. It was a useless thing, this small wooden tyforndor. Very carefully he placed it inside his tunic.

Across the sky scudded soft white clouds . . . the harbingers of change, for the thunderheads were massing behind them. The wind had been steady, and for two days they had sailed close to the heavily forested Selnessor peninsula, to keep them clear of the westward flow of the Trulden current.

This morning, Fenobar and Sig leaned on the railing and watched Shundor harbor unfold as the pilot angled them past the breakwaters.

Fenobar was too hot in this southern climate, and tried not to fidget. He was wearing a light tunic under his mail, which would not last a two-day before the armor rubbed holes in it. The sleeve along his bad arm had been padded expertly by Lor, the sailmaker. Lor had also made a summerweight undertunic for Sig, which had pleased the Demon very much.

Over their shining armor, they were both wearing green getar silk surcoats. Fenobar touched the embroidered badge at his shoulder—his identity. A surge of self-confidence went through him.

Sig flung out a five-fingered hand, pointing toward the line of distant docks. "I see the harbor master coming!" The Axe in its harness at his back moved and caught the sunlight on its curved double blades.

Fenobar squinted and could make out nothing. As his ears were sharper than the Demon's, Sig's eyes were better than his, at least in the daylight. His new self-confidence suddenly began to ebb and he tried to still the sudden nervousness which had come to shiver his belly. It was ridiculous to feel this way, he told himself. He had gone over this time and time again with Belam. He looked around for the brown-crest and saw the smaller male approaching him, dressed in a green tunic and carrying a blank stick book.

Belam flattened his crest in greeting and came to stand to one side of him. Just then the door opened to the main cabin and Keltain, at the head of her sister-group, stepped onto the deck. They had been keeping to themselves for the last several days and Fenobar had rather missed their company. The sister-group had gotten into the habit of inviting him and Sig to sit with them of an evening. He dipped his crest in their direction. Among them was one important change, the reason they had not had him to their cabin. Sorlain, she of the white fur, was wrapped about in veils, until only her golden eyes showed. Thus she was proclaiming her readiness to accept the male of her choice. She was closely accompanied by

Mertis and Bril, who had put off their colored silks in favor of the green and white of Clan Bektar.

Sorlain's hot, interested eyes met Fenobar's and he gulped. Her sister-group closed up around her, putting a solid wall between them. That denial was a relief of sorts and Fenobar resolutely turned his attention back to the coming meeting. The lookout shouted down that the harbor master was on his way.

The harbor master's vessel was slender and narrow, rowed by six muscular darkcrests. It skimmed quickly and easily toward them, like a bug skating over the surface of a pond. The harbor master was as yet only a whitecrested form seated in the prow. Behind him stood another. The long tannish crest above the shining helm proclaiming him the harbor master's sholstan.

The sailors tossed the ladder down as the harbor master came alongside and a heavily built mailed whitecrest clambered up, followed closely by his tancrested sholstan. Having already seen the Chalig flag at the mast, he was not prepared to find Fenobar's white crest waiting for him on deck, nor could he possibly have expected anything like Sig to be standing at Fenobar's back. The Shundor harbor master and his sholstan took one look at that round, crestless head and froze with shock.

Fenobar took ruthless advantage of the harbor master's confusion to get a low docking fee and sent him on his way without disabusing him of the notion that something terrible would happen to him if he upset the Demon. It was no surprise, therefore, to discover they had been given one of the better docking slips, adjacent to the water tank, food stalls and merchants's row.

Belam was entering all this on the book stick with

one foreclaw. His crest was fluffed up and there was a smug tilt to his ears.

As soon as the ship was made fast, Fenobar prepared to go ashore. Accompanied by Belam and Sig, he strode into Merchant's Row. Here, the cargo master was invaluable. Fenobar would never have found the right buyers for their goods, but Belam led the way confidently down the long, narrow street, where darkcrests sat under their House signs, calling aloud the wares they wanted to buy. A wave of silence accompanied the trio from the *Wave Dancer* as they moved down the row.

Belam came to a halt in front of a house with a yellow thorn stick painted over the door and clicked his finger claws together at the darkcrest. "My Lord would speak with yours!" he said grandly, setting down the cargo samples he had been carrying. Dipping his crest to Fenobar, he stepped back out of the way.

From the small room under the House sign, a large whitecrest emerged. He had small, shrewd eyes and they lingered on Sig's badge before he sat down behind the table to finger the fabrics and taste the foodstuffs. Ignoring the Demon's presence, the merchant got down to business. He was willing to take everything they had to offer. He was a good bargainer, very good. Not even Sig's presence spoiled his concentration.

But he had met his match in Fenobar, and Belam was quite cheerful as he totted up sums on his book stick. Fenobar picked up the small sack of coins and gems the merchant had left behind as his interest price. It always belonged to the whitecrest. Belam returned to the ship with the merchant's agent to see to the removal of the cargo, while Fenobar and Sig walked on out of Merchant's Row into the marketplace.

"What is the purpose of these gold rounds and these jewels the merchant gave us for our cargo?" Sig asked. He was peering into the small sack Fenobar had given him to carry.

"Haven't you ever seen money before?"

"No." Sig poured some of the contents out into his hand. "Is this really money? I've heard of it, but we don't use it at home. We use work hours."

Shaking his head over his sholstan's irregular education, Fenobar slowly worked his way through the crowded bazaar, looking for the things Keltain had told him to buy. After years of listening to Black Fentaru, he knew better than to make the final decision himself. A steady stream of darkcrests were sent back to the *Wave Dancer* to show wares for her approval. Her business finished, they were free to find Armorer's Lane.

Sig had walked through the crowd with wide eyes, twisting this way and that in an effort to see everything at once. The crowds were doing their best to ignore Sig after the news had run ahead that he was part of a war band. The badge was read, the mark on his wrist noted with a kind of silent amazement. But conversation had a tendency to sink where he passed, and more than one glance was shot after his departing back.

Armorer Lane was filled with the heat of forges and the clanging of hammer against metal as white-crested and palecrested males worked over their anvils, for in this craft alone the darkcrests were excluded. Unlike the marketplace, this was a street where the warrior kind congregated, and for the first time Fenobar noticed how many of them were young, unkempt Chalig warriors with a sullen, defeated look to them.

Fenobar leaned back against the counter of the stall where Sig, entranced by the quality of the leather work, was looking at sword harnesses. Idly he studied the passing crowd. In addition to the Shundor and Chalig warriors, there were a great many outclan Selnessor, whose badges bore a wide variety of clan insignia.

He was wondering why so many strangers should be wandering through the streets of Shundor, when he felt someone staring at him. Turning his head slightly, he found a rangy Chalig palecrest standing nearly opposite him on the other side of the lane, half in the shadow of a sword seller's awning. This warrior, perhaps ten years older than Fenobar, was gazing fixedly at him, or rather, at the badge on his shoulder. The warrior was of a light reddish brown, crest somewhat pinkish, but long and with a healthy shine to it. His ears were notched from old fights, and a sword scar ran lengthwise down his jawline. The Chalig had been on the road a long time, for he had painted his armor black to protect it, and his surcoat was dirty and torn. But his weapons were well cared for and he held himself straight and proud. The Chalig lifted puzzled eyes to Fenobar's face. The badge on his shoulder bore the same white flower of Bektar as Fenobar's now did.

Well, that explained his interest. He was probably wondering who Fenobar was and was too far away to make out the smaller details of his badge.

Sig nudged Fenobar. He was holding a green baldric with gold tracing. An axe harness. "Do you think we could buy this for the Axe?"

Fenobar flattened his crest and ears in shame. They had not been showing the Axe any proper respect. For days it had hung in a makeshift harness

Sig himself had cobbled together out of scraps of leather. Perhaps this harness, which was a thing of beauty, would in some way erase his neglect. When the bargaining was finished and Sig was covering the Axe's distinctive head in a green and gold hood, Fenobar sought the Bektarri palecrest again. The place across the way was empty, and his gaze shifted about until he found the warrior had drifted to a place against a shield maker's stall not far from him. Fenobar caught the warrior's eye and tilted his crest at the crowded street. "Why are all these outclan Selnessor in Shundor port?"

"They are looking for warriors," the Bektarri palecrest said in a slightly husky voice. "They have had the coughing sickness in the east. I have heard it has killed fully a third of their war bands."

Fenobar moved down to the shield-maker's stall, the palecrest obligingly moving to make room for him. He picked out two stout, blank shields, nothing fancy. As he dickered with the shield-maker to make the changes needed for his bad arm, Fenobar was peripherally aware that not far away a young white-crest, with an equally young war band at his back, was offering to challenge one of the eastern Selnessor. It was a lessor challenge, a test of skill, one warrior to another—the kind of challenge a palecrest would make to the whitecrest of a war band he wishes to join. That alone would have revealed the young commander's desperation and need for protection even without the added shame of seeking that protection from an outlander. The young Chalig's voice was shrill, lacking conviction, broadcasting all too clearly his loss of self confidence. Fenobar stopped his haggling and turned to look, as did a large number of other warriors up and down the street.

The loss of their clan Spirits had brought the Chalig

lower than warriors had any right to be. Fenobar turned his head away, unwilling to be a witness to this degradation. Even if they were his enemies, they should not be brought to begging for the lowest place in another clan just so they could have the protection of a Spirit.

The Selnessor whitecrest also heard that desperate note, and it made him cruel. He would not challenge. He turned away as the Chalig whitecrest pleaded with him, losing yet more honor. The youngster must have been very desperate, for he went after the Selnessor and challenged yet again. The Selnessor said something in a low, sneering voice and the young whitecrest went for his sword. The Selnessor was ready for him, and the Chalig had not cleared his sword sheath before the older warrior's sword darted for his throat. The body slumped to the ground, and as darkcrests came with water to wash the blood from the cobblestones, the dead whitecrest's war band carried his body away.

Fenobar turned back to the merchant to conclude his deal and up and down the street, chatter and dickering resumed. Finished, Fenobar turned to the Bektarri warrior. Flicking his crest at the spot where the young whitecrest had died, Fenobar said, "That was not well done."

The warrior's eyes were hard. At Fenobar's words his crest lifted slowly erect, a danger sign. "It was not necessary to humiliate him before the killing. I have been here five days and seen that one dishonor these cublin commanders for the joy it offers him. And not only him . . . all those eastern Selnessor. Surely if offends the honor of the Gods as well as this Clan for him to behave like that, yet no priest, no ranking whitecrest, strips him of honor for it. The Chalig may be the butt of Tyvai, but we deserve

better than to be killed like dornfor in the streets!"
He turned, shamed and angry, and started to walk
away.

There was an air of responsibility and intelligence
about the palecrest which reminded Fenobar forcibly
of Stells. On an impulse he said, "Would you come
and share a pitcher of wine with myself and my
sholstan? I would learn more concerning these
Selnessor."

The tall warrior stopped, turned and looked hard
at Sig. After a moment he said, "It would be an
honor, my Lord."

CHAPTER SIXTEEN

Except that the older warrior avoided Sig's eyes, and kept Fenobar between himself and the Demon as he led the way to a nearby tavern, he handled Sig's presence well, and Fenobar was pleased.

"It is not a grand place," the palecrest said, by way of excusing the old building, which had a decided drift to leeward. "But the wine is excellent."

The room was full of young Chalig whitecrest warriors with their retinues. The groups of four and five hunched over the crude tables, filling the room with a low murmur. The sound ceased as Fenobar led the way to an unoccupied table along the far wall with Sig and the palecrest at his back. The center of the long, low room was empty except for the posts holding the roof up, and the red lines between those posts told him the empty space served as a challenge circle.

He settled down on the mat behind the table, his back against the wall. As the Chalig warrior and Sig took places on either side of him, he thumped the scarred table for service. The conversation around them picked up to a sharp buzz as those less informed asked enlightenment of their neighbors. Sig nonchalantly put his elbows on the table, resting his chin on clasped hands in such a way that the red triangular burn on the inside of his wrist was clearly seen.

A darkcrest servant scuttled out of the rear of the establishment, wiping his hands on a dirty apron. He took one look at Sig, dove for a back room and refused to come out.

"I thought you said I would be invisible," Sig said, mildly amused.

"To those who count," Fenobar said, "you are."

Without saying anything the Chalig palecrest went to the bar and brought back earthenware cups and a pitcher of wine. He set them on the table in front of Fenobar. Fenobar shoved a ruby across the scarred table to the Chalig—payment for their drinks. It was perhaps a large gesture to make with their slim funds, but he was feeling expansive.

Sig looked critically at the jewel lying untouched beside the Chalig's red furred hand. "Is that going to be enough for wine? It's just ordinary corundum— red, at that."

"Ordinary . . . ??" Both the Imkairans turned to stare at the Demon. "Have you seen a lot of these?" Fenobar finally asked.

"Oh, yes," Sig said offhandedly, being more interested in studying the crowd. "They're all over the place at home."

Chewing over this nugget of information, Fenobar rather absently poured wine for all of them.

At the first sip, Sig's grey eyes lit up. "This tastes just like the merryberrry juice we make back home."

The Chalig gave Sig a mistrustful glance and leaned

back, away from the Demon, who was nearly opposite him.

Fenobar flicked his crest toward the warrior. "I am
Wrong-hand Fenobar, of Fen, of the Monghanirri.
And this is my sholstan, Sig."

"I am called Soonkar, of Bektar," the warrior replied in his husky voice. He pointed a claw in the
direction of Fenobar's badge. "How does an outlander whitecrest come to bear the device of my
Clan?"

"I'm paying off a debt," Fenobar said, sipping
appreciatively at the wine.

"Then you are not here looking for service among
the Selnessor?" There was a hint of eagerness in the
other, imperfectly concealed.

Fenobar's crest dipped to one side in wry humor.
"No. I have a place among the Bektarri for the next
year, at least."

Soonkar's eyes shifted to Sig. You will be taking
that behind my Clan walls? his expression said. His
eyes lingered on the Axe at Sig's back and widened
briefly with a kind of thoughtful speculation. Fenobar
was taking a drink and missed it. Soonkar's eyes
traveled to Fenobar's still uneven crest, down to his
left hand, half hidden by the sleeve of his undertunic.

Calmly, Fenobar raised his twisted hand, showing
it clearly, and let it drop. "Yes, that is why I am
called Wrong-hand."

Soonkar's crest drooped in embarrassment and apology. Studying the crude cup he held between his
hands he asked, "Would you be needing warriors?"

Startled, Fenobar blurted, "Why?" Which was not
what he meant to say at all.

Soonkar's ears flattened. "Do you really need to
ask? From all over Chalig territory, the younglings
have come . . ." He hesitated. "And some warriors

not so young . . . to seek a place among the Selnessor. The Selnessor delight in seeing how low we are willing to abase ourselves in order to join with a Clan that has the protection of a Spirit. So far has Thenorig brought down the proud Chaligirri that we must barter what little honor we have left to eat crumbs from the tables of the Selnessor!"

"Was your commander one of those swept up in Thenorig's net?" Fenobar asked, feeling the Selnessor was not a safe topic.

"He died at the taking of our town." Soonkar sipped at his wine. "I was his sholstan. Freed of the bond that would have forced myself and the war band into Thenorig's retinue, my whitecrested clankin somehow overlooked a chance to attach what was left of our war band to their own retinues, and add yet more starving mouths to Thenorig's tail. For which kindness I will always hold them in honor," he finished calmly.

"You speak of 'our war band.' Have you kept together, then?" Fenobar refilled the cups. It was Sig's job, but Sig was absorbed in the activity of the tavern, as wide-eyed as a cublin at the Spring Festival.

"My troop has been together for many years and they trusted my judgment still, after our commander died, so that we were not as desperate as a younger group of warriors to have a whitecrest at our head. We also thought it would be easier for us to be taken on by a Selnessor whitecrest if we did not already have a commander. But we have found none among them to our liking."

And am I to believe you have suddenly found a commander to your liking in *me?* Fenobar thought. I know what you want—a chance to get home again. But he kept those thoughts behind his teeth. What he actually said was, "So you are sholstan. The troop obey you then, as if you were whitecrest?"

"Hunh!" Soonkar snorted in derision. "Not *exactly* like a whitecrest, but they obey."

"Fen." A certain note in the Demon's voice claimed Fenobar's attention as if Sig had shouted his warning aloud. He followed Sig's eyes and saw that a tall Selnessor whitecrest, helm bronzed after the eastern fashion, had come lounging in through the door. He carried an aura of wealth, power and elegance around him like a cloak and was as out of place in that tavern as a war tatarra in a herd of ghaido. Sig's instincts were not astray. Languidly he approached their table, giving them enough time to read his badge. The lower right-hand corner had been crossed with the white line of favorite son. His status was high in his House.

The Selnessor stopped in front of Fenobar and flicked his crest in an insultingly brief greeting, ears twitching in mockery. "They tell me you are wrong-handed. A one-armed warrior belongs in the temple. I will do you a favor and take this, the last of your war band, from you so you will be free to choose that haven." And he nodded his crest toward Sig.

"You are mistaken," Fenobar said quietly. He had had long practice in keeping battle fury down in the face of insults, and knew better than to let himself be baited into rashness. He stood up slowly, shorter than the other, but slim and deadly. He moved out from behind the table, chosing to go behind Soonkar rather than Sig. "You are mistaken," he said again. "Sig is not the last, but the first. And I have already served my time in the temple."

Sig calmly poured himself another drink. "I am right-hand sholstan to the Commander Fenobar." He looked up the Selnessor's length and explained politely, "That means that it you succeed in killing him, I will have to cut your heart out."

The whitecrest gave the Demon an affronted stare and Sig smiled gently into his outrage, adding to the insult.

Trying to recover his aplomb, the Selnessor spat. "Kill me? I think not. After the cripple is dead you will be taken to Selne, a gift for the High King, and kept caged for all to stare at!"

"That would not suit me at all, since I, like my commander, have already served my time." Sig stood. Lazily he reached over his shoulder and the Axe appeared like magic in his long-fingered hands. He lounged around the table toward the Selnessor, his actions, if not his words, pure whitecrest. For a startled moment, everyone in the tavern, including Fenobar, thought he intended to attack. But Sig merely leaned his wide shoulders against the nearest roof support, thumbing one of the honed edges on the double Axe head, his strange direhawk eyes fixed unwaveringly on the Selnessor commander.

Listening to this exchange, Fenobar was filled with a strange and heady delight. Only in the ancient story of Lykalt and Rinwar had he ever heard of a palecrest offering to fight a whitecrest for killing his commander. It was the stuff of which legends were made.

The Selnessor caught the movement as Fenobar's crest fluffed. He stepped back, his hand going to his sword, and thereby lost status, for the other two had not moved. The roomful of Chalig murmured their amusement, and everywhere crests lifted and fluffed. He met Fenobar's amused eyes and lost his temper. The whole scene had been taken away from him, making him look like a fool. Shrugging off his shield, because Fenobar did not have one and they would say he had taken unfair advantage of a cripple, he snarled his challenge once more at Fenobar.

Drawing his sword and moving with the swiftness that had kept him alive in Bokeem, Fenobar leaped for the other. The Selnessor was not as good as he thought he was, and the fight was very short. He could not anticipate Fenobar's right-handed style and his blocking was clumsy. Like a thing alive, Fenobar's sword stabbed and flickered, hunting for an opening. Then the Selnessor failed to block a deadly blow and Fenobar's weapon cut deep into his side, driven with all the force of a powerful right arm.

Blood fountained upward as the Selnessor whitecrest sank to the floor, even as his tancrested sholstan jumped forward to support him. He died without a word spoken, but his green eyes rested with hatred on Fenobar until death filmed them over.

The Selnessor sholstan stood above the body of his commander, staring defiantly at Fenobar. "By right I am honor bound to you, but I tell you plain, I will not serve with a crippled commander who needs a Demon of Undoing to fight his battles for him."

Fenobar considered killing him for those words, but having been spoken they would either be believed, or not, by those present. No killing would change that. He showed his teeth to the Selnessor in a feral grin. His sword pointed at the dead whitecrest. "If this one had the training of you, what makes you think I would want you? Go."

Rage stiffened the Selnessor sholstan's crest and one hand started for his sword, but Sig made a warning movement and the Selnessor palecrest thought better of starting anything. Hoisting his commander's body over his shoulder, the Selnessor sholstan left.

"My Lord." Soonkar stood up. "I have eyes to understand skill when I see it. The Demon did not move during your kill. He did not help." He stepped close to Sig and muttered for those round ears alone, "Except you scared him witless with that talk of cutting out his heart." He continued into the center of the challenge square. "If my Lord be willing, I challenge to a test of skill. If you are pleased with me, I would be honored to take oath of you."

Fenobar studied the Bektarri warrior for a long, considering moment. Soonkar did not have to say this, nor ask a skill challenge of him where all those ears which had just heard the Selnessor's accusations could hear. He was protecting a future Commander's honor, which would be his honor if he was taken on. "I accept your skill challenge. But I do not do such things in the middle of a tavern. We will find a challenge circle and do it properly."

Some time later, having stopped to collect Soonkar's troop of six from the extremely humble quarters they had found for themselves, Soonkar and Fenobar were standing beside one of the challenge circles in the temple garden. The circles were separated one from the other by bushes and trees, for these were places for private ranking challenges on a neutral ground. Some distance away they could hear the clatter of weapons and loud calls as other combatants were urged on by their war bands.

"About my troop," Soonkar started hesitantly. He turned to look at the six Bektarri warriors drawn up stiffly in a line behind them.

"I accept them."

Soonkar frowned. "You know nothing about them."

Fenobar sighed to himself. He had rather hoped to get out of having to fight all of Soonkar's troop one by one and passing judgment on them. He was not yet in the best fighting shape and he was afraid if he got too tired he would look bad. But if Soonkar had something on his mind, it would be best if he heard the ex-sholstan out.

With a clear, careful analysis of their strong and weak points, Soonkar described each member of his troop. When he came to the sixth and last warrior under his command, he hesitated. "Bartic . . . thinks too much. But there have been times when his ideas have helped us. For that reason I have kept him, although he is the least and will always be the least in any troop he is in. Also, he has been wounded recently. It will take months for him to get his full strength back."

Bartic was grey, with curious white stripes on arms and legs. His light grey eyes were focused somewhere past the two Ranking males and there was a tenseness about him that spoke of fear. He stood a little crookedly, favoring the side where his mail had been badly repaired. If he were dismissed, what kind of place could he find in another war band without Soonkar to speak for him? Fenobar didn't hesitate. "If his ideas have helped you in the past, they may help me in the future. We take him as well."

Soonkar dipped his crest to Fenobar in respect and formally repeated his challenge. Fenobar as formally accepted and they took their places within the circle. Sig came to help Fenobar adjust the straps on his new shield, which they had picked up on their way to the garden. That settled to his satisfaction, they saluted each other and began.

If Soonkar seemed clumsy at first, it was because he was facing a right-handed opponent. Nevertheless, he was quick to find a way of countering Fenobar's blows. The younger, faster whitecrest put him through the basic sword moves, pushing the warrior harder at each pass, forcing him to show all his skill. And, though he did not realize it, showing *his* skill to Soonkar.

After a few minutes of this, Fenobar had learned two things. The Chalig warrior was proving to be quicker than Fenobar thought he would be, and he had not been well taught. His shield work was especially bad. He had no conception of using it as a weapon at all, but merely as something to hide behind. But this was no real surprise. From his own years in Bokeem, Fenobar knew that the masters there had a low estimation of the ability of the average palecrest to learning anything beyond the more basic slash and hack style of sword-play.

Soonkar was taking a very long time to be overcome by fesen, and the longer he held onto his temper, the higher he rose in Fenobar's opinion. But finally Fenobar managed to tip him over the edge into the blood madness. This was the final test. Fenobar crossed swords with the Chalig, locking them together at the hilts. Eye-to-eye with the palecrest, he ordered him to cease—to stand down and lower his sword.

Soonkar's ear flicked sideways, as if he were listening for another voice, but then his eyes focused on Fenobar's head. Fenobar could see the struggle in the other as he pulled back from the berserker rage. Sanity came back behind those red-gold eyes, tension went out of his muscles, and he took two paces back, somewhat dazed, and lowered his sword.

"Put your weapon away," Fenobar commanded, and the Chalig did, with a smooth, practiced gesture.

Fenobar sheathed his own sword, very satisfied. This Soonkar was a warrior worth having by anyone's standards. He approached the warrior, reached out his good hand and took the Chalig's throat in his hold. "You are mine. You have yielded to my authority."

"I am yours, as long as you have the strength to hold," Soonkar replied in the approved manner.

Then it was time to take the troop through their paces, much as he had Soonkar. The evaluation Soonkar had given them was accurate. They were all solid warriors, slow to raise fesen—and all with those same fatal flaws of sword-learning he'd already noted with Soonkar. It made no difference. They were willing to come with him, to put up with Sig's presence, and he took them all.

On the way back to the ship the Bektarri sported fresh burns on their wrists, and Fenobar had a rosette pattern of triangular brands on the inside of his left forearm. He was feeling a little lightheaded from the pain, but overall quite happy. He had a war band at last. Now all he had to do was keep them.

Behind him he heard Sig say, "Walk with me, Soonkar."

And the Chalig's wary reply: "But you are war band First and Sholstan. We are not near in status."

"Tatarra dung!" was Sig's forthright answer. "I may be sholstan, but we both know in the eyes of the troop you are the war band First."

There was a moment of palpable surprise, and then Soonkar's husky voice, still cautious. "I do not say you are wrong, but I do not claim that rank. There must be peace within a war band or all goes awry."

Fenobar's ears perked up at that remark. This Soonkar was one of the more sensible palecrests, but you could not demote a warrior and expect him to sit easy under it. There was no point in creating unnecessary stress between Sig and Soonkar when, Tyvai knew, there was enough there already. It was time to step in and make things official. "Sig is sholstan of choice," he said quietly over his shoulder. "You, Soonkar, will be war band First."

"As you command, my Lord," Soonkar agreed. "But it seems an overmany leaders for so small a war band."

Keltain and her sister-group, with the exception of Sorlain, were busy within a large knot of eager darkcrests holding samples of their wares when Fenobar led his war band aboard the *Wave Dancer*. She looked up and her green eyes widened. A second later she was pushing through the males with murmured apologies and coming straight toward him. Courteously, he waited.

She gave him a flick of the ear in acknowledgement, but it was to Soonkar she went. Taking his hand, she searched that scarred, reddish face. "Brother, I had not thought to see you again."

"As you see," Soonkar replied, a trifle stiffly, his ears held at an embarrassed angle.

"There are other sister-groups among the Family, besides me and mine, who will be pleased to see you among us again." Keltain's ears were demurely lowered.

Soonkar's ears went back a little, but there was a suspicion of fluff to his pink crest.

Keltain turned over the hand she was holding, pushed up mail and undertunic, and looked at the fresh brand on his wrist. "So." Her green eyes went to Fenobar's arm. "Not many would take so many hurts at one time," she commented. Letting go her brother she faced Fenobar. "You have gained much honor among the Bektarri this day. This increase in your prestige will add to Sorlain's pleasure. She has instructed me to ask you to the main cabin tonight after dinner."

This could not mean what it seemed to mean, Fenobar told himself as he went to the cabin he shared with Sig. Not for him the attentions of females or the siring of cublin. His arm had seen to that.

Dinner was a festive affair shared with Sig and Soonkar and eaten on the deck outside the cabin where they had more room. Served by attentive darkcrests, there were delicacies Fenobar and Soonkar had not tasted in many months, and Sig, never.

Sig brought one of his seaweed cakes to the table, and although Fenobar warned Soonkar it tasted like old shield leather, the Bektar warrior ate several pieces with a thoughtful expression on his scarred face. "It's good," he murmured.

"The first couple of times, yes," Fenobar agreed. "And after that I wouldn't use it to wrap three-day fish in."

The last dish was cleared away. Belam appeared, holding a new undertunic over his arm. The other two gave Fenobar a speculative look.

"Should we wait up for you?" Sig asked slyly.

Fenobar's ears dipped. "I don't know why they want me . . ."

"Oh, don't you?" Sig murmured.

Had they been alone when Sig gave him that provocative sideways look out of his direhawk eyes, Fenobar would have thrown a bone at him. But there was nothing to do but try to be as dignified as possible and ignore his sholstan's mischief as Sig helped him change into the clean undertunic and his armor.

When the door to the stern cabin was opened to Fenobar's scratch, it had been changed. Curtains were drawn over the working place at the back of the room and under the lantern hanging from the ceiling, Sorlain was reclining among a pile of the brightly colored pillows, scarves draped loosely about her body. The soft yellow light was reflected in her golden eyes. Her scent filled the air with a heady fragrance.

His heart thudded heavily. He could not take his eyes from her. Keltain and the other two of the sister-group who had been standing beside the door started to leave. Keltain said, "Have a sweet time, sister." But it didn't really register with him. He took a long, slow pace forward, drowning in Sorlain's bright welcome. The sister-group quietly closed the door behind them, leaving the two of them alone. The light burned, but not as brightly as those eyes, coming closer to him. A hand rested lightly on his sleeve. Her fur was silky against his as she helped him out of his armor.

What he didn't know, she taught him.

Several days passed in a hot blur. Then he woke one morning to find Sorlain gone, leaving him in a nest of soft pillows. Stretching mightily he heard someone enter. It was not Sorlain, but Keltain. She carried a tray holding a pot and two cups for the morning brew. She set the tray down on the low table and gracefully curled up nearby, pouring out a cup of singali. She handed it to him.

"Sorlain is well content. She says you are like a pumnor of the high mountains. And Mertis has had another seeing. The whitecrest cublin Sorlain bears will make our Family and the male House first within the Clan. And the Bektar Clan he will make only a little lower than the Royal Clan."

"That is a fine seeing," Fenobar said politely, not really hearing her. It was over. He remembered Sorlain's lustrous eyes, the touch of the fine-boned hand, the pearly opalescence of her claws, the curve of shoulder and thigh, and the feel of his fingers on the soft white pelt. He set his cup down. "I must rejoin my warriors." He got up and collected his gear from the corner, where someone, probably Sorlain, had hung it.

Keltain wrapped her arms around updrawn knees and looked up at him while he dressed. "Soonkar told me what your Demon did when you faced that Selnessor whitecrest. He is making up a song about it. He hopes you will not mind, but he has been used to being a sholstan and it seems to him to be a song worth making. Your Demon knows nothing of songs, and he has asked Soonkar to teach him. That is very strange, I think. What is stranger yet, is that Soonkar *is* teaching him."

His ears twitching with inner laughter, Fenobar settled his sword harness. "It must be trying for Soonkar. Sig has many good qualities, but a good voice is not among them." He hesitated, darting her a quick glance. "What was Soonkar's rank in Bektar before Thenorig came?"

"He was sholstan to the favorite son of his House, who was mate to my mother's sister-group. Their second mate," she added after a slight pause. "My sire died full ten years ago.

"His Male House is the male side of my Family. The Ranking whitecrest was my mother's sire and was fourth after the King. Our Family, both the male and female houses, are sailors. We run the fishing fleet and the larger merchant vessels, like this one. Also, the Ranking male is always the harbor master.

"Soonkar is mate to my cousin's sister-group within our Family. If he were not full blood to myself and Sorlain, he would have been mate to my sister-group." She put her head on her knees, her ears at half droop, as if the loss of this opportunity distressed her. "It is good you have brought him back to us."

Fenobar was at a loss for words, once more, with this unaccountable female. No male would have admitted such strong feeling for another. Tilting his crest at her politely, he went to find his sholstan and his war band First.

A sharp wind caught his nose as he closed the door behind him. Lifting his head he sniffed deeply, clearing the closeness of the cabin from his lungs. They were at sea and had been for several days, judging from the shape of the coastline. Those who described the time of mating as a kind of madness were right. Madness, indeed, that he had not even known they had left port! The sky was that early morning grey before the sun comes over the horizon, and the only sounds were the creaking of the rigging and the high calls of the sea birds circling behind the stern looking for scraps. He walked toward the forward cabin which he shared with Sig and heard the Demon's deep, burring voice on the far side, where there was shelter from the wind.

He edged along the narrow space between the rail and the cabin to find Soonkar and Sig seated side by side on the deck, with their backs to the wall. Between them sat a large jug and two mugs of singali.

Sig looked up as Fenobar's shadow fell over him and grinned his Demon welcome, his head very white against the dark wood behind him. "So you're back! Have a cup!" he said, handing his commander his own freshly poured mug.

Soonkar had scrambled to his feet as soon as he saw his commander and was standing there, crest at a respectful angle. "No, Sig!" he said promptly. "It is not fitting that the commander should drink after one of his war band. I will get another cup." He disappeared around the other side of the cabin.

Fitting or not, Fenobar accepted the cup and settled down beside Sig, sipping the hot brew. It tasted better than the cup Keltain had given him in the cabin, perhaps because he had regained his freedom. "What's the matter with Soonkar? He seemed in a terrible hurry to get away from my company." He handed Sig his cup back.

Sig chuckled, a peculiarly Demon sound of laughter. "He thinks you might be angry with us."

"Why?"

Sig laughed aloud, showing his flat white teeth, and he was still laughing when Soonkar came back. He continued to chuckle all the while Soonkar filled and handed Fenobar the cup he'd brought.

"I can guess he has not yet told you, then." Soonkar's voice was resigned.

Sig lifted his cup to Fenobar. "You fell like a sheet of titanium. I've never seen anyone so wrapped up in a female before."

Fenobar blinked slowly at him. "It is the time of mating. It is not so with your folk?"

"Hmmmm. Only at the beginning. I'm told it wears off after a while."

"You are told?" Soonkar asked familiarly, from the other side of Fenobar. "Don't you know?"

"I've never been in love," Sig answered honestly.

Fenobar exchanged a puzzled glance with Soonkar behind Sig's back, but refrained from asking the obvious. "Did you try to speak with me? I thought I remembered you at the door once . . . and wasn't there a lot of noise another time?"

Sig threw his head back and pealed out a sound of enjoyment no Imkairan could hope to match for sheer range and volume. "Keltain wouldn't let anyone close to you and Sorlain. Every time I even glanced in your direction she would raise her hand and stick out her claws. To make sure I got the message, she spent an hour honing them where I could see her doing it."

"That was only because that first night you insisted on singing some demon song to them and clanging shields together on the cabin roof beside the skylight," Soonkar mumbled.

"Ritual harassment of the newly mated couple . . ." Sig replied to Fenobar's look of astonishment. "How can you have a proper wedding without it?"

Fenobar's crest went limp. "It's not done! Sig! You must leave the mated ones alone. I was counting on you and Soonkar to make sure we *were* left alone."

"Well, you were. By everybody but us," Sig replied frankly.

"Don't include me in that," Soonkar said firmly. "You did it all by yourself."

"Another male isn't supposed to come anywhere near a mated couple," Fenobar said in a strangled voice. "Soonkar, didn't you tell him that?"

"Yes, my Lord, but he wasn't in a mood to pay attention," Soonkar replied unhappily. His pink crest was at half tilt.

"Sig," Fenobar was shaking, thinking of the close call his sholstan had had, "you must never, never do that again. She could have killed you and been well within her rights."

"How was I supposed to know?" Sig replied reasonably. "No one said anything until afterwards."

"Anyone else would have known that a female standing guard with a drawn sword meant *something*," Soonkar replied irritably.

"She was at the door. No one said anything about

the window." The Demon spread his five-fingered hands in a purely Demon gesture.

"Bah!" Soonkar said. "You are being willfully stupid."

Fenobar waited for fesen to rise between his warriors, but Sig only laughed and poured himself a cup of singali. The talk turned to the weather and Fenobar relaxed against the wall, ears twitching as he listened to them. They were easy together in a way he had seldom seen top-ranking war band mates. It was a good feeling to share in this relaxed talk. It was security of a kind he'd never heard about before. Only a Demon of Undoing could have created it.

CHAPTER SEVENTEEN

They sailed north up the Selnessor peninsula for another day, the Belt Mountains gradually flattening out into dusky green plains. There was a rising sense of expectation among the crew and the Bektarri warriors. The palecrests crowded along the rail and pointed out landmarks to each other, and Sig and Fenobar sat outside their cabin door, exchanging brief looks and feeling a little left out. At mid-morning the *Wave Dancer* sailed into Bektar Harbor, when the sun was shining and the air was crisp. It was the beginning of autumn. Fenobar breathed deep of the cool air, glad to be away from the Olknessor heat.

Bektar Harbor was small and isolated. Keltain had not told him much about her Clan and now he understood why. They were few in number and evidently not very prosperous, even in the best of times. There was a seedy look to the buildings along the wharfs, that was the neglect of decades rather than years. There were only two other large ships at anchor and they both looked old, even to his untrained eyes. The rest of the small craft rocking at the docks, Soonkar said, were fishing boats.

The *Wave Dancer* sailed into the harbor in grand style, all sails belled by the wind, and the water curling bravely back from her prow. Smartly drilled, the crew pulled down the sails, while the pilot threw himself against his rudder pole and slid the *Dancer* alongside the deepwater dock. A stream of cublin, females and darkcrests poured from the city walls onto the quay, eagerly catching at the ropes the crew threw.

In a shorter time than he'd thought possible, the *Dancer* was firmly tied to the dock and the gangway put out. It seemed to Fenobar, surveying the crowd, that the entire clan must have come out to see the *Wave Dancer* come home.

At the foot of the wharf, the Elder Sister-Group stood waiting, their white and green robes a cluster of stillness among the general crowd movement. Keltain and her own sister-group came down the gangway, the darkcrests automatically giving way before them. Fenobar gave her time to tell the Elder Sister-Group about Sig and then came off the ship, conscious of his war band behind him, and especially of the Demon's round head shining in the sun at his shoulder.

Fenobar was greeted with self-contained courtesy. Sig was ignored. Not even by a look did the females suggest the Demon was not Imkairan. The cublin were not so disciplined, and a knot of wide-eyed youngsters trailed along with them to the King House, where they dared not enter.

Entering into the main hall, the females made directly for the long flight of stairs which led to the upper quarters. The lower floor, which was the King's private domain, was dark and dusty. Fenobar stood a moment, looking around at the dark corridors, and found the silence oppressive. He signed to Sig and

Soonkar to wait in the hall outside the King's quarters, and continued alone up the broad stairs in the wake of the senior and junior sister-groups.

The upper chambers where the females lived was all light and bustling activity. He was bowed into the meeting room at the top of the steps by a darkcrested servant, tactfully discouraged from going any further into the female quarters. This was as far as a warrior was permitted in the female quarters. This room was as cold and unused as the male quarters below. Walking over to the window, he stood looking down at the plaza in front of the King House. Only a few individuals were crossing a place which was the male heart of the Clan, where they came to practice and learn. It was as desolate as a graveyard, and the wrongness of it made him feel ill. It was how Fen must look now.

Servants entered the room behind him and busied themselves. They withdrew and he turned around to find the place transformed with bright pillows, lights, a three-sided table, and the homey scent of singali brew.

Keltain came into the room as the last of the servants was leaving. She had changed from her white silk tunic to one of light ghaido wool in green, which he thought was unseemly short. She saw him still standing by the window. "You've never been in the female chambers before, have you?"

He shook his head.

"It is proper for you to be seated before the sister-groups arrive." She motioned to the table as she knelt down along one side.

Fenobar removed his helm and tucked it under his bad arm, slanting his crest in her direction. He crossed to the table and settled himself at one angle. It could not be said, of that strange little table, that anyone could sit opposite another. Not knowing what else to do with his helm, he set it on the rug beside him.

Keltain folded her hands in her lap and peeked up at him, her green eyes catching the light for a moment.

There was no more conversation. They simply waited, eyes on their folded hands.

Minutes passed. Then, finally, out in the hall, Fenobar's listening ears heard footsteps approaching, and in moments the Elder Sister-Group came in. They were old—as old as his teachers had been in Bokeem. They seemed to fill the room with their fluttery long green robes, though there were only four of them. Groaning a little, three of them found places among the pillows piled against the wall, muttering among themselves. The Foremost knelt at the remaining side of the table, her movements stiff and awkward, accompanied by several grimaces of pain. In her youth, her fur had been a medium brown, but age had turned her face white and sprinkled the rest of her coat until she was brindled. The flesh had fallen away from her bones, leaving her nose quite prominent, but there was a youthful sparkle to the intelligent green eyes. She looked from Keltain to Fenobar, studying them both as she poured out the singali and handed their cups to them.

"So," she said, folding her hands around her cup. "Keltain, tell me of the trip."

The rustlings and shiftings among the pillows stilled as Keltain started to speak. In a clear, unemotional voice, she told them how she had failed with her trading until she fished Fenobar and his Demon of Undoing out of the Trulden current just south of the Smoking Lands and made a bargain with him to serve the Bektarri for one year. She handed over a bundled of record sticks, showing the ship's accounts.

The Foremost ran her fingers across the marks and

handed the sticks over her shoulder to the rest of the group to read. The old females murmured, heads together, running their fingers across the incised marks passing the sticks hand to hand. Finally they were returned to the Foremost with their verdict. "We are pleased with this whitecrest's work."

"He is crippled," Glaim commented. A warning.

"We need someone to take care of the contracts, not to fight!" one of the others replied sharply.

Another said, "I want to know about this Demon he has running at his shoulder."

"Yes," Glaim said slowly, studying Fenobar. "What about this creature you brought with you?"

Silently Fenobar held out his right wrist, where the long thin scar of the Sig's kalnak showed clearly. "He is my sholstan."

She nodded as if satisfied. "See that you keep him under control. The work we would have you do would be done by the King, if we had a King. Keltain's Male House has offered you honor place with them, but I want you close by where I can keep an eye on you and not have to send a messenger the length of the town to bring you to me. You will live, therefore, in the King's quarters."

Fenobar made a movement of protest at these words.

Glaim shook her ears at him. "I know. Keltain has told me you refused the Kingship, and I'm not giving it to you now. It is merely an arrangement which suits me to make."

She sat back a little on her heels, preparing to rise. "Tomorrow morning, in the plaza, you will meet the Clan. Tobeh, the darkcrest in charge of your household, will bring you at the proper time. Bring that Demon of yours so the Clan can get a good look at him. We wouldn't want our darkcrests to come

upon him suddenly and turn him into fish bait out of
sheer hysteria." She levered herself to her feet in
stages, groaning a little, and led the sister-group out.

Keltain slapped the table and looked triumphantly
at Fenobar. "That Demon of yours must be on our
side. This is going to work out very well."

"For whom?" Fenobar asked wryly. But he asked
his question of an empty room, Keltain was already
gone.

Darkcrested servants were set to cleaning the King's
chambers, dispelling, by sheer activity, the generally
dreary coldness of the lower levels. The war band
was waiting patiently for him to return, crouching on
their heels in the middle of the hall, where the
servants had to constantly go around them. Sig had
wandered into the main banquet room, and was studying the murals with his usual air of absorbed interest.
A darkcrest, seeing him there, backed hurriedly out
again and left him to his solitary meditations.

Fenobar collected his war band together and let
Soonkar show the way to the warrior barracks attached to the back of the King House. Pushing open
the bronzed door, Soonkar stepped into the large
empty hall ahead of Fenobar, moving aside only
when he was sure no danger was lurking. The place
was as lifeless as the King's chambers in the House
had been. The fireplaces were cold, and the beds,
facing each other along the walls, each with their
ghaido wool-stuffed mattresses rolled up to the head,
made Fenobar shiver. He had never seen a barracks
that was empty.

Soonkar and the other Bektari palecrests went pok-
ing and prodding cheerfully among the things left
behind by the hastily departed warriors and finally
chose for themselves the highly sought sleeping places
near the fire. They were home and they were content.

A group of darkcrests came through a small side door and introduced themselves as the barracks servants. By the time Fenobar and Sig had walked the length of the hall to the outer door, the darkcrests had lit fires, spread mattresses and were well on their way to spoiling the warriors in their care.

"Let us hope we have such a welcome awaiting us!" Fenobar joked to Sig, as they started back to his quarters. But a short distance from the barracks, they espied a door in the King House, quite small and unimportant looking. With a sense of guilty adventure, Fenobar and Sig opened it and sidled inside, to find themselves in the dark audience chamber. Sig struck a light to one of the candles in the wall sconce and they carried it with them, inspecting the murals, wall hangings and the ornate raised chair where the King sat to dispense justice. "The King's sholstan stands at his left," Fenobar told the Demon.

Sig put his hands on his hips. "The dimensions of this place are the same as that of a challenge court."

"No mistake," Fenobar replied. "This room was the challenge court in the old days when the King had to take and hold the chair by killing his rivals. The Kingship is nominally open to all whitecrest males of the clan. But now usually the King breeds for his successor. If the cublin is both intelligent and strong, there is usually little disagreement about him becoming the new King."

They found another door out of the audience chamber behind one of the wall hangings. Fenobar sniffed the air once and confidently led them to the kitchens. There, their sudden appearance from a small stairwell beside one of the fireplaces put most of the kitchen staff into considerable disorder. Fenobar tilted his crest regally at everyone, plucked a pair of hot meat pasties off a platter and, handing one to Sig, departed, with his sholstan solemn-faced behind him, to check out the King's private quarters.

Fenobar threw open a set of double doors and stopped on the threshold. "This is the King's working room . . ."

"A study?" Sig was at his shoulder, looking eagerly over his head. There was a fire newly lit in the fireplace. The walls were covered with stick books and maps, and a huge table was littered with papers, books, brushes, paints, as if the King had but a moment before he stepped out of the room. The illusion wasn't dispersed even after Fenobar ran his fingers across one of the maps and left a trail in the dust, and Sig, picking up one of the paint pots, remarked that they had all dried out.

Another set of double doors was set in the east wall and when Fenobar pushed these open he found himself in the King's sleeping chamber. A fire burned in this room, too, and the hangings of green and yellow over the huge bed were silk. The rug was deep and delightfully warm under his toes. The walls were covered with tapestries, and between them hung antique swords and other arms. A door led to a smaller chamber where a servant might sleep. Fenobar sighed and folded up bonelessly among the green pillows. "Sig, call a servant for me, will you?"

When the darkcrest entered, Fenobar ordered him to remove everything from the King's chamber, including the bed. "I will keep the carpet, but I prefer something less ornate to sleep in. You will also have the servant's chamber prepared for my sholstan."

The darkcrest—Tobeh, Fenobar remembered his name to be—merely bowed and left to carry out his instructions. In the few moments of quiet before the place was invaded by an army of darkcrests, Fenobar sighed deeply. "Sig, I could get awfully used to this during a years's time."

The Demon folded up beside him on the carpet, hands clasped loosely between his knees, and stared into the fire. The Axe, as always, was across his back.

When he didn't say anything, Fenobar looked anxiously at him. There was a sadness in the other and suddenly Fenobar remembered that moment on the cliff after the tyforndor had trampled their raft into kindling and Sig had nearly howled for the longing in him to return home. *But he is my sholstan now,* Fenobar told himself. *Mine . . . as long as I need him.* Which meant forever. But a coldness had come to settle at the bottom of his stomach. For it came to him that the bond between a sholstan and his commander was of the old order and Sig was change incarnate. Someday, Sig was going to follow his longing back to his own clan. The bond would not hold him.

Two months later Fenobar was working in the study. He had already cleared up the most pressing matters, put his mark on hundreds of book sticks, and pleased the Elder Sister-Group enormously by his grasp of problems and willingness to work. From that he gathered the former King of Bektar—Beklor—tended to spend most of his time on the practice field. He was trying to puzzle out the former King's individualistic style of record-keeping and not making much headway. Beklor had had only a very slight grasp of accounting principles and Fenobar could not seem to find out what he had done with all the money he took in.

He ran his hand through his crest and felt the long, silky hairs with pleasure. It had grown in very nicely, just as Sig had told him it would. A darkcrest came in with another pot of hot brew, taking away the one that had gotten cold while he worked over the clay table Sig had made for him.

Seeing him struggling with the old King's numbers, and the way he kept throwing wooden sheets into the fire in disgust, Sig had said he needed something he could use more than once or he was going to cause the destruction of an entire forest. The clay table was so large he could copy several book sticks worth of information on it.

He heard a door open and slam shut. The noise announced Sig, who never would wait for the porter to open to him. Heavy, impetuous steps came up the stairs three at a time. Fenobar lifted his head, waiting to see if Tobeh would make it to his door before Sig did. Tobeh's bare feet were a pitter-patter in the hall as he darted out of whatever room he had been working in to intercept the sholstan.

"That's all right," he heard Sig's burring boom. "I've got it; no need to fash yourself." There was a rap of knuckles against the wood, Sig's individualistic way of announcing himself, and without waiting for permission, he opened the door. He was wearing his new armor, helm made especially for his round head, with a place in the top to stick a twist of dyed tatarra tail, which Sig mostly forgot to put in. The Axe, as always, was slung across his back.

Sig looked over at Fenobar, one hand still on the door handle. "You busy, Fen? I have to talk to you. It's important."

Fenobar's crest fluffed, as it always did when he saw his sholstan, and he nodded a silent invitation to sit down at the empty mat across from him.

But Sig didn't sit. Instead, he took the Axe off his back and held it out to Fenobar, its head still concealed by the green and gold hood bought in Shundor. "How many obsidian, two-headed war axes are there in existence?"

"Why do you ask?" Fenobar asked, stalling for time. He had a suspicion what was coming next.

"Because I was stopped in the street just now by that doddering old whitecrest priest, Tengli. He reamed me out for carrying a Clan Spirit around like it was so much dirty laundry."

"Tengli!" Fenobar repeated, recalling the old priest's carrying voice. "How many of the Clan heard him?"

"The war band, with whom I was training, a group of cublin, a couple of sister-groups, and some darkcrests carrying wood. I give it ten minutes before it's all over town. And Soonkar—Soonkar, mind you— was right there, heard the whole thing and didn't even blink!"

"Sig . . . you . . ."

"Don't 'Sig' me! Soonkar *knows*. He must always have known. After Tengli left I asked Soonkar how many obsidian, two-headed war axes there were. And you know what he told me? That except for the one I carry there is only one other, the Black Axe of Monghan. Three thousand years old if it's a day!" Sig was shouting by this time. "This is the most well known weapon on the entire continent! Fen, what were you thinking of to have me carry it all over Shundor Port?"

"They can't *know*," Fenobar said calmly. "No one was told the Black Axe of Monghan was removed from the Clan. The Spirits are *never* taken away from the temple, Sig."

"That old priest knew, and Soonkar *knows*, Fen. If *he* could figure it out, how many other warriors recognized it? Half the Chalig in Shundor must have seen it."

"They can't know," Fenobar repeated.

Sig took a deep breath. "What will be the first sign that you're wrong?"

"When warriors start arriving at our gates to challenge me for rank."

"We're in big trouble then, Fen, because the first boat-load of them sailed into the harbor twenty minutes ago."

Feeling very cold, Fenobar slowly stood up, threw the book stick he'd been studying end-first into the clay table. "I'd better get my armor on."

Sig followed him into the bedchamber, done over in green juras cloth, to help him. "What are you going to do?"

"I will go to the audience room and wait. After they have talked to the harbor master, which at the moment is Keltain, and affirm that Bektar has no King, they will challenge me. When I am dead they will make you part of their war band, and with you goes the Axe, which they will promptly take away from you."

"They will all challenge you?" Sig sounded stunned.

"Until I lose. Then they will challenge whoever holds you."

"You said once the Axe was meant to hang in the temple at Mone. Couldn't you put it under the protection of the God Shaindar, here in Bektar?"

"Hang it in a *Chalig* temple?" It was nearly a shriek.

"Sorry," Sig muttered. "I forgot. But why would they want the Axe? It's a Monghanirri Clan Spirit. What good can it do some other Clan?" He was lacing Fenobar's undertunic, and when he was finished, he helped Fenobar wriggle into the mail shirt.

"These who refuse to seek the protection of the last Chalig Spirit, Thenorig's Red Banner, do so because they detest Thenorig so much they'd rather wander the Void without protection than crawl to him out of fear. If they could join another Clan, they would. Better by far to take to themselves another Spirit and return with it to their Clan. For most of them it has been over three years that they have been without Clan Spirits and they are getting desperate. The Axe has great power and has only two warriors to protect it. The commander who gains it, gains much."

"You have more warriors than two to protect the Axe. It was not only because of the Axe that my troop and I asked to join your war band." The harsh voice belonged to Soonkar. He was standing in the open door to Fenobar's bedchamber, ears back and crest at half tilt, helm under one arm.

Fenobar and Sig both looked around, startled.

The palecrest took a step forward into the chamber. "Sig was right that I knew the Axe for what it was. I did want to join your war band for that reason. But then you killed a Selnessor Lord, one-handed as you are, and did it easily. Such a one, I told myself, would be a fast-rising commander . . . and you were coming to Bektar. So I stood by you and asked for the skill test. But it was when you agreed to take my entire troop, even Bartic, that I realized how wisely I had chosen. Since then you have risen steadily in the eyes of the Elder Sister-Group and in mine as well. You have brains to go with your sword-learning.

"Sig will stand at your right when you face these challenges. He does not have to, but I know him well enough to know he will do it. I ask your permission to stand at your left. I do not have to, but I wish to show these outlanders how high your war band holds you."

Fenobar was about to agree to this when Sig spoke, his words soft and deadly. "I will do more than stand at his side. I will fight, too."

"No, Sig," Fenobar said, turning to look him straight in the eye. "These are ranking challenges between whitecrest. I must do it alone."

Sig bowed his head a moment, then raised austere direhawk eyes. "They will not have me or the Axe for the plucking. When you go down, I will fight them until I, too, die."

Through the stones that seemed to fill his stomach at the thought of the Demon's death, Fenobar said, "But you will not fight with the Axe."

"I will not fight with the Axe," the Demon agreed. "It will hang on the wall behind the King chair and I will use a steel war axe from the warkip, like I have been doing in our practice sessions."

"It is waiting for you in the hall in Kagruf's hands. The war band stands behind you," Soonkar said, eyes alight and crest fluffed. "We will show these outlanders the fighting mettle of the Bektar warriors."

Fenobar buckled his sword harness around him and took his shield from Sig. He had regrets, but this was no time to voice them.

A servant padded to the doorway behind Soonkar. "My Lord, the harbor master sends word that ten whitecrests and their war bands seek an audience with you. She sends her deepest apologies."

Carefully, Fenobar tucked his helm under his bad arm. "I am ready. Sig?"

"Pardon, Lord," the servant bobbed his crest at Fenobar nervously. "They are already here and are awaiting you in the audience chamber. Tobeh is taking their names and rank."

Fenobar barely acknowledged this as he headed for the door. Sig slipped the Axe over his shoulder and fell into place a half pace behind Fenobar's right shoulder, while Soonkar took his place at Fenobar's other shoulder a half step behind Sig.

The rest of the war band were waiting for them in the hall. Kagruf handed Sig a plain but sharply honed double-headed war axe. Sig swung it experimentally and raised one eyebrow at the tancrested warrior. "This is not the one I usually practice with. It feels like it was made for me."

Soonkar flicked his crest at the Demon. "It was. A warrior fights best with a weapon made for his length of arm and strength. We had this made especially for you, knowing there would come a time, one way or another, when it would be needed."

In Fenobar, fesen was rising, but there was gladness, too. The war band was solidly united. How many other war bands could claim to have more than the ritual of the bond mark holding them together?

Head high, crest fully erect, Fenobar strode into the audience room, ignoring the gathered outland warriors as if the long room echoed with emptiness. He swung around to face those warriors when he was in front of the King chair, his war band taking their place behind him. Sig left his side a moment to place the Black Axe on the pegs behind the King chair, where once the Bektar White Branch had hung. He came back to his position with his new war axe in both hands, as once before, confounded the commander with his willingness to take part in a matter that the law said did not concern him.

There was a gasp from the assembled warriors as they got a good look at the Demon. A mutter ran through the ranks as Soonkar, taking his cue from Sig, drew his sword, and the rest of the war band after him, spreading out so they were unmistakably between the outlanders and the Axe.

Four of the war bands stood out from the others and, studying their waiting commanders, Fenobar knew he faced the toughest of all the warriors who wanted the Axe.

The were scrutinizing him as thoroughly as he was them. They were missing nothing of his youth, slight build, or bad arm. With the merest lift of lip he bared his teeth at them. An overconfident whitecrest was a dead whitecrest. Let them relearn the lessons of Bokeem!

Tobeh pattered out from among the warriors to one side of Fenobar, well out of the way of any sword swings, and called the first name. From among the four whitecrests gathered to the fore, a heavy-shouldered warrior stepped forward, at least ten years from his time in Bokeem. There was a brutal look to the strong face, and nothing in the yellow eyes but contempt. Arrogantly he took another step forward, and tilted his crest to Fenobar. "I am Loosmig, and I was among the First Rank of my Clan. I am the Ranking warrior here. Join me as a bond ally, you and your war band, and you will be assured always of high standing."

The offer hadn't been entirely unexpected. No warrior wants to fight if he can gain status in some other way. It would be the sensible thing to join this Loosmig. But Fenobar had promised to keep the Axe safe, and as long as he was alive, the Axe would remain the Black Axe of Monghan—not the Black Axe of Chalig. He pulled his sword and heard it swish overhead with a clear, eager sound. "I cannot join you. Now or ever."

"Do you claim King right?"

"No."

Another warrior, just as big, a bit greyer than the first, took an eager step forward. "I am Elsnor. I claim the King right of Bektar."

"It will do you no good, my Lord. I am promised only until the midsummer relap harvest, and then I will be on my way. And the axe with me."

Elsnor mumbled something about it not being worth it under his breath.

"Who claims King right over Bektar?" Sharp and furious the words rang through the chamber and old Glaim, her sister-group hard on her heels, strode forward past the assembled warriors to stand before the rather shame-eared Elsnor. She poked a clawed finger into the warrior's chest. "You do, do you? Without consulting the Elder Sisters first? It makes no difference. We will have none of you outlanders, so you can just forget about getting your rumps on the King chair."

"This is a warrior matter, old one," Loosmig said contemptuously.

"That's Honored Old One to you, rat crest. You've been out in the sun so long it's boiled your brains so you have forgotten your manners. What is this warrior matter that is so important you stole a ship and came all the way from Shundor to our poor little Clan?"

Loosmig met her fierce eyes without flinching and said nothing. It was another of the warriors, a younger one, made exceedingly nervous by this exchange, who called out insolently, "We want the Black Axe of Monghan."

"And our little youngling has it? Is this what you are saying?" She looked slowly around at them, her old eyes piercingly aware. "Well, we know why you want it, don't we? It's easier to steal a Clan Spirit than to go to Thenorig and fight *him* for the return of your own. No wonder Mad Thenorig has been able to reduce the Chalig to dust!"

She paused to let that gibe sink in before continuing. "It is warrior right, I agree, to settle this matter of the Axe among yourselves, and if it were not for an important matter which has come up, I would let you cut each other into tagris meat. After you hear my news perhaps you will find something else to do with your swords."

Stumping to the step on which the King chair sat, she mounted it and turned to look at that assembly of warriors. "Before we, the Elder Sisters of this Clan, permit you to continue with your ranking challenges, one among you must lead the rest in a matter of Clan honor." She looked over the silent, sullen faces under jerking crests. "As you all know, Clan Honor comes before warrior right. For the one among you willing to take on the Clan Honor of Bektar there is great honor awaiting you."

"From *this* Clan?" Loosmig sneered. "There is more honor to be had in the lowest ranking house of Gamlor than in the Kingship of Bektar."

"You don't know how glad it makes me to know you do not covet Bektar," Glaim replied, "as I strongly suspect any cublin of your siring spend their days sitting on the dung hill, snapping at flies."

There was a stir of flickering ears around the room before she continued. "The great Honor I speak of is one all the Tribe will give to the one among you willing to take it. Only the royal High King himself could have more honor than the one who does this thing." She paused, waiting; and sure enough, one of them had to ask.

"What Honor to the Bektar would be so great as that, Foremost?"

"Mad Thenorig is coming here and we need a Hero to go and kill him."

There was a long, long, unbroken silence as no one moved except to look at each other out of the corners of their eyes.

"I will do it," Fenobar said at the same time as Loosmig. They glared at each other, crests twitching.

"You?" And Loosmig wrinkled one lip as if he found the very sight of Fenobar repugnant.

Fenobar nodded, slowly. Their eyes locked and held.

"It is challenge, then?"

"Body to body, claw to claw," Fenobar replied, handing his helm to Sig.

"Time?" the other asked.

"Now," Fenobar replied. Fesen was beating through him, and like always as battle heat rose, sight narrowed. Hunter's vision. There was only the brutal, scarred features of his opponent for him.

Loosmig, his crest bound by his helm, saluted his willingness. "Place?"

Fenobar's show of teeth was as wide as one of Sig's grins, and entirely without humor. "Here, below the Axe." Let his ancestors be witness to what he was going to do.

"Is it winner take all?" Loosmig's eyes were calculating.

"No. It is for my own reasons that I chose to fight here. If you live through this challenge and still want the Axe, you will have to ask my sholstan for it."

Fenobar stood naked on the outside of the white line marking the Challenge Circle in the old floor. Battle madness was climbing and he no longer wished to talk.

Distantly he heard Sig whisper to someone behind him. "But Loosmig is so big! Isn't there anything we can do to help Fen?"

Now *that* was a sholstan! Fenobar felt a warmth suffuse him that had nothing to do with fesen.

"No," Soonkar whispered back. The single syllable was uncompromising. "A whitecrest must do it alone, or lose so much honor that cutting his throat is the only way out."

He was not going to fail. Fenobar's left hand flexed, flattening. The ka-rah-teh Sig had taught him was

clear in his mind. Sight narrowed still further until
the only thing real to him was the raging desire to
find his challenger and sink his teeth into his throat.
A voice was telling him to hold off, that it wasn't
time yet. He did not want to listen, shook off an
urgent hand on his arm. His head swayed back and
forth, searching. . . .

"Help me, Sig!" Soonkar whispered frantically. "He
isn't listening to me."

Soonkar's voice annoyed Fenobar, irritated and set
up an itching of pain along exposed nerve endings.
He growled . . . and lashed out with his good hand.

A wider, five-fingered grip came down on his shoulders. The deep voice was speaking softly into his ear,
filled with those odd burrs and lilts so different from
any other voice, soothing and comforting. That voice
was a white line through his battle fury, a way out if
he chose to follow it, the only thing left he could
attend to. Sig was saying softly, "Not yet, my Lord.
Not yet."

Then Fenobar's enemy was in front of him, on the
far side of the challenge circle, but as yet outside the
white lines. The other's tattered ears were laid tight
to his skull, eyes narrowed almost shut. For a moment Fenobar watched the play of muscles beneath
the Chalig's light brown fur, only a fraction darker
than his own. Loosmig stepped inside the lines, and
at the same moment, Sig loosed his hold on his
shoulders with one last word. "Win!"

Like an arrow released from the bow, the slighter
Fenobar hurled himself across the intervening space.
He wasted no time clawing, biting and slashing. In
truth his good hand played little part in what happened next. He kicked the whitecrest flat onto his
back as he sprang into the high, flying leap he'd
practiced with Sig. He came down on his good arm

and rolled to his feet so fast he was just a blur of
motion. As he came up, Loosmig was just scrambling
his feet under him. Fenobar gave him the necessary
second to stand upright and then deliberately stepped
within the circle of his arms, going for the Chalig's
throat with his good hand and striking upwards under his ribs with his stiffened, crippled hand. The
Chalig's breath whooshed out of him and his eyes
grew round and glazed.

Fenobar stepped back, snarling softly, and watched
as the Chalig took one stiff step, another, and then
fell forward on his face and lay limply on the floor.
He was dead, had been dead from the moment Fenobar
hit him.

The warriors packed around the Challenge Court
moved back several steps, staring first at Fenobar,
who was so wrought up with unexpended energy
that he was pacing back and forth within the challenge square, howling. One by one they began to
drift away.

"Wait," called Glaim. "How many of you are going
with him to face Mad Thenorig and regain your Clan
Spirits?" The drifting grew more focused, became a
decided rush for the door. Her ears twitched with
amusement.

CHAPTER EIGHTEEN

When Loosmig's war band, having carefully weighed all aspects of the matter (which mostly meant asking themselves if they could tolerate Sig's presence), came to ask if they might join Fenobar's war band, he was in no shape to listen to them. It was Soonkar who met them outside the King's chambers (rather to their relief) because Sig was with Fenobar, talking the still wrought up Fen into some kind of calm.

Slowly his soothing words penetrated the place fesen had taken Fenobar and he came back to himself with a sigh and bone-crumbling weariness. He collapsed among the green pillows in front of the fire and accepted the cup of hot singali brew Sig handed him. Fenobar's hand shook, spilling some of the singali on the pillow beside him. Sig blotted up the spill with an old surcoat and settled down cross-legged beside him. Together they stared into the fire.

"Why did you say you would fight Thenorig?" Sig asked after a while.

Fenobar sighed and pulled at his crest. "It would

be pleasant to say I did it after careful consideration. But the truth, Sig, is that pride and pure rank lust got the better of me. I wanted to succeed where my sire had failed."

Resting his chin on folded hands, still gazing into the flames, Sig said, "Well, whatever your reasons, it gave us some breathing room. And sent those outlanders off with their shields thumping behind them." He lifted his head to meet Fenobar's eyes and a snort of laughter escaped him. "You should have seen how they slunk away when Glaim asked which of them would accompany you to battle Thenorig and claim their Clan Spirits!"

Fenobar looked up at the Axe hanging above the fireplace where Sig always hung it. "Was it a good choice? Those who would have taken the Axe from us today would at least have also kept it from Thenorig. And I have pledged to take it right into his hands. Tyvai help us, Sig. I don't know if I can beat Thenorig."

"You will do what you did today. It will be done."

"You've never seen him. Thenorig is huge! And he has enormous prestige and status. No one less than a King has ever beaten a High King—especially not one who wins like Thenorig." He muttered this last nearly under his breath.

"Open the door!" A clear and commanding voice was suddenly raised in the hallway. "No, Soonkar, I must speak to the Commander, now!"

Soonkar scratched at the door first, before warily putting his head around it to look in. "My Lord, the Harbor Master Keltain would speak with you."

"She may enter," Fenobar said wearily.

Keltain, with her sister-group at her back, pushed past Soonkar and strode into the sleeping chamber. Sorlain, Bril and Mertis, all in lightweight armor, took positions beside the door, leaning on their spears. Keltain came all the way to where Fenobar was still crouched before the fire, sipping his singali. He barely looked up, and his crest stirred weakly in a token dip of respect.

Sig, in the far corner beside the bed, where he was hanging up Fenobar's armor, turned to watch her.

She hunkered down beside Fenobar. "I am sorry these outlanders took you so by surprise. I thought to give you more warning of those challengers, but my messenger was delayed by Tengli the Priest."

Fenobar put his cup down and looked at her in surprise.

Keltain put out one silver-tipped claw and drew it lightly down his leg. "You have much honor with our Family, warrior. My sister-group and I saw your challenge fight. It was well done from beginning to end.

"None of those so-called warriors have stayed around. No. I am wrong. Soonkar asked me to tell you that Loosmig's war band is asking if there is room in your war band for them. For the rest," she made a dismissing motion with her head, "they are all aboard ship and heading out into the ocean at next tide. And good riddance to them."

"We couldn't feed that many extra stomachs, anyway," Fenobar said. "There isn't enough food in the warehouses."

Keltain tapped his knee. "I have also come on orders from the Elder Sisters. They wish to speak to you on this matter of fighting Thenorig."

"Sig, my armor." Fenobar climbed slowly and a little unsteadily to his feet.

Glaim leaned back on the throne, tapping her long

claws on the arms as she studied him. Fenobar was standing before her in the audience chamber of the female quarters, the furthest he'd ever penetrated into that forbidden territory. Behind him was Keltain's sister-group, and in the left-hand sholstan position stood Keltain herself. He wondered wearily if it was a mistake or if she actually meant something by it.

Glaim stirred, motioned with one hand, and from among the crowd a female stepped forward—a very young female, little more than a cublin. Her tunic was dirty and she herself was nearly dropping with exhaustion.

"Tell the warrior the news you have brought us," Glaim ordered quietly.

With a deep breath, the female started to talk in a high, rapid voice. "My Family has an outlying farm. Early, before dawn it was, a warrior came into our yard and collapsed. He had been running most of the night. He told us to send word to the Clan that Thenorig knows we hold the Axe of Monghan and he wants it and any males who are here with it." She stopped as suddenly as she had started, cast a frightened look around the assembly, and retreated back among the bright tunics.

"It is harvest season. I do not want this . . . High King," Glaim spat, "to forage over the lands of the Bektarri. He did so once before and we were living on fish and tree bark all winter. We *will not* go through that again. Therefore, warrior, I ask, in the name of all the Elder Sisters of all the Families, that you go to meet this Thenorig on the borders of Bektar, instead of waiting, as is the custom, for him to arrive at our gates."

Fenobar wondered briefly if Sig had infected the Bektar Elder Sisters with law-breaking. He took a deep breath. "I will do as the Elder Sisters of Bektar command."

"Foremost." It was Keltain speaking, behind him. "Foremost, I and my sisters wish to accompany Fenobar of Fen to this challenge with Thenorig."

"Is there some reason for this, granddaughter?"

"We have a . . . proprietary interest in his future. He has promised himself to us until midsummer. When he becomes the Hero of Chalig, surely it will be a great honor for Bektar if he remains here full time?" This was said with a challenging look of her green eyes.

"I hold by my bargains," Fenobar said stiffly, secretly amazed she could be so sure he would win this fight.

Glaim nodded. "Yes, it would be great Honor for Bektar. We should all go, to see his rank lust does not get the better of his word and send him off like a dorfnor in heat to claim his position within the Royal Clan."

Fenobar's ears were flat to his head, and if he had dared, he would have growled at the Foremost.

Fenobar returned to his study, closing the door quietly behind him, walked over to where Sig was reading, and dropped down on the rug in front of him. Sig looked inquiringly up from his work and put the book stick to one side. "I am to fight Thenorig, the day after tomorrow," Fenobar said as one facing his doom. "Thenorig knows about the Axe and he is coming to destroy it. If I die, the Elder Sister-Group has pledged to help you get it to Mone."

"I see . . ." Sig said after a moment. "Have you decided what you will do with Thenorig's retinue after you win?"

Fenobar stared at him. Then his crest went limp

with fright. He forced it back up. "No." His left hand started to jerk. "When I beat Thenorig I will have more warriors than the High King. He will want them back. I have heard about the Chalig High King. He has only lost once in his life and that to Thenorig. And if I kill him I will be the Chalig High King. They will never accept a one-armed warrior as High King. I will have to fight his sons, one by one, through the entire Clan, and after them, the Clan closest in rank to the royal clan. I will spend the rest of my life—and it won't be a long one—fighting off challengers." His hand was jerking madly by now and he hung on to it with his other, forcibly holding it down. "I am a whitecrest. It is my destiny to lead warriors, to fight, to command. But, Sig, to you alone I tell this thing. It is hard to face a future where you know you cannot win."

Sig reached out and covered Fenobar's hands with his own. "We will find a way out of this."

"How? There are only two ways to go. Fight Thenorig and win. Or fight Thenorig and lose. I cannot lose because then I will lose the Axe as well." His words were heavy and hopeless, but even so the spasming in his bad arm lessened.

Sig let go his hold. "We will find some way out of this."

Fenobar looked earnestly into those direhawk eyes. "Sig, don't use your power on my behalf. You are pledged to me and to use your power to overcome my challengers would be great dishonor."

Sig's lips twisted wryly. "I can guarantee I won't use any power."

When they rode out of Bektar's land gate two days later, Fenobar, Sig and Soonkar mounted on three of the few war tatarra left to the Clan, they headed a procession made up not only of the fifteen warriors now in Fenobar's war band, but most of the Clan. Female, darkcrest, young and old kept determined pace with them. They reached the border near sunset, just a scant hour after the scouts reported that Thenorig's war band had settled down for the night a few miles from the Bektar border.

The Bektar folk set up their own camp. The talk around the campfires that night was hopeful but subdued. In his own tent, Fenobar paced back and forth.

"You will tire yourself out," Sig cautioned him.

"Does it matter? Ruin is staring us in the face! Gods! I would give up Clan and Tribe if only I were shown an answer!"

"To what, my Lord?" Soonkar ducked under the fastened back flap into the tent. His red-gold eyes were tired, and his pinkish crest looked mussed, as if he, too, had not been sleeping well in the last few days.

Fen and Sig looked at each other, then Sig shrugged. "You might as well tell him."

Sounding very young in his own ears, Fenobar said defensively, "I do not want to become the next Chalig Hero." He rather thought Soonkar would sneer at him for saying such a thing, but Soonkar only flicked a tired ear. "It's a little late to be changing your mind."

"It is not fighting Thenorig . . . !" Fenobar choked, crest jerking as fesen rose.

"It is what comes after," Sig explained hastily to the war band First.

"So. You have thought on that also and like it as little as I. It is good to know your mind has not become clouded with ranking fever. It is good to know, though a little late in the coming. Well. A

short life and a full one, as my mother always said."
Soonkar deferentially tilted his crest at Fenobar. "At
least they will sing about us around the nightfires."

"Soonkar," Sig asked a little desperately. "Can't
you think of any way we can avoid Fenobar getting a
challenge from the High King?"

"No. Once he kills Thenorig, his fate is sealed."

"We'll see about that," Sig muttered, but he spoke
in his own language and the others did not understand.

"What am I going to do about that whistle?"
Fenobar said suddenly into the silence that had fallen
between the three of them.

"What whistle?" Soonkar and Sig asked at the
same time.

Fenobar blinked. "Haven't I ever told you how
Thenorig wins his fights?"

They chorused their negatives, and Fenobar told
them in detail about Black Fentaru's challenge fight
with Mad Thenorig. Of how the Chalig had fallen
onto the ground and mewed like an infant and how
Black Fentaru, shocked, had stepped out of the Challenge circle and lost the fight. "And this is why he
has never killed any of the Chalig Kings, but taken
them into his war band," he finished.

Soonkar sat silent, crest jerking and claws working
in and out on his knees.

"Why not let the darkcrest whistle?" Sig asked,
bewildered. "If you are prepared for it, it shouldn't
bother you."

Fenobar stared at his sholstan, thinking. "I cannot
take the chance," he said at last. "Black Fentaru was
the victor of many challenges but Thenorig's keening
blew him clear out of the circle. I cannot hope to do
better than that. Even if I did not step out of the
circle, no warrior can lift a claw to an infant."

"But he is not an infant," Sig replied, stubbornly refusing to accept this explanation.

"The commander is right," Soonkar said. "His best chance is to kill Thenorig quickly, before the darkcrest whistles." He started to add something and stopped, turning his head away, clearly perturbed about some thought.

"But what if I cannot kill him quickly?" Fenobar had all-too-clear memory of the monstrous size of the Chalig High King. "What if I only hurt him and the darkcrest whistles before I can finish it?"

Sig shrugged. "It can't be hard to keep Thenorig's darkcrest from whistling. All we have to do is gag him."

Soonkar turned to stare at the Demon, as did Fenobar, but Soonkar's look held relief while Fenobar's was only amazed. "If it were that simple, why has no one ever done it?" Fenobar asked.

"Perhaps none of those defeated Kings ever thought to pass the word along. After all, it's a pretty embarrassing way to lose your rank. Even Fenobar couldn't bring himself to talk about it until now."

Soonkar was showing all his teeth as he said to Fenobar, "I will be glad to see to the gagging of this darkcrest, my Lord." And from the tone of his voice and tilt of crest, that gagging would be none too pleasant for Thenorig's darkcrest.

In the thin grey light before dawn, Soonkar rode off with the malin to deliver Fenobar's challenge. Fenobar waited, not in the hot sun, but in his tent, sipping water and popping meat chips into this mouth. To pass the time he had Sig lay out paint and brushes and began designing a badge for himself for when he became the Hero of the Chalig, and another for when he became King of the Chalig.

Sig ducked under the flap and poured himself a

mug of water from the pitcher sitting on the table beside his commander. There was a bright look to his grey eyes that Fenobar had come to recognize as the rise of Demon fesen. "Soonkar and the war band are returning."

Fenobar put down his brushes, wiped his hands and rose leisurely to meet Soonkar as he dismounted outside the tent entrance. "I gave the message, my Lord. Thenorig will come in an hour. Or whenever they can shove him up on that patuz of his and send him in the right direction."

"Why, Soonkar," Fenobar murmured, eyes gleaming. "I don't think you have a very high opinion of the High King." But his left hand twitched and he hid it hastily in the material of his tunic.

"Bah!" said Soonkar, helping himself to a handful of meat chips.

Sig was looking at Fenobar's drawings, leaning over the boards, with his hands braced among the little paint pots.

An hour later excited howls poured forth from the entire Clan as the High King was sighted coming toward them. A warrior came pounding up to the tent to give Fenobar the news in a more formal manner. Fenobar didn't move until they told him Thenorig, followed by hundreds of whitecrests and their warriors, were almost at the challenge circle already prepared on a small knoll not far from where the Bektarri were camped. Only then did Fenobar stroll from his tent, Sig and Soonkar at his back.

The whitecrests with Thenorig, Fenobar saw with a little gulp, were all Kings. They stood grim and silent, drawn up on one side of the challenge circle. On his side the females, cublin and darkcrests of Bektar were gathered around in a loose semi-circle, noisy and excited with anticipation. To the fore was a quiet gathering of his helmed and mailed war band. As Fenobar stepped forward to the edge of the challenge circle, he happened to look up . . . right into the golden eyes of his sire.

Black Fentaru stared in disbelief and turned to the Chalig beside him. "I told you not to get your hopes up, Lemark. Though you must give him honor for making the attempt. And I say it not just because he is one of my begetting."

There was no time to consider just what kind of right-handed compliment Black Fentaru was dealing. Sig was helping him out of the white juras tunic which was all he was wearing. The Demon, more nervous then Fenobar had ever seen him, was saying, "Whatever you do, don't let him get a hold on you and don't try to stand up to any of his blows. He'll cut you in half. Be careful."

"Easy for you to say," Fenobar muttered. His left hand twitched. He tried to flex it and work the cramp from the fingers.

Thenorig was pushed from among his whitecrests by overly willing hands. He looked, if anything, more tattered, scarred and miserable than he had on the challenge circle at Fen. But as he stumbled over the markings to take his place, to Fenobar he looked as solid and unchallengeable as a brick wall in motion.

Fenobar stepped to the curbing, curling his toes around the hard edge, and felt all his confidence ooze out of him. It was a peculiar feeling. In Bokeem he had been forced to fight. And defeat, when it was inevitable, had not seemed too terrible. But it was only now that he understood why. Then he had been among his peers, knowing there would come a day when he could defeat most of them. He had never fought anyone who outranked him as much as Thenorig. He felt that awesome Rank, that clan high status, like a strong weight against his sword arm, pressing down on his mind like a stormcloud and robbing him of fesen. "Challenge rank high, and die," was the old saying. It took on a personal meaning for him now, when it was entirely too late.

He took a deep breath, steadying his faltering courage. He could still do it. Sig fought without fesen. The kah-rah-teh was supposed to be used without fesen. How often had Sig told him that? He could win if he kept his wits. Old advice came back to him from the practice grounds of Bokeem. *Study your opponent.* He lifted his eyes to Thenorig's huge bulk standing awkwardly just outside the circle. It did not seem as if Thenorig knew why he was there. He simply stood, stolidly, without fesen. The remains of his crest lay flat to one side—appeasement. His little eyes were red and mad.

Fenobar spared a half second to look around for Thenorig's browncrest. He was standing a little apart from the Chalig warriors, nearly among the darkcrests of Bektar, looking sleek and self-satisfied. His crest had been braided and dipped in perfumed oils. He wore a fine silk tunic with the King badge on the chest, uncrossed by the staff of a darkcrest servant. The Chalig's little pale eyes were on Fenobar with all the gleeful satisfaction of a vulture awaiting a long-denied meal.

Sig was still near the circle, watching Fenobar. Soonkar was not among the retinue—had apparently already taken his sack and the gag and gone to stalk the little Chalig among the crowd on the far side of the circle. There was no point in waiting any further.

Fenobar cautiously stepped across the line and Thenorig charged. Fenobar ducked easily under a clumsy grab, setting himself to wear the other down by his speed and agility. But Gods! He'd forgotten how long a reach there was to those arms. Fenobar did not have much maneuvering room. None at all for mistakes.

He dodged to one side. Thenorig hesitated and Fenobar leaped into the air, kicking him in the side with both feet. Thenorig rocked back on his heels for a moment and then came after him, bellowing madness, while Fenobar scrambled out of the way on hands and knees. Had he hurt Thenorig? It was doubtful.

He had a glimpse of the perfumed browncrest: his eyes were wide with dawning worry. One hand was hovering towards his mouth and Soonkar was nowhere near him.

He would have to end this now, before the brown Chalig whistled. Fenobar circled, flexing his left hand, trying to keep one eye on the browncrest and one on Thenorig. He was not ready for this, wished he had more time. He brought his left hand up, saw that it was not flat and stiff but slightly curved. The Chalig browncrest lifted his fingers toward his mouth as if he'd made up his mind. There was no time to set his mind or hand the way Sig had taught him. He gathered what energies the enervating weight of Thenorig's terrible status had left to him and flung himself at the huge Chalig, punching his left hand up under Thenorig's tremendous ribcage. It was like striking a rock. Thenorig stepped back, one hand going to his chest; he stared at Fenobar and then, with a roar, bulled in after him. Fenobar dodged clumsily, his left hand numb and broken. He had failed!

The Chalig browncrest lowered his hand. There was no need to whistle yet, his eyes said. He was enjoying the game. As long as he did not whistle, Fenobar still had a chance. He tried another kah-rah-teh move, this time grabbing one of Thenorig's arms. He was supposed to twist and throw the Chalig off his feet, but Thenorig was immovable and it was Fenobar's footing that slipped. He hung a moment on that tremendous muscular arm, meeting the confused look in the Chalig's small red eyes with one of his own. Thenorig lifted his arm and Fenobar felt like a burr clinging to a mountain.

As he let go, Fenobar twisted, and for a moment one of the faces in the crowd came into focus. Dark, grim . . . Black Fentaru. And over the King's shoulder another dark face, amazingly similar. Stells? Fenobar looked up and almost failed to dodge a wide, swinging cut at his head. It *was* Stells! Somehow he had gotten back to his post at Black Fentaru's shoulder.

Fenobar danced past Thenorig, slashing this time at the Chalig's exposed side, and drew blood. Thenorig roared with pain. Spinning quicker than Fenobar thought possible, the Chalig reached for him and Fenobar had to scramble away. But one of those shield-sized hands caught at his arm—going, like an animal, for the source of his pain. Grabbing Fenobar's hand, he squeezed. There was a small crunching as the bones in his wrist broke. Fenobar kicked blindly and Thenorig let go with another squall of pain.

Twist. Shuffle. Dodge. Around and around they went in a death dance that had taken on all the choreographed moves of a long-standing ritual. Fesen still would not rise in him, but its absence no longer seemed so devastating. Oddly enough, the sense of Thenorig's unassailable status likewise no longer weighted him. Perhaps, he thought wryly, it was because with both wrists broken his own survival was the only thing of any real importance to him. There was now only one way he could win. He considered what he would have to do to become the Hero of the Chalig and wondered how much personal honor would be left him at the finish. Repugnance for the step he would have to take made his lip curl in a silent snarl. And sudden recollection set him looking hastily for Soonkar.

The battle plan had changed. If Soonkar gagged the browncrest like he was supposed to do, he would seal Fenobar's fate for certain. He darted glances at the crowd and still couldn't locate Soonkar. Sig was still close, looking pale and strained. Fenobar maneuvered close to his sholstan and tried to speak for his ears alone. "Don't let Soonkar do it."

Sig's face screwed up anxiously and he held one hand behind his ear as a sign he had not heard. Fenobar, his newest fear growing with every moment, threw himself into a roll and as he passed the Demon yelled, "Don't let him do it!" And came to his feet facing the Chalig browncrest who was looking distinctly sleepy. Behind the browncrest the crowd shifted, parted, to let Soonkar through. There was a fixed look of intense pleasure on Soonkar's long face.

Thenorig lunged. Duck, shuffle, dodge. Fenobar resumed the dance, and when the browncrest came within his view again Soonkar was standing behind him, arms raised high, holding open a heavy sack. Behind him there was a moment of turmoil. A gold, earless head rose above the Bektarri as Sig reached for his malinmate, yelling something which was lost in the crowd noise.

Thenorig lunged, out of step in the dance they had made together. Fenobar whirled, shifted desperately to find Soonkar. Before he could, sharp as a pumnor's challenge scream a whistle shrilled peremptorily above crowd noise. Thenorig promptly collapsed onto the ground, curled up and keened. A sigh of disappointment rose from the gathered Chalig whitecrests.

Fenobar stopped in his tracks and slowly straightened up. Behind the bored Chalig browncrest Sig's bright head heaved beside Soonkar's pinkish crest. The two of them, locked in a silent, furious struggle for the sack, fell, and disappeared from sight among the throng.

Fenobar was left staring down at the mewling Thenorig. He was not so much shocked as embarrassed, if that was the right word for the urge to squirm away from such a debased sight.

The crowd grew silent, waiting.

Fenobar looked down at his feet. He was still well within the circle. He had not stepped out. He was not going to step out. Hundreds of whitecrest eyes were fixed on him and the scent of the crowd had gone from despair to hope. But he had not yet won. He would not win until Thenorig was dead. Bile rose, stinging the back of his nose.

It was one thing to rip out a warrior's throat in the heat of battle madness, quite another to do it cold. His hands were useless. He could not use his claws. But it had to be done—there was no other way to rid the world of Mad Thenorig. Revulsion in every line of his body at what he was being forced to do, Fenobar knelt on one knee beside the Chalig. Lips pulled distastefully back from his teeth, he prepared to chew his way through the matted fur at Thenorig's throat.

Then the browncrest was tugging at his shoulder, absurdly braided crest flapping limply, screaming, "No! You can't do that! Thenorig always wins!"

"Not this time," Fenobar said grimly, spitting out a mouthful of brown fur.

There was a concerted roar from the massed warriors. "Hold, warrior!" someone was saying, and pulled the darkcrest off his shoulder. "The challenge has been interfered with. One has struck a dishonorable blow when his lord was down. The fight goes to you."

Fenobar looked up in time to see a priest negligently tossing the browncrest out of the circle, into eagerly waiting Chalig whitecrest hands. He spat out another mouthful of fur. "You sure about that?"

But the question was lost in the tumult as Chalig voices roared their freedom. Sig was at his shoulder, helping Fenobar get to his feet. "Gods be thanked I didn't have to go through with it," Fenobar muttered into his sholstan's ear. "I don't think I'm ever going to get the taste of him out of my mouth."

From somewhere a cart was being drawn forward, and the priest was preparing to step up into it, where he could be heard over the crowd. Sig was bending over Thenorig, stuffing a rag into the Chalig's mouth. "I don't know about you, but I can't take much more of this noise."

Fenobar watched, bleary-eyed from pain and fatigue but noticing, as he noticed everything about Sig, that there were claw marks on his throat and that his surcoat was slit across the front in three parallel cuts, so that the mail showed through. It was a good thing, he thought distantly, that Sig had worn his armor.

Soonkar, standing not far away, didn't look too good either. One eye was swelling shut and he seemed to be limping. In one hand he still held a twisted and rent sack and he seemed to be looking with regret at the browncrested Chalig in the hands of the whitecrests on the far side of the challenge circle.

Sig was still bending over Thenorig, running fingers, their tips oddly dark, through the sparse white hairs of the Chalig's crest. He stiffened and swung around on one knee to Fenobar. "Look at this!"

Fenobar leaned against Sig's shoulder and looked. Sig spread the crest hairs so that Fenobar could see to the roots. They were brown. For the first time that morning fesen sang along Fenobar's nerves. Rage swept away pain and weariness and he turned on his heel. "You, priest! Come here NOW!"

The priest stopped his speech and looked down at him, startled at being spoken to like that. Fenobar's crest jerked. "Now!" he repeated, and the Demon, behind him, pulled his war axe as if he were willing to make sure the priest came. Five priests shouldered their way into the challenge circle, crests jerking with wrath, offended by this speech to their royal High Priest, and ready to teach this outland upstart a sharp lesson, even if he was the Hero of the Chalig.

Fenobar stepped back, pointing at Thenorig. "Examine his crest!"

One by one the High Priests bent over Thenorig and examined his head. When the last one was finished with his inspection, he walked over to the Royal High Priest, who had not moved from his place in the cart, and spoke to him in an undertone.

Then the Royal High Priest, whose verdict was law, raised his hands high. "In the eyes of the God and Clan there is no bond between the Chaligirri and this Thenorig. *He is outcast*." There was a dead silence from the assembled Imkaira. Then a deep voice boomed out one word. "*Why?*" It was Black Fentaru who spoke. Fenobar would know that voice anywhere.

"Yes!" another king shouted. "Why now?"

"Why?"

"Why?" The word was cried aloud by more, until thunderously the land rang with it.

"Because the High King is a DARKCREST!" It was not the Royal Priest who shrieked that sentence out in a voice thickened with hate and repulsion, but another.

There was stark silence from the ones who heard. And the shouting died as the word was passed back to the waiting multitude of warriors. But before then, there came a long, low growl from the massed Chalig Kings around the challenge circle and then they surged forward, neither one nor another in the lead, but like a wave going over a rock.

Fenobar scrambled away from their fury, helped by Sig. When the Kings pulled back, each held a bloody chunk of meat in his hand and of Thenorig there was nothing left but a pool of rapidly congealing blood.

The Royal High Priest still had not moved from his place on the back of the cart. Now he raised his arms again. "For a defiler . . . the law is *defilement*! The Kings dropped their handful of meat onto the earth and with their feet, ground it into the dust, raking dirt over it with their toe claws.

"The name of Thenorig is anathema. No cublin henceforth shall bear his name. His line is to be removed from the living!"

The Red Banner was brought forward by a three-hand of rather recently battered priests of Thenorig's clan—they who had stolen the power of the Chalig Clan Spirits. The Red Banner was ripped from their hold and cast into Thenorig's blood. "This is the Red Banner! Let its dishonor be removed by the blood of he who brought it low!"

The Royal Priest held it up, dripping with gore, so that all might see. Then he folded it reverently, touched it to his crest, and handed it to the other priests. "Burn it!

"Each High Priest among you shall take the Clan Spirit of his tribe from the trophy cart and return with it to your clans." He looked around at the unmoving Kings. "Go!"

Slowly, disbelievingly, the whitecrests started to walk away, not yet used, perhaps, to the idea of their freedom. But they walked faster and faster, gathering their clan warriors as they went, until they were running.

One group of whitecrests and warriors came forward into the Bektarri lines. The Bektarri broke into triumphant howls, then scattered to their fires and tents to start celebrating.

At last there was no one left at the challenge ground but Fenobar, his war band, a handful of Fenirri warriors and the Royal High Priest, who was getting down off his cart. Black Fentaru had been staring hard at his son for a long time. When there was nothing else to claim Fenobar's attention, and he had, perforce, to look at his sire, Black Fentaru said ominously, "Where is the Axe?"

The Elder Sister-Group had left the jubilant Bektarri and were coming toward them. Behind the old females was Keltain, bearing a heavily wrapped but unmistakably shaped object. "It is here," Glaim said composedly, stopping in front of Black Fentaru and looking him up and down. "So. You are our cublin's sire. He has the look of you when his blood is up."

Black Fentaru's crest jerked, his only answer to this bit of impertinence. Stells came forward with eager hands and took the Axe tenderly from Keltain. Fentaru glared at his son. "The Axe was supposed to have been taken to Mone. Instead, you carted it all over the continent. You, with that thing at your shoulder."

Fenobar flicked his crest. "This is my sholstan,

King of Fen." Fenobar was strangely untouched by his sire's anger. Tiredly he said, "I have kept the Axe safe and fulfilled my duty to the Clan."

"I suppose you think you will bring that monster back with you to Fen? It is even uglier than Stells told me it was. I tell you clearly, I will not have it behind my clan walls."

"And am I to return to Fen, my Lord?" Fenobar asked.

"Yes, of course. You are still Temple Commander."

"I have just defeated Mad Thenorig, and I am no Temple Commander of yours."

Black Fentaru stared into his eyes. "I see you are not. But just what are you, youngling? Do you think these Chalig will honor you for what you have done? You shamed them in the face of each other and the world when you told them Thenorig was darkcrest. Do you honestly think they will want your face around to remind them of that fact?"

Fenobar opened his mouth and shut it again, bewildered. As hurt and as tired as he was, things were moving too fast for him. He swayed and Sig moved up behind him, lending him the support of his shoulder.

The High Priest stepped up, jerking his whitecrest for attention. "I'm afraid your sire has the right of it, youngling. We will always honor you for what you have done, but there can be no place for you among the royal clan. You have, I think, earned a boon from us, and that will have to suffice."

"You give me honor," Fenobar said dazedly, wanting nothing more than to go to his tent and be alone.

Glaim cleared her throat. "As a matter of fact, we were about to offer the youngling a place with us."

"With you?"

"As King."

"Ah," said the High Priest, relieved. "Then we will make him a Chalig with high Clan right—provided there is a House among the Bektarri . . . ?"

"The House and Family of the White Ship," Keltain said promptly. "We take him in as favorite son. He *and* his sholstan," she said with a meaningful glance at Black Fentaru.

"Then that is settled. I will send him his badge once we get back to Chalne." The Royal High Priest strode off as if glad to get away.

Black Fentaru was giving Fenobar a strange look, and over the King's shoulder Fenobar could see Stells, also giving him that strange look. Solemnly, the King of Fen saluted the new King of Bektar and turned away. Stells lingered long enough to say, "Shaindar be with you, youngling. And the Demon, too, of course."

There was a moment when no one met anyone's else's eyes. Then Sig said, "The commander is hurt."

"I have already sent for a priest to attend to him," Glaim said composedly. "Take him to his tent. And youngling, let me know in the morning if you truly wish to become King of Bektar. I know we are a small and poor Clan, and perhaps you might still claim for a boon the Kingship of some other, more prosperous place." She went back to the fires and the celebrating, her sisters behind her.

Soonkar came up on the other side of Fenobar and between him and Sig, they half carried, half walked Fenobar back to his tent. He was only vaguely aware of Keltain hovering, first on one side and then on the other. Behind them all, trailing along in a disorganized knot, was the rest of the war band.

At the tent Keltain sent the war band away to celebrate with the rest of the Clan. Soonkar would not have gone, but he knew Sig wouldn't let anyone else near Fenobar—he had that look about him, like a female pumnor with one kit. Keltain squatted down beside the pillows where Sig had laid Fenobar. "I hope you say you will become of our Clan and tribe," she said softly. "My sisters and I . . . we want you to become our group mate."

Then the priest was there and she had to leave.

A long while later, Fenobar opened groggy eyes. There had been something in the drink they gave him before setting his wrist that had cut the pain of what they had done to him considerably. It was dark inside the tent, and outside he could hear the shrilling of night insects and the distant clamor of the still-celebrating Bektarri. Somewhere close by was the warm scent of sajawa. Sig was with him, guarding him.

He reached out a hand to push himself up among the pillows and was mildly interested to see that hand swathed in bandages, with only the tips of his fingers showing. He looked at the other hand. That too was bandaged. "I'm not wrong-handed . . . I'm no-handed." He twitched his ears madly, feeling more than a little bit drunk.

"You are awake, then?" Sig asked, moving in the darkness, only his silhouette visible against the stars outside the open tent flap. His arm came around Fenobar's shoulders, raising him, and a cup of water was held to his lips.

The cup was withdrawn and Fenobar turned his head contentedly on his sholstan's shoulder. "Sig?"

"Yes?"

"Did you wash the paint off your fingers?"

There was a shocked silence, then cautiously, the Demon said, "You saw that?"

"And how adroitly you painted the roots of Thenorig's crest."

In a small, hesitant voice, totally unlike himself, Sig asked, "Are you angry?"

Fenobar sighed. "It is no light thing to think oneself a Hero, and then find out you have been relegated to the status of pest control."

Sig's arm tightened painfully around Fenobar's shoulders. "You did not want to be Hero and have to fight the High King," Sig said stubbornly, as if he had the thing by rote.

"True." Fenobar stared up at the sagging tent overhead, thinking, *My Demon, you have done it to me again. But I wouldn't give you up for a hundred Kingships.* It was getting terribly hard to think. "Sig, do I want to be King of Bektar?"

"Yes." No indecision there.

"Do I want to be group-mate to Keltain and her sisters?"

There was a rich chuckle of Demon laughter. "You can answer that better than I can. But I would hazard to say yes."

Content, Fenobar closed his eyes.

THE KING OF YS
POUL AND KAREN ANDERSON

THE KING OF YS—
THE GREATEST
EPIC FANTASY
OF THIS DECADE!

by Poul and Karen Anderson

As many authors that have brought new life and meaning to Camelot and her King, so have Poul and Karen Anderson brought to life a city of legend on the coast of Brittany . . . Ys.

THE ROMAN SOLDIER BECAME A KING, AND HUSBAND TO THE NINE

In *Roma Mater*, the Roman centurion Gratillonius became King of Ys, city of legend— and husband to its nine magical Queens.

A PRIEST-KING AT WAR WITH HIS GODS

In *Gallicenae*, Gratillonius consolidates his power in the name and service of Rome the Mother, and his war worsens with the senile Gods of Ys, that once blessed city.

HE MUST MARRY HIS DAUGHTER—OR WATCH AS HIS KINGDOM IS DESTROYED

In *Dahut* the final demands of the gods were made clear: that Gratillonius wed his own daughter . . . and as a result of his defying that divine ultimatum, the consequent destruction of Ys itself.

THE STUNNING CLIMAX

In *The Dog and the Wolf*, the once and future king strives first to save the remnant of the Ysans from utter destruction—then use them to save civilization itself, as the light that once was Rome flickers out, and barbarian night descends upon the world. In the progress, Gratillonius, once a Roman centurion and King of Ys, will become King Grallon of Brittany, and give rise to a legend that will ring down the corridors of time!

FRED SABERHAGEN

Fred Saberhagen needs very little introduction these days. His most famous creations—the awesome Berserkers—are known to SF readers around the world. He's reached the bestseller lists several times, most recently with his "Book of Swords" series, and his novels span the territory from hard science fiction to high fantasy. Quite understandably, Saberhagen's been labeled one of the best writers in the business.

These fine novels by Saberhagen are available from Baen Books:

PYRAMIDS

A fascinating new twist on the time-travel novel, introducing a great new series hero: Pilgrim, the Flying Dutchman of Time, whose only hope for returning home lies in subtly altering the history of our own timeline to more closely reflect his own. Fortunately for us, Pilgrim's timeline is a rather more pleasant one than ours, and so the changes are—or at least are supposed to be—for the better. Learn why the curse of the Pharaoh Khufu (builder of the Great Pyramid) had a special reality, in *Pyramids*. "Saberhagen's light, imaginative and enjoyable adventures speed along twisting paths to a climax that is even more surprising than the rest of the book." —*Publishers Weekly*

AFTER THE FACT

This is the second novel featuring the great new series hero, Pilgrim—the Lost Traveller adrift in time and dimensionality. His current project: to rescue Abraham Lincoln from assassination, AFTER THE FACT!

THE FRANKENSTEIN PAPERS

At last—the truth about the sinister Dr. Frankenstein and his monster with a heart of gold, based on a history written by the monster himself! Find out what happened when the mad Doctor brought his creation to life, and why the monster has no scars.

THE "EMPIRE OF THE EAST" SERIES

THE BROKEN LANDS, Book I

A masterful blend of high technology and high sorcery; a unique adventure in a world on the brink of ultimate change; a world were magic rules—and science struggles to live again! "*Empire of the East* is one of the best science fiction fantasy epics—Saberhagen can be justly proud. Highly recommended."—*Science Fiction Review*. "A fine mix of fantasy and science fiction, action and speculation."—Roger Zelazny

THE BLACK MOUNTAINS, Book II

East meets West in bloody conflict on a world where magic rules, but technology is revolting! "*Empire of the East* is the work of a master!"—*Magazine of Fantasy and Science Fiction*

ARDNEH'S WORLD, Book III

The gripping climax of the "Empire of the East" series. "Ranks favorably with Tolkien. Exceptional in sheer unbridled zest and imaginative sweep."
—*School Library Journal*

*   *   *

THE GOLDEN PEOPLE

Genetically perfect, super-human children are created by a dedicated scientist for the betterment of Mankind. As the children mature, however, they begin to wonder if Man *should* survive . . .

LOVE CONQUERS ALL

In a future where childbirth is outlawed and promiscuity required, one woman dares fight the system for the right to bear children.

MY BEST

Saberhagen presents his personal best, in *My Best*. One sure to please lovers of "hard" science fiction as well as high fantasy.

OCTAGON

Players scattered across the continent are engaged in a game called "Starweb." Each player has certain attributes, and can ally with or attack any of the others. But one player seems to have confused the reality of the world: a player with the attributes of machinelike precision and mechanical ruthlessness. His name is Octagon, and he's out for blood.

You can order all of Fred Saberhagen's books with this order form. Check your choices and send the combined cover price/s to: Baen Books, Dept. BA, 260 Fifth Avenue, New York, New York 10001.

PYRAMIDS • 320 pp. •
65609-0 • $3.50   _____
AFTER THE FACT • 320 pp. •
65391-1 • $3.95   _____
THE FRANKENSTEIN PAPERS •
288 pp. • 65550-7 • $3.50   _____
THE BROKEN LANDS • 224 pp. •
65380-6 • $2.95   _____
THE BLACK MOUNTAINS • 192 pp.
• 65390-3 • $2.75   _____
ARDNEH'S WORLD, Book III •
192 pp. • 65404-7 • $2.75   _____
THE GOLDEN PEOPLE • 272 pp. •
55904-4 • $3.50   _____
LOVE CONQUERS ALL • 288 pp. •
55953-2 • $2.95   _____
MY BEST • 320 pp. • 65645-7 •
$2.95   _____
OCTAGON • 288 pp. •
65353-9 • $2.95